A Time in Ybor City

A Time in Ybor City

Cuban Tampa in the 1930s

A Novel

Ron Kase

Published by Race Street Books Writer's Cooperative, Philadelphia, PA 19102
Racestreetbooks1@gmail.com

3rd Edition

Front cover photo by Kenneth Kase depicts the Tampa Bay Hotel, completed in 1891, which presently is Plant Hall of the University of Tampa.

ISBN: 1544098456
ISBN 13: 9781544098456
Printed in the United States of America

Acknowledgements

The fine writer Frank McLaughlin edited the novel's original manuscript. His magical touch honed by years of writing and editing turned sentences around and gave life to ordinary paragraphs. The places in the story that touch on George Gershwin's and other marvelous composers' music were expanded and improved by the expertise of Mike Giorgio, composer, arranger and fine musician a part of New Jersey's glorious music men tradition. Alice Pianfetti the great adventurer and writer proofread and copy edited the several manuscript versions making them better.

Advance readers Deborah Solomon and Cathy Losos bravely waded through the book's unedited draft encountering errors, typos, and misspellings, but they hung on and provided sound criticism, which I happily followed.

I was fortunate to discover Race Street Books Writer's Cooperative and their juried process of selecting books for publication. I appreciate their guidance during the publishing process along with the Auden Trust's support of my travels to Cuba. Our usually drama free wonderful family has made it possible for me to think and write, and enjoy retirement from a mostly satisfying career, without many interruptions. We are my wife Kathleen, daughter Betsy, sons Kenneth and Jonathan, grandson Jonah, son-in-law David and me. We're small in number, but big in spirit.

Ybor City, pronounced *E' bore City*, is a section of northeast Tampa, Florida founded in 1886 by Vincente Martinez Ybor as the Cuban cigar making center of the United States

Negro, the accepted designation in 1934 of a person of African descent

Colored, referring to anyone "with one drop of Negro blood" as specified in the hiring practices of the U.S. Government under President Woodrow Wilson that forbade the government's employment of any "colored" person over a certain basic job level. The "one drop" rule was adopted by eighteen states, and was the rule of law identifying persons as colored and therefore not entitled to all legal protections until the United States Supreme Court struck down the acts in 1967

Forward

This is a work of fiction, historical fiction, which is filled with peril for a writer. Henry James held that "Any attempt to write about a period more than 50 years removed from one's own was worthless and should not be attempted." Of course, James couldn't have anticipated the great store of knowledge that was developed and made available to anyone with curiosity and the tenaciousness to sift through the depth of information and evaluate its worthwhileness.

All of the historic events and facts referenced in this book are accurate according to the accepted research. The novel touches on some of America's wealthiest families, the Clarks, Plants and Warburgs, and parts of their stories as woven into the book are true. In 1934, George Gershwin did spend most of the summer on Folly Island, South Carolina working with DuBose Heyward on their epic opera "Porgy and Bess." The rest, as they say, is history. Gershwin was an exceptional man talented in so many areas and unusually sensitive for his time to the issues and achievements of members of minority populations.

Henry B. Plant's colossal hotels; the Tampa Bay and the Bellevue still exist in some manner. The Arabian Nights inspired, Tampa Bay Hotel, completely intact, is the administration building on the picturesque campus of The University of Tampa, but sadly the Bellevue, after the demolition of about one half of the gigantic structure, will be turned into condominium units. References to places in Tampa, Manhattan, Cooperstown and Havana are absolutely accurate, and most importantly, the images of Ybor City portrayed in this book are based on the research of Florida historians. Many of the episodes attributed to known people are based on facts and records. The Cuban culture of Ybor City was the beginning of the close relationship between Cuba and the United States that ended in 1960.

The value of one dollar in 1934 the year the Great Depression bottomed out is equivalent to almost $18.00 in 2016. Wages in the cigar factories of Ybor City remained considerably higher than the average factory worker's earnings in any other part of the United States.

A new era of U.S./Cuban relationships began in January 2015 when President Barack Obama announced the desire to re-align the attitude of the United States toward its close neighbor the nation of Cuba. The process of normalization will take several years however due to intractable attitudes of some people in the governments of both countries.

Chapter 1

Ybor City 1934

"My father met Vicente Martinez Ybor in Cuba in 1880. Ybor was a Spanish Grandee, successful in the tobacco business in Havana, but unhappy with the unrest in the Spanish colony. The Cubans are a combination of European and Caribbean people with an African influence from slaves imported to work in the sugar fields and sugar mills tossed into the mix. Decades of inter-marriage produced fiery revolutionaries who regularly fought for the island's independence. The turmoil caused Cuba's cigar making factories to close and the cigar makers to move to Florida, ninety miles across the sea. The move also avoided the tariff imposed by the American government on finished Cuban cigars. My father, James Flynn, an American, was the port agent for the Plant Steamship Line that sailed between the struggling Port of Tampa and elegant Havana with a stop in Key West. He accepted the tobacco shipments that Ybor sent to his cigar factory in Key West, Florida's most southern point."

"After almost twenty years of manufacturing cigars in Key West, Ybor, tired of labor problems and demands for Cuba's independence led by sympathetic cigar workers, moved his operations to a place near Tampa, Florida where on the forty acres he purchased he could build a large efficient factory something not possible to do in tightly packed Key West. The Tampa Board of Trade helped Ybor buy his first factory site and he quickly purchased an additional one hundred acres, which he re-sold or leased to rival tobacco manufacturers for cigar production. Due to its humid climate, which was perfect for cigar making; Tampa rapidly became the Cuban cigar center for North America with almost one hundred factories turning out all grades of Havana cigars. The section that held most of Tampa's cigar factories became a separate community known as Ybor City."

As Flynn reminisced, he smoked a *Perfecto Garcia* clear Havana cigar. He held it up and said, "It actually helps me think," and then continued with his story. "Ybor City was distinctly Cuban even though other ethnic groups also populated the community; it was the Cuban culture that dominated every aspect of life. Prior to the Spanish-American War the call for Cuba Libre was led by the patriot and leader of the Cuban independence movement Jose Marti during his many visits to Ybor City."

"In fact," continued Flynn, "Cuban cigar workers established patriotic clubs that raised large sums to pay for the revolution fermenting in Cuba and supported and armed groups of fighters that sailed from Tampa to Cuba to harass the Spanish colonial government. When a free Cuba was established in 1898 after the Spanish-American War; the business of cigar making again became the main focus of Ybor City's residents." For some time, Flynn had clipped newspaper articles about his beloved Ybor City. They rested in a file cabinet drawer, and he thought maybe someday he would write the definitive history of the place.

Reported by Victoriano Manteiga editor of *La Gaceta* October 14, 1923. (Translated from the Spanish) "The cigar makers mainly live in cottages with one long hallway from front to back known as shotgun houses, and they have sprung up by the hundreds among the cigar factories, and by 1900 a commercial center had grown rapidly in Ybor City with Seventh Avenue a wide street its main thoroughfare. Restaurants, clothing stores, bakeries and social clubs catered to the array of Cuban cigar rollers known as tabagueros who are among the highest earning factory working people in America. At first, all the cigar rollers were men, and women did the less skilled stripping of the tobacco leaves. As time went on, women joined

the ranks of cigar rollers and kept up with the men who had dominated the field. There was so much work available that the Cubans
were joined by Spaniards from Cuba, and later directly from Spain.
Italians primarily from Sicily who had migrated as part of the great
wave of Italian immigrants in the early days of this century, and had
found their way to New Orleans had now settled in Ybor City. Also,
Romanian Jews directly from Europe set up retail businesses catering
to the cigar workers.

There is a small red light district at the town's edge at 19th Street
that attracts only the unmarried males of the community living in
boarding houses because Ybor City is a family town where everyone knows about everyone else. The El Dorado on Eighth Avenue a
square two story brick building is the gambling center of the cigar
making community. Cigar makers are gamblers by nature and the El
Dorado offers card games, craps and roulette wheels, and the favorite of Cuban gambling *bolita* along with a busy bar even now during
Prohibition. The cigar workers and their families are out every night
after work on Seventh Avenue dressed up and spending money in
the clothing stores, restaurants, and bars. English is rarely heard on
Seventh Avenue except in the stores. Spanish and some Italian are
the languages of the cigar workers. Cars and trolleys go back and
forth on the busy congested street while happy people move to the
Cuban music that's heard all over Seventh Avenue. It's as if Ybor
City was actually a part of Cuba that just happens to be in Florida."

"My father must have impressed Mr. Ybor because Ybor sent a telegram to him
in Havana offering a job in Tampa. We moved to Florida a few weeks later after
my father gave notice to the Plant Steamship Lines. He became the shipping
manager of the Ybor cigar empire that employed three hundred cigar rollers.
He dealt with the railroads, the Post Office and the first trucking firms in West
Florida. He devised water proof packing for the regular ocean going shipments of
hundreds of wood boxes of Clear Havana cigars to Hunters & Frankau London's
oldest cigar retailer and distributor.   At times he also accompanied Mr. Ybor

when he met with Tampa's political and government people. Because my father had worked for Henry B. Plant he had status in the city Plant helped create."

"Growing up here we all learned about the history of Ybor City because it surrounded us all the time," Flynn reminisced. "By 1920 about 12,000 men and women worked in the factories of Ybor City producing clear Havana cigars. Cigar use was so popular in North America that when the cigar workers periodically went on strike for higher wages, which at times became violent, it became a national issue, and cigar prices climbed and people hoarded their supply of Cuban smokes."

"Let me explain," Flynn said, "Clear Havana premium cigars are made primarily in Tampa, and contain tobacco grown only in Cuba, which is acknowledged to be the world's best leaf and filler. Each hand rolled cigar features a double layer of leaf tobacco that holds the cigar firmly together. The wrapper leaf has to be perfect; free of blotches and imperfections. Its color uniform and carefully matched with the filler tobacco blend selected for ease of draw and coolness of smoke. Cigar making is an art, and a means of individual expression."

Alongside the cigar factories were Ybor City companies that produced the cedar cigar boxes, and designers and printers making the distinctive graphics pasted onto the inside of the cover of every cigar box. However, the economic gains didn't make up for the disturbances experienced by Tampa's old line residents brought about by the immigrant cigar factory workers.

Reported in the *Tampa Morning Tribune* January 12, 1906 "Even the most orthodox Christians of the people of Tampa draw the line. Ybor City's Cubans seem to have very little decency in their composition. You can at any time of the day if you promenade along the streets of Ybor City see children from all ages one to seven years playing around in garb which nature gave them with a little additional covering of dirt or cheesecloth, generally the former. Tampa people recognize the fact that the ideas and habits of the Cuban population in our midst are quite different from theirs. But at the same time there is a limit to even these things, and on Sunday circuses staged outdoors by Cuban performers, musicians and public cooking of food disrupt the Sabbath by the attendance of large crowds of cigar worker's families."

Reported by Ramon Valdespino editor of *La Traduccion* May 7, 1923. (Translated from the Spanish)"The most popular and respected people in Ybor City are the lectors who stood in the center or sat on a raised platform in every cigar factory and read to the cigar rollers while they worked with razor sharp chaveta knives cutting the rolled tobacco. The lectors speak Spanish, English and sometimes Italian. They read newspapers and novels in Spanish, and Shakespeare and other classics in English. Their booming cultured voices provide a rhythm that helps the rollers produce perfect cigars all day long, and also helps to prevent boredom. Lectors auditioned for their jobs much like stage actors and opera tenors because they are paid by the workers in the same manner that began in the last century in Cuba. Lectors often wore white suits, wide-brimmed hats and have a grand almost imperial presence. They are all men with the exception of one woman lector who is Puerto Rican and dresses like a man. The only black Cuban lector is Facundo Accion; the community's leading intellectual. The lectors are celebrities, and are acknowledged by slight bowing of heads by the cigar workers, and offers of free drinks everywhere in Ybor City. To show approval of the lector's performance in the factories; a cigar roller tapped the base of his chaveta on the work bench. The lectors reinforce Ybor City's uniquely Cuban culture and provide an intellectual atmosphere missing in every other kind of factory anywhere else in America. Also because they have listened so long, and so intently to the lectors some of the cigar rollers can recite passages from Shakespeare and Miguel Cervantes without having an ability themselves to read or write."

Flynn had translated the articles from the Spanish language newspapers. His Spanish was as good as any of the Cubans or even the Spaniards in Ybor City. He was a keen observer of the tumult surrounding the cigar factories and thought about collecting more articles and publishing a book in order to record the unique dynamic combination of Cuban and European cultures. He noted, "The fight for Cuban independence from Spain had been a daily issue in Ybor City prior to 1898, and Cubans traveled back and forth from Tampa to Havana at the slightest excuse on Plant System steamers often bringing money collected from the cigar rollers to finance the Cuba Libre movement. The end of the Spanish-American War and Spain's defeat provided an opportunity for Cubans to return home, but most stayed in Florida after raising families and establishing roots through jobs, businesses, and membership in the social clubs that were a central part of their lives."

Chapter 2

The Queen of Ybor City (1934)

The proprietress of Ybor City's Excelsior Hotel, Consuelo Middleton Davis, arrived in Tampa in 1932 after being widowed and then fleeing Charles City, Virginia because the pain of losing her beloved husband from a hunting accident she said was too much to bear. Consuelo was a self-described grand dame of Charles City due to her family the Middleton's, prominent cotton brokers out of Savannah, Georgia. And most importantly, her husband Arlington Davis was a grandson of Jefferson Davis of Tennessee, president of *the Confederate States of America.*

Consuelo cut a striking figure throughout Ybor City a place notoriously open to different kinds of people where a mixture of ethnic groups, races, and gender benders lived in happy confusion fueled by steady work in the cigar factories, and locally distilled Cuban sugar cane and pineapple alcohol called *mamba* that never stopped flowing even during Prohibition.

Consuelo covered her beautiful 5'-7" height in silk sheaths that reached barely to her knees. She avoided the flapper style of fringes and bows decorating the short silk dresses, but the sheaths were daring enough to make men anticipate with pleasure her arrival anywhere in Ybor City. It was rumored that Consuelo didn't wear under garments and that her shapely breasts moved freely beneath the silk covering them. Occasionally one was rewarded with a glimpse of her nipples shaped like pencil erasers pushing against fabric. She enjoyed the attention from the men walking and talking in groups along Seventh Avenue the busy shopping street. Storekeepers leaned out of their open store fronts to catch a glimpse of one of Ybor City's main attractions.

Seeing Consuelo from either her front or her back was equally pleasurable. Walking along Seventh Avenue in Ybor City, Consuelo greeted all whom she approached, and was completely aware as she smiled to herself of being admired as she walked away. The sheath dresses exactly fit to draw attention to her perfectly dimensioned rear perched on top of long elegant legs. Her hair was bobbed, and black as coal and combed to one side like the women in the movies who were threats to the blond sweethearts trying to hold on to their men.

As beautiful as her body and demeanor were, Consuelo's most striking feature was her flawless face containing classic features and large all-knowing green eyes. However, Consuelo's most discussed feature in the homes, bars, and clubs of Ybor City was her smooth skin and its unusual light olive-caramel color. Some said that Consuelo claimed her ancestors were French Corsicans inter-married with Sicilian Moors that had escaped the Spanish Inquisition centuries ago. Others maintained that Consuelo's great grandmother was the Indian prin-cess Sacagawea who guided the Lewis and Clark Expedition a century earlier. While those who thought they knew the inside story insisted that Consuelo was the illegitimate daughter of President Warren Harding and Nan Britton a beau-tiful mixed race woman from Marion, Ohio.

Consuelo loved all of the rumors and enjoyed being an object of curiosity among the Ybor City inhabitants since she had first taken up residence. Her local fame had spread and brought important visitors to the Excelsior Hotel, and her spoken Spanish had improved to the point that she could be mistaken for a Cuban. She was wealthy and generous and had become powerful in the cigar making city to the point that no one any longer wondered about who she was and where she had come from on her way to Ybor City.

That was all to the good because Consuelo Middleton Davis had never been in Charles City, and wasn't a widow of a man called Arlington Davis. She had always thought *Consuelo*, from the George Sand novel, was an exotic first name so she adopted it. Middleton was the brand of a powered preparation containing a pinch of opium that helped relieve menstrual cramps when mixed with a bit of whiskey. And Davis, Consuelo couldn't even remember exactly when she first saw it on a Civil War statue in a park somewhere in the south. It had been a while since she traveled from Cooperstown, New York to Florida, encouraged by the wealthy older gentleman who admired her quick brain, her straight forward manner and, especially, her sensuous face and body, which delighted him during their highly sexual affair that had bloomed during their three years together. With his support and generosity, and the influence of some other powerful people Consuelo became the queen of Ybor City.

Completing the errands that had taken most of the morning including leaving a generous cash contribution at the L'Unione Italiana to the Sacco & Vanzetti Fund for the defense of Italians wrongly accused of crimes, a meeting with the bank manager to learn about the new Federal Deposit Insurance Corporation, and a stop at the Segundo bakery to buy freshly baked Cuban bread, Consuelo returned to the Excelsior Hotel located on Ybor City's busiest street; Seventh Avenue, before the noon sun became unbearable. It was the end of July, the hottest month in the Tampa Bay area. Consuelo had thought about closing the hotel for the summer months as there really wasn't a sufficient number of guests to warrant staying open during the days the humidity was soaring, and the nation's economy was failing. But she felt a loyalty to the hotel's staff members who were Cubans except for Harvey Sparks the front desk manager. He was the all-around major-domo and kept the place running smoothly as he had done for the previous owner. The hotel was a successful business because it catered to Cuban businessmen visiting Ybor City to make arrangements for tobacco importing, cigar wholesalers from New York, Chicago and Boston, and passengers making ready to embark on ships leaving from the Port of Tampa. This morning Harvey was tending the brass and black walnut reception desk, and was agitated not unusual for him, and relieved to see Consuelo.

"Thanks be to whatever is holy Miss Consuelo," Harvey sputtered. "You cannot guess what is going on here."

Consuelo who rarely showed her emotions was curious but not alarmed smiled at Harvey and said. "All right I'm listening."

"Not five minutes ago I was talking on the telephone to Mr. Henry Plant. He wants to speak with you. Can you imagine Henry Plant calling here? I asked if I could be of service, but just nice as could be he said he would like you to telephone him at your convenience, if you have the opportunity, and then he thanked me for my courtesy and gave me his phone number for you."

Consuelo placed the call from her small office that was built between the hotel and her cottage. It was actually a hallway with a window joining the buildings for Consuelo's convenience, but a desk and file were moved in and an office was created. The office had two undulating Westinghouse fans to keep air moving, which provided an illusion of cooling. Consuelo had learned about Willis Carrier's air conditioning, and had written to the inventor offering to be his first customer in Florida, but hadn't heard back from him. The Tampa telephone operator successfully contacted Henry Plant who cheerfully greeted Consuelo. "CC are you well? What has the dismal state of the nation done to you?"

Consuelo replied, "Oh Hank it's so good to hear your voice. You remind me of the times at the Tampa Bay Hotel. I'm well and as happy as I can be without Daniel in my life, and I try not to think about what's going on in the rest of the country."

"Well we must hope this man Roosevelt will live up to his promises; even though he's a Democrat. Hoover and the Christian temperance people put us into this situation. I believe it's the end of the Republican Party. They will never have another president in office. Good riddance."

"Hank are you at the Bellevue?"

"Yes, that's the reason I called. Amy and I have had the pleasure of hosting George Gershwin, the wonderful composer from New York, at the hotel. We had attended the New York opening of his "Strike Up the Band" and later saw "Of Thee I Sing," which was a bit shocking, but we did enjoy the show. Gershwin and I have a mutual friend, the banker Charles Rosenthal, a Ladenburg Thalmann partner who goes to all of Gershwin's first nights. Hmm I'm getting off track. I telephoned because George Gershwin wants to learn something about Ybor City and the cigar rollers, the lectors, the mish mash of immigrant life there, and I suggested he stay for a while at your lovely hotel if of course, you can accommodate him."

"I'd be honored for him to stay here especially after his being with you at the Belleview. Daniel and I saw two Gershwin shows on Broadway. "Lady Be

Good" and "Girl Crazy." We also met Ruby Keeler. Mr. Gershwin is most welcome. We'll try to accommodate him."

Plant was pleased. "Excellent, thank you. My car will deliver Mr. Gershwin prior to noon tomorrow. He is not an early riser."

"Goodbye Hank. I hope to see you again sometime."

"That would be lovely. Thank you and goodbye."

Consuelo sat back in her leather executive chair that Harvey Sparks had somehow acquired. The possibility of seeing Hank Plant again was unlikely, but Consuelo felt good that he had called. Plant was partly responsible for Consuelo's acquisition of the Excelsior and the adjourning cottage, and he had urged America's most famous music man to be a guest of her hotel. Harvey's nerves would be wrecked.

Chapter 3

Folly Island, South Carolina - June 1934

The two lane road wound from Charleston to the Ashley River ferry. Then across Wappoo Creek through James Island, and spilled out onto Folly Island, George Gershwin's destination in June of 1934. The composer had worked for over a year on what would become the great American opera, "Porgy and Bess." Gershwin, born in Brooklyn, New York into a Russian immigrant Jewish family, had no knowledge at all about the lives of penniless Negros residing in the Deep South and speaking the Gullah dialect. However, he had read and loved the 1925 bestselling novel "Porgy" by the distinguished southern writer DuBose Heyward, and had contacted him. Gershwin was intrigued by Heyward's dignified characterization of the Gullah people. Heyward, a son of Southern white plantation aristocracy nevertheless treated his fictional Negro characters with intelligence and respect for their difficult lives; a rarity in Depression-era America.

Heyward's ancestor had been a signer of the Declaration of Independence representing South Carolina, but the family had lost their land and possessions during the Civil War. DuBose and Dorothy Heyward had struggled financially ever since DuBose had given up a successful insurance business in Charleston to devote himself full time to writing. The Heywards had met at the MacDowell Colony in Peterborough, New Hampshire and married after spending their third summer together. MacDowell was a summer residential retreat that invited America's outstanding writers and visual artists to work, think, and reside in their own cottages without distractions, and without any cost to them. Meals were offered in a dining hall, but trays of food would be brought to the cottages for those who wanted seclusion. Dorothy was a successful playwright with three Broadway productions to her credit. She had studied writing at Columbia University and Harvard, and among her friends were the writers Eugene O'Neill and Thomas Wolfe.

Dorothy had written a play called "Catfish Row" based on her husband's book "Porgy," which had been successfully produced on Broadway by the Theater Guild in 1927, but the Guild had changed the production's name back to "Porgy." Heyward had personally coached the New York based actors in the Gullah patois. Gershwin after reading "Porgy," became obsessed with the story and wanted nothing more than to make it into the opera he believed America was ready to embrace. It took five more years for the work on the opera to begin, and two more to finally complete the score by working at Heyward's beach house in South Carolina for almost two months without interruptions.

Gershwin learned from Heyward that the Gullah Negros were descended from slaves especially recruited in Sierra Leone, the rice coast of the African continent. A higher price was paid for slaves captured from the region because they were skilled rice farmers, and were sought after by the South Carolina and Georgia rice growers. Heyward was charmed by the language spoken by the Gullah people a combination of English, and African Krio that produced a Creole dialect that was smooth and musical to one's ear. Heyward skillfully incorporated the dialect into "Porgy," which had attracted Gershwin since he could envision a grand stage production along with a full orchestra playing his music, as he read Heyward's story. Now he was on his way to work with Heyward at his Folly Island summer home to complete "Porgy and Bess," which had been stalled several times over several years due to Gershwin's many commitments to compose music for shows, reviews and motion pictures that had produced the delays, which frustrated Heyward.

Heyward had been pursued by Al Jolson, the song and dance man known for his racist performances in blackface, who wanted to produce and act in a movie based on "Porgy." Not wanting to cheapen or dilute "Porgy's" message, Heyward rebuffed Jolson's agent who kept raising the amount Jolson was willing to pay for the book's rights, while he waited patiently for Gershwin to begin work on their opera. Heyward would only work with George Gershwin. He knew Gershwin was the best composer of their time, and since hearing Gershwin's *Rhapsody in Blue,* there wasn't anyone else he could consider for a collaboration. Dorothy and DuBose were adamant that the opera would cast only Negro performers, and no whites in black face as was the usual practice.

Heyward hadn't been idle during the years waiting for Gershwin to commit his talent to "Porgy and Bess." He had worked in California collaborating on the writing of two outstanding screen plays in Hollywood for the classic films "The Emperor Jones" and Pearl S. Buck's brilliant story of emerging China, "The Good Earth," but was demoralized by the experience. Heyward was reserved, a poet slight in stature, he found the newly rich and powerful people running Hollywood's motion picture studios brash and even threatening. Dorothy Heyward remained angry about Gershwin's long delay in beginning the opera based on Heyward's book. She was unhappy that Gershwin was coming to Folly Beach because she believed that he would crush her husband by his presence as Irving Thalberg had done in Hollywood.

Gershwin and his cousin Henry Botkin had left New York in early June after a grand sendoff at Pennsylvania Station, catered by Longchamps Restaurants, where they boarded the Atlantic Coast Line train Havana Special that ran along the east coast with a stop in North Charleston. Botkin was a painter and wanted to make paintings of Gullah people going about their lives on the small barrier islands. They were met in Charleston by Paul Mueller who had driven from New York City in Gershwin's Buick bringing two sets of luggage, George's golf clubs and Botkin's easel, paint box and a dozen canvases. "Paul," exclaimed Gershwin, "I'm so pleased to see you. When did you arrive here, and have you seen Heyward?"

Mueller, Gershwin's Negro valet, and the organized force that allowed him to accomplish as much as he did every day was devoted to Gershwin. "I got here the day before yesterday and went straight out to Folly. I stayed at the Heyward's help's house. I got your place all ready."

"You'll move in with Henry and me. How's our place," asked Gershwin suspiciously? He lived in an elegant Riverside Drive penthouse apartment that looked over the Hudson River that was decorated with beautiful contemporary furnishings and his collection of fine artwork. "And Paul, see if you can find a golf club that will allow me to play as a paying guest from time to time, one with members that have seen a Jew before."

"Yes, sir. They'll love me showing up at the front door. I'll ask around. The cottage Mr. Heyward got for you is pretty nice. It's right on the beach. Just don't drink the tap water. It feels oily and probably tastes like that. I got jugs of drinking water in the car. Everyone on Folly brings water from Charleston. Imagine that buying water in jugs?"

They spent most of June and July on Folly Beach. Their cottage was a single story raised cedar shake house with big windows that allowed the Atlantic winds to circulate below and through the structure. When the breeze from the ocean abated, however, mosquitos and sand flies were everywhere. Gershwin, who almost always wore a suit, starched shirt and tie except on the golf course, dressed casually and even walked barefoot on the sand beach that stretched between the cottage and Heyward's large two story house. Cousin Harry wore bathing suits all day even when sketching and painting on nearby James Island with its Gullah Negro population.

When the members of Charleston's aristocracy asked Gershwin at the dinner parties he, Botkin and the Heywards attended regularly, what he was doing on Folly Island he answered rather formally, "Porgy & Bess' is my serious attempt to put into operatic form a purely American theme. It will be infinitely more sophisticated than anything done before." When a Charleston hostess asked, "Why a Negro theme?" Gershwin's answer didn't endear him to anyone that evening, "Because the white man is more unemotional, dull and drab." Gershwin believed what he said. He was able to see beyond a person's skin color. His respect for and connection with anyone was based on their passion, intelligence, and talent. Yet somehow he understood the plight of Negros living in a place they hadn't chosen and were made to feel unwelcome to the point that they lived in fear. Upon reading Heyward's novel "Porgy" Gershwin, without any hesitation understood the people of Catfish Row even though his

knowledge of Negro life was limited to the actors, musicians, and writers living in New York's Harlem section beyond 96th Street in Manhattan. On occasion, Gershwin had gone uptown to sample the famous Harlem nightlife. He frankly enjoyed the crowded clubs and the great jazz musicians playing their brand of music almost to dawn. He was introduced to the beautiful Negro actress Ethel Moses by Emil Mosbacher Gershwin's close friend a bond broker, and an investor in her shows and movies. Known as "The Bronze Venus" Ethel Moses with Mosbacher and Gershwin arrived at the Savoy Ballroom on Lenox Avenue and 140th Street in Harlem late one Thursday evening.

The Savoy Ballroom was a giant place devoted to couples dancing to the great big band music of Chuck Webb, Count Basie and Tommy Dorsey. The Savoy was a famous racially integrated ballroom that was half-owned by Moe Gales a distant cousin of Gershwin. After dancing the new Lindy Hop for most of the night to the beat of the hit song, *Stompin' at the Savoy,* Mosbacher left to get some sleep before the bond market opened the next day. Gershwin and Ethel Moses, mostly unnoticed in the crowded ballroom that held two thousand dancing couples, decided they were hungry.

They left the Savoy and drifted for a block to the Radium Club that began serving breakfast at 4 am. After their orders of ham and eggs sunny side up with hash brown potatoes, fried okra, pancakes with maple syrup, and raisin bread toast along with hot coffee arrived and covered their table with plates, Moses and Gershwin couldn't stop laughing at the amount of food in front of them. Later, as the sun was coming up while walking Moses to Striver's Row, Harlem's most elegant address, she took Gershwin's arm and held on until they reached her home. A brief kiss ended their evening together.

Heyward and Gershwin worked every day on Folly Island in the cottage's living room using a rented Cunningham upright piano. Like most composers and lyricists, Gershwin and Heyward absorbed their surroundings. They used the sights, scents, and sounds from their lives, and transferred those memories into words and music. They also drew inspiration from each other. As they brought their own history to "Porgy and Bess," the memories that made up each man's time were drawn upon and shared in an open vulnerable manner. By listening to Gershwin's playing his music, Heyward heard notes woven into

a mosaic of sound and form that crossed all musical genres. The musical phrases turned into compositions and drew out Heyward's lyrics that beautifully married to the song. On Folly Island, during what was to become a famous summer, they wrote the lyrics and melodies for much of the production including; *Summertime, A Woman is a Sometime Thing, Honey Man, Oh Little Stars, My Man's Gone Now, Leavin Fo' the Promis Lan, I Got Plenty of Nuttin, Bes You Is My Woman Now,* and *I love You Porgy.* They worked slowly and carefully respecting each other's creativity. When Gershwin played their music on the piano people gathered around outside the cottage keeping time.

Gershwin, used to the comfortable living and exciting times in Manhattan, was sometimes frustrated by Folly Island life. Exclaiming to Heyward one day when he wanted to talk with Ira his brother and collaborator, "Imagine, there's not one phone on the whole island. How do you stand it?" Heyward just smiled and reminded Gershwin that they were going to Charleston that evening for a dinner at one of Charleston's aristocratic homes and that a telephone would certainly be available. Gershwin enjoyed the visits to Charleston for sightseeing, shopping and dinners in the fine houses along the Battery and Meeting Street. He would play the latest Heyward-Gershwin music on the piano and was always the center of attention. He and Harry were exotics from New York, artists, cultured Jews, and of course Gershwin was the nation's most famous music man. Brother Ira did visit once but stayed in Charleston at the charming old South style Mills House as did Gershwin's friend Kay Swift on one occasion.

As much as could be accomplished that summer on Folly Island was done by Heyward and Gershwin. Gershwin planned to return to New York and complete the score so that rehearsals could be scheduled in the early months of 1935. However, at some point, he decided to take a detour to Tampa, Florida to meet with Henry Plant at the urging of his friend and banker Charles Rosenthal. Gershwin was seeking an "angel" to invest in "Porgy and Bess" so that he would not have to worry about the production's financing. The Theater Guild's directors Lawrence Langer and Theresa Helburn had some concerns about the tremendous costs associated with the rental of Broadway's Alvin Theater for rehearsals for at least six months prior to opening night. Also, the salaries of the large cast, orchestra, stage hands, set designers, lighting crew, and carpenters were also issues for the producers. The Theater Guild was Broadway's most distinguished producer of plays and musicals, and had been seeking a purely American themed production at the very moment the original "Porgy" manuscript arrived in 1926. The new musical version by Gershwin and Heyward eight years later would cost many times more. If Henry Plant would underwrite the production Gershwin would have one thing less to worry about as he finished the staging and orchestrating.

Chapter 4

The Belleview - Biltmore Hotel 1934

On the last Monday of July Gershwin said goodbye to the Heywards. He was grateful for their hospitality and for the smooth collaboration by DuBose. Gershwin had worked with several able collaborators including his brother Ira but felt the experience of working with Heyward exhilarating. Dorothy, on the other hand, still believed that Gershwin's love of being the center of attention would overshadow DuBose's contributions to the project. She regularly warned her husband about Gershwin's need for the limelight. However, the summer passed without any displays of artistic jealousies or creative temperaments flaring.

At the North Charleston railroad station, he waited for train No. 95 the Pinellas Special that headed in the direction of Tampa and terminated on a private rail siding close to the Bellevue-Biltmore Hotel in Belleair, Florida. The elegant resort hotel built on Old Clearwater Bay off of the Gulf of Mexico in 1895 by Henry B. Plant was the largest wood structure in the world and the headquarters of the Plant family's Florida Empire.

Cousin Harry waited for his train to New York City. He was tanned and pleased with the art he had made on Folly. Paul Mueller had packed the Buick with their luggage, the paintings, and the acquisitions Gershwin had gathered in Charleston. He enjoyed shopping for clothing and decorative objects and had found both in abundance. "Paul be careful," Gershwin warned. "Drive slowly, but get out of the South as soon as you can." Mueller was stopping in Baltimore to visit family on his way to New York, but he understood Gershwin's warning.

"Don't worry about me, Boss. Are you sure you don't want me to drive you to Tampa?"

"No, Heyward says the roads to Florida are terrible. Thankfully you take US 1 from here to home. Be especially cautious in the small towns, and when you find a place to eat; have them make up sandwiches so you don't get hungry." They were aware of the "whites only" policy Mueller would encounter from Charleston to Baltimore. Gershwin's train was the first to arrive. He shook hands with both men and boarded No. 95 for the overnight trip to Florida's west coast.

He arrived at the Bellevue after stops in Thomasville, Georgia, Tallahassee, Dunnellon, Florida, and Tampa where he boarded the waiting Pinellas Special train for the last leg of the trip. Gershwin was familiar with fine surroundings. He had stayed at the grand hotels in Hollywood, Havana, the Bahamas, Europe and Palm Beach, but he wasn't prepared for the grandeur of the Bellevue. He stood still taking in the immense white wood structure that sat gracefully on sloping land above a beautiful bay. As big as the hotel was, the building itself covered twenty acres, it was perfectly proportioned, and fit comfortably into its location. The hotel's four hundred suites had annually housed Thomas Edison and Henry Ford among the many famous people from the time it opened in 1897 through the Roaring 20s. Today, however, there wasn't any activity around the hotel as it was summer and practically no one traveled to Florida during the hot months. Hotels were closed to guests and maintenance was done on the buildings, furniture repaired, carpeting replaced and swimming pools emptied and painted. Even the golf course was unused. Florida resort living meant long wintertime stays with trunks shipped ahead by Railway Express from families in New England and the Midwest accompanied by servants, formal dining and tennis whites. The wealthiest came to the Bellevue and the Tampa Bay Hotel by private railroad cars.

Two Negro men wearing green uniforms with the Bellevue Hotel name stitched on their jackets appeared at the train stop and took charge of Gershwin's luggage. They directed him to the main entrance and disappeared into a side door. Before reaching the steps of the portico the front door burst open and a tall man in tennis clothing hurried through to greet him. "Mr. Gershwin. I'm so sorry. I was playing tennis and the time got away from me, and I was doing well against our new young pro, Don Budge who I believe you'll be hearing about. I usually don't greet a distinguished guest in this manner," he said referring to his white trousers, shirt, and tennis shoes.

Gershwin smiled, "Mr. Plant I presume. I'm George Gershwin."

"Yes, of course you are. Come, please have a drink to cool off. Mrs. Plant, Amy, will join us for lunch." They entered the massive long hotel lobby and strolled to a bright palm filled dining room with windows open onto the bay, which allowed a steady breeze and kept the room comfortable. Over the elaborately carved bar were colored glass windows that Gershwin recognized as the work of Louis Comfort Tiffany.

Amy Warren Plant an attractive woman, who Gershwin guessed was about thirty-five with her husband a few years older, entered the tropical themed room. Plant made the introductions while informing Gershwin that they had attended the opening nights of two of his Broadway shows and loved his music. "Somehow Charles Rosenthal is able to secure tickets for your productions that even the ticket scalpers can't supply." Gershwin smiled because Rosenthal asked him for the show tickets for the Plants and other prized clients. The Plants actually called Manhattan home and lived in the house built by Hank Plant's father Morton on Fifth Avenue at 86th Street. Gershwin, who prized his Riverside Drive penthouse understood that the Plants were part of a strata of New York society than he could never hope to enter even with his great professional and financial success; as theirs was achieved only through birth.

Amy engaged Gershwin immediately. "Mr. Gershwin, I majored in musicology at Sweet Briar in Virginia and, although I only play a little piano now, I had a wonderful education in music.

"Hank interrupted, "Nonsense Amy, you're fine at the piano especially when you sing; *Someone to Watch Over Me*. I'd wager Mr. Gershwin would enjoy hearing you."

Amy's indulgent wife smile said enough, but she went on to say, "Hank, I'm sure Mr. Gershwin does not want to listen to an amateur sing Gertrude

Lawrence's song. It was so emotional and she sounded so lonely I cried when she sang it." Gertrude Lawrence had skillfully handled the Gershwin classic in the musical "Oh Kay" perfecting the downward chord changes that parallel the melody in the song's verses to the soaring melody in the bridge. It was one of Gershwin's best use of melody in a popular ballad, which evoked longing for love.

After two rounds of sidecar cocktails, shrimp salads with deep fried hush-puppies, and creamy vanilla ice cream laced with rum soaked pineapple and coconut shavings for dessert, they agreed to meet for dinner at 8 in the private dining room. Then Gershwin followed the assistant manager who arrived at their table to say that the hotel's best suite was ready, and did Mr. Gershwin desire to have his luggage unpacked?

Hank Plant was the third generation of Plants benefiting from the fortune amassed by his grandfather Henry B. Plant after the Civil War. The first Henry B. Plant was responsible for building the *Plant System* of rail lines throughout the southern states that linked up to his steamships that sailed between Tampa and Cuba. His Southern Express Company was the leading transfer company in the states south of the Mason-Dixon Line. He also built two of the largest hotels in the world; the Tampa Bay and the Bellevue-Biltmore, and six additional resort hotels that catered to wealthy Victorian era travelers. The first Henry B. Plant was responsible for financing and building the Port of Tampa, which made the city a major shipper and receiver of goods along with Savannah and Charleston.

Morton Freeman Plant, Hank's father, amassed an even greater fortune by investing in street car and subway lines in Connecticut and New York including the city's first subway system, the Interboro Rapid Transit Company. He also built and operated the illustrious four hundred room Griswold Hotel in Groton, Connecticut, and was responsible for the downtown development of Groton and New London, Connecticut. He was a founder of Connecticut College for Women, and part owner of the Philadelphia National League baseball club, and an investor in several banks in New York City and Florida. He loved sailing and was a commodore of the New York Yacht Club, and a charter member of the Ardsley Country Club in Westchester for his golf and tennis.

In 1913 Hank was eighteen when his mother Nellie died from pleurisy. The family had lived on Fifth Avenue's "Millionaire's Row" since 1902 among the

Vanderbilts, Astors, the Payne Whitneys, Sinclairs, H.O. Havemeyer, Henry Clay Frick and the Livingston Beekmans. A collection of the nation's wealthiest families. The Plant mansion on 52nd Street was an outstanding example of Italian Renaissance design built on a corner parcel sold to Morton Plant by William Vanderbilt. It was a beautiful building among other beautiful buildings that rivaled the mansions along the Cliffwalk in Newport, Rhode Island.

Later, during dinner in the Plant's private dining room, Gershwin, who was usually candid, asked Hank Plant why he and Amy were in Florida at the summer's hottest time. "We're here to transfer ownership of the Tampa Bay Hotel, which we closed after last season, to the City of Tampa. The era of the giant resort hotel with its staff numbering in the hundreds can no longer be maintained. This place is another example of that. We employ twenty gardeners for example. They will stay on because I'm committed to keeping the hotel's appearance the way my father and grandfather had kept it. The nation has had a depression since 1928, and there's no sign of recovery." Plant's voice became lower as he spoke, and a sadness over took him. "It's similar to the time father sold our home on 52nd Street because the Vanderbilts said that Fifth Avenue had become commercial. It was 1917 before the war ended. Father actually traded our home to Pierre Cartier the French jeweler for a string of matched pearls for my step mother Mae Caldwell."

Gershwin was astonished by Plant's admission. "I've been in the Cartier building. That was your home? I had assumed it was built for Cartier." Gershwin was quite curious as to why Morton Plant had agreed to trade his home for jewelry, but instead asked, "Are you staying on here?"

"We'll leave for home in a few more days. There's a lot to do this year with maintaining the hotel. Wood buildings don't do very well in this climate. I'll sign the contract with Tampa tomorrow, and another major problem will disappear. I understand the city plans a university on that site incorporating the hotel and reserving one wing for the Henry B. Plant Museum. I believe Grandfather would like that." He hesitated and then continued. "My father was mesmerized by Mae. They married less than a year after mother died, and Mae had been divorced only a month. His wedding gift to Mae was $8 million, and a new house on Fifth Avenue at 86th Street. Unfortunately, father died the following year. I have suspected that Mae was somehow responsible." Plant looked directly at Gershwin for the first time since he began speaking about his father. "Forgive me, but you're easy to talk to. I usually don't share the family's history, and I hope it won't be put to music for a new show."

Hank Plant appeared weary as if the responsibilities on his shoulders were more than he could bear. He alone controlled all of the Plant family's myriad interests. He didn't have siblings or cousins to share any of the burden he felt in continuing what his grandfather and father had built during times that rewarded wild speculation. Plant enterprises were losing money due to the national financial crisis left by Herbert Hoover. Prohibition had ended, which might help the overall economy, but the remaining Plant hotels in Florida had to be closed along with the Griswold in Connecticut. Plant Line railroads should be merged with other rail lines for efficiency and Plant Steamships, which were still profitable should have been replaced some years ago with newer more efficient vessels.

Gershwin smiled and assured Plant that his secrets were safe. Amy Plant pretended she hadn't heard Hank accuse his stepmother of involvement in her husband's death. Even though Mae had married twice after being widowed and recently was widowed again, Amy didn't want to think that Mae, whom Amy believed was entertaining, was a murderer.

Gershwin had eaten sparingly. He rose and took off his suit jacket, loosened the silk tie and strolled to the Steinway piano across the room. He unbuttoned his shirt cuffs folded back the material and sat on the bench staring at the ivory keys for just a moment. He began playing the beautiful sweeping Gershwin style overture from "Porgy and Bess," heard for the first time by anyone outside of the small group living around the rented cottage on Folly Island. For a few minutes he seemed lost in the music, and in love with the music. When finished he stood. Amy and Hank applauded lightly, and Gershwin said, "Allow me to tell the story of 'Porgy and Bess.'"

Chapter 5

Cooperstown, NY 1929

The little village at the head of Lake Otsego in New York's "Leatherstocking District" was the home of the aristocratic Clark family the co-owners of the Singer Sewing Machine Company one of the nation's largest industrial companies that produced home sewing machines used by every woman in America who sewed or mended clothing, linens, curtains and furniture covers, as well as the large industrial sewing machines found in thousands of factories in America and Europe.

Clarks had lived in Cooperstown since the time of the Civil War building Fernleigh a stone mansion as their first estate in 1869. The second generation of Clarks living in Cooperstown purchased more than 10,000 acres of property in and around the town. Three parts of the Clark family established 'gentleman's farms" called Red Creek Farm, Iroquois Farm, and Fenimore Farm each producing specialty fruit or vegetables in fields and groves surrounding elegant stone residences.

In 1898 the family commissioned the architect Ernst Flagg to build a grand building on Cooperstown's Main Street for the YMCA. Flagg had designed the first Singer Building in New York City for the Clarks, and later in 1908 the new Singer Building on Broadway at Liberty Street in Manhattan. The new Singer company structure was an iconic Beaux-Arts architectural triumph towering sixty-four floors over the city. For a single year, it was the world's tallest building. More decorative than practical, its twenty-five story tower distinguished the building from all others in the city, but its limited floor space was inadequate for business offices.

The Clark family's generous support of Cooperstown's institutions enabled a network of health and cultural organizations develop and prosper in the small gem of a sophisticated country town. The leading beneficiary of the Clark beneficence was the Mary Imogene Bassett Hospital named for a young doctor who settled in Cooperstown in 1893 to practice medicine, had a successful career, and was a beloved physician. A patient, Edward Severin Clark, offered to finance the building of a hospital with Dr. Bassett as Chief-of-Staff. The hospital opened in 1922, but wasn't able to sustain itself after Dr. Bassett's untimely death, and closed in 1925. Strangely, an alliance between Dr. Henry Cooper a descendant of author James Fennimore Cooper, and Stephen C. Clark both of whom happened to be living in New York City at the time resulted in the re-opening of Bassett Hospital in 1929.

The hospital was quickly re-established and admissions increased due to the new medical staff's fine reputation, many of whom were graduates of Columbia University's College of Physicians and Surgeons, which attracted patients from as far as one hundred miles away. Advertisements in local newspapers listed open positions in the hospital including a Female Ward Auxiliary who kept the ward sanitary and helped the nurses in any manner that might be required. Among those answering the advertisements was a Mulatto woman called Carmella Chase known as CC. She was well known in the town as a competent and trustworthy cook and cleaner. She was born north of Cooperstown twenty-nine years before. CC's mixed heritage: Cayuga tribe, African, and her father, the English travel writer Anthony Dodd Chase who had visited the area while preparing a guide to the Northeastern United States for the German publisher Langenscheidt, produced an especially attractive person with a sharp mind and quick wit. CC was hired by the hospital and assigned to the main female ward that housed sixteen patient beds in a large room with no privacy what so ever. She was provided with three uniforms consisting of dark blue dresses that almost reached the floor, light blue aprons and blue caps. CC was expected to wash and iron one set every night after her shift was over.

One of the great advantages of working in Bassett Hospital was the medical plan given free to employees, an innovation that would not be emulated until decades later.

Working on the ward five days a week, while demanding, was also satisfying for CC who hadn't worked for a large organization before. She easily adjusted to her status on the bottom rung of a hierarchy with physicians on the top, akin to the gods on Mount Olympus. Even nurses stood up whenever a physician entered the room. A physician's order was never questioned and patients weren't allowed to read their own medical charts, which were hung at the foot of the beds. Nurses wore white caps with stripes or shapes that set them apart. The caps represented the different nursing schools affiliated with hospitals in New York and New England that the women had attended.

The Female Ward's day head nurse, there were three one each, shift was the ward's straw boss similar in authority to a master sergeant in the army on whom even the officers depended to keep everything running smoothly. CC's head nurse was Mary Margaret Griffin a graduate of Our Lady of Lourdes Hospital School of Nursing in Binghamton. Nurse Griffin wore her starched cap with a single black stripe proudly and ignored the complaints from the other nurses regarding the comb that steadied the cap on one's head for an entire shift and also tended to pull out tufts of hair when it was removed at day's end. CC only heard from nurse Griffin when she was being given an order to do something that usually involved the cleaning up of bodily fluids. Not even a good morning or a good night was ever addressed to CC by nurse Griffin. Therefore when another nurse informed CC that nurse Griffin asked to see her after the shift ended CC was surprised and worried throughout the last two hours of the day trying to imagine what it was she had done incorrectly.

At 4:00 pm after orienting the evening ward auxiliary CC entered the nursing office located at the south end of the room. A large window allowed the nurses to look at the patients without actually hearing them. CC had rarely entered the office so she was unsure what to do until the head nurse looked up from the chart she was writing in and almost smiled. She asked CC to sit down in the chair at the desk's side. CC complied, and wondered if she was going to be fired, and that was the reason nurse Griffin almost smiled.

"CC I want to ask you something," nurse Griffin began. "The hospital's board of directors will hold their annual weekend meeting soon, and Mr. Clark asked me to suggest someone, a woman, to serve and clean up the food and beverages at the meetings. Someone discrete who can be trusted not to repeat what she might overhear. Would you like to do that?"

CC was shocked that nurse Griffin actually thought she was trustworthy enough to work for the board members, but she recovered enough to ask, "Will I be paid?"

"Of course," Nurse Griffin replied. "The event is two weeks from now in the Clark's new West Hill Manor, and you'll wear a maid's uniform, black with a white apron and black stockings."

The two weeks passed quickly and CC picked up the uniform, bought stylish shoes, black stockings and prepared to meet the rich and powerful people who controlled Bassett Hospital and other important places. Friday, after her shift ended at the hospital, CC walked the two blocks to West Hill, and was admitted by a butler who showed her to a dressing room on the second floor with a bathroom attached. CC undressed and washed carefully. She applied new makeup and put on clean underwear, a black slip and the black stockings held in place by garters. With the black uniform and white apron on her slender frame, CC looked at herself in the room's full length mirror and thought she looked like a French postcard.

In the kitchen, CC received admiring looks from the men bringing in the food and the bootleg liquor for the weekend. She also received instructions from the family butler and began to familiarize herself with the dining room in which the long table was set for twelve diners. At about 7:30 the board members began to arrive at West Hill. CC took coats to the cloakroom and served whiskeys in the library. Promptly at eight Stephen Clark, board chairman, announced that dinner would be served and, much like orderly children, the board members, all men, filed into the dining room. Mr. Clark had introduced himself and Dr. Mackenzie, the hospital's medical director, to CC before they were all seated. Dinner was served by CC and the butler, and after the table was cleared the formal meeting began. The entire weekend was a series of presentations both financial and medical. CC was at each session emptying ashtrays, serving whiskey, coffee, sandwiches, pastries, and hand rolled cigars from Tampa's Ybor City.

Throughout the weekend the men of the board cast approving looks at CC but looked away after she noticed their attention. However, one individual held his stare until CC looked away. He was Daniel Clark a cousin of Stephen who was obviously intrigued by the beautiful light brown woman whose dancer's legs were sheaved in black nylon that he imagined had garters clinging to lovely thighs. On Sunday morning the last session was held after breakfast at the Otesaga Hotel, a 1909 wedding cake type of building, on the lake where the out of town directors stayed. CC dressed in her regular clothing assisted with the meeting's closure. As she was about to leave the hotel; Daniel Clark openly approached her and offered his business card saying, "Please call me at your earliest convenience. I have a proposal for you to consider." He tipped his hat and walked out the door to his waiting chauffeured automobile.

CC stuck the card in a pocket and walked to her small apartment in a house on Chestnut Street near the hospital. She was tired, not from the physical work over the weekend, but from being on stage in effect as the only woman in the company of twelve wealthy men. She hoped that her performance had been well received, but she really knew that it had been a success. CC undressed, put on pajama bottoms and happily got into her bed where she promptly fell asleep for the rest of the day.

The next days were a blur as the Female Ward was full to capacity and CC was kept busy ministering to the patients and the nurses. She worked overtime two evenings because the evening auxiliary was ill. By Friday CC was exhausted and wanted only to go home, bathe and sleep. However, she discovered Daniel Clark's business card in her pocket and decided to call him just to see what he wanted.

After lunch Friday, CC found a phone booth in the lobby and inserted a nickel to make the call, which would change her life. Daniel Clark answered his phone and seemed pleased that it was CC calling. They agreed to meet the next day for a lunch in the Otesaga Hotel dining room, which would make them an unusual couple due to CC's mixed racial background. She thought about that but realized that a Clark family member can do just about anything in Cooperstown and that the Clarks probably own the Otesaga, which she discovered was the case. The hotel, a Federal style brick, and wood building had opened in 1909 on Otesaga Lake, which James Fennimore Cooper referred to as "Glimmerglass" in his novels.

Lunching in a luxurious hotel dining room with an American aristocrat was an experience CC never imagined she would have. However once she was escorted to Daniel Clark's table, and he stood to greet her, and the maître d' hotel held out her chair to seat her, she felt comfortable in the new surroundings. CC had dressed for the occasion in a shimmering silk dress that had been given to her by the wife of one of the doctors at the hospital who appreciated CC's helping out whenever the couple hosted a party for the medical staff. She also wore a cloche hat pulled close to her face. Daniel Clark took in CC's appearance and smiled as he ordered lunch for both of them. He saw this beautiful woman close up for the first time just a week ago and she had been on his mind ever since. Since Prohibition was raging they were not offered cocktails but lunch, consisting of cold sea food salad, hot popovers, and ice tea, was delicious and the conversation between CC and Clark was pleasant and natural. Mostly it consisted of questions asked by Clark on a wide variety of topics ranging from politics to ambitions and CC's two years as a student in the New York State Teacher's College in Albany where her classes in elocution, European and art history, and Western civilization, stirred up her curious mind, and fired up her ambition that set her apart from family and friends. CC answered everything in a polite and intelligent manner, which encouraged Clark to continue the conversation for nearly two hours.

Clark revealed that he was a widower age fifty-eight and in excellent physical condition. He lived alone in a twelve room Greek Revival style house a few streets from the hotel. He was wealthy as was every member of the Clark family and wasn't worried about the terrible state of the national economy because the Clark fortune wasn't invested in the stock market. Instead, he insisted that sewing machines and the thread to make them operate would never go out of fashion because women loved to sew and mend, and it was taught to girls in high school home economics classes throughout the country. That would not change, he insisted and would expand as Singer sewing machines were being sold in twenty-four countries. He also talked nostalgically about his time in Scotland at the million square foot Singer plant in Clydebank which he helped run for two years. At this point, CC asked, "Mr. Clark what is it you want to ask me?"

Clark seemed surprised that he hadn't covered that point. "Miss CC, I am offering you a position in my home as the housekeeper. You will be in charge of the cleaning staff, the cook, laundress, gardeners all who come in daily and the general operation of the house. I will expect you to live in your own section of the house, but spend time with me when I'm home, which is much of the time except during the harshest part of winter." Clark stopped and sipped his ice tea with mint sprigs before continuing. "I observed you throughout last weekend, and admired your calm in charge manner, and frankly I also admired your beauty, which today your silk dress has made even more evident. I want to have a beautiful woman in my life right now, but I won't marry again because I desire a simpler relationship."

"Do you mean you would discharge me if I don't agree to your demands for a sexual relationship," she asked lightly? "Is that one of the housekeeper's duties, not that I mind?" CC looked into Clark's eyes and then smiled. "I think you're a handsome man, Daniel," calling him by his first name. Clark was becoming aroused just from the conversation with the elegant light brown woman, and he realized that she would turn him inside out sexually, and he could not wait for it to begin.

Clark attempted to gain the upper hand in the conversation, but when he looked at the smiling CC he could only think about kissing her slightly open mouth. "You will be paid one hundred and fifty dollars each week, subject to review in two months. You will have no living expenses and my car will take you wherever you need to go. When will you move in?"

CC who was paid thirty-five dollars a week as ward auxiliary said, "I have to give notice at the hospital. I believe two weeks is customary."

"Nonsense." Clark had regained control of the situation and wanted CC to move into his home much sooner than two weeks. "You may give one week's notice, and that's the way it shall be. I want you to be running the house and you and me getting acquainted as soon as possible. In fact let me show you around the house today as the staff doesn't come in on weekends."

They drove away in Clark's black Packard automobile. Charles, Clark's driver didn't even seem to notice CC until Clark introduced her as the new housekeeper. The car drove under the portico at the side of an impressive stucco house in the Mediterranean style. Charles got out and unlocked the house before opening the car doors for CC and Clark. "He lives over the garage in an apartment," explained Clark as Charles drove around to the rear of the house. They entered a sunny solarium filled with rattan furniture, green plants and Persian silk wall murals depicting bright flowers. "This is my favorite room," Clark said smiling at the thought of having an exotic woman in his home.

"It's beautiful, restful," agreed CC. They seemed to drift together now, lips finding lips, tongues discovering tongues until CC broke away to use the bathroom off the main hall. Once on her own she thought about the situation. It was perhaps an opportunity for her, but for what? She wasn't sure, but would find out the extent of Clark's attraction to her. CC slipped out of her brassiere, which she actually didn't need. Her breasts were firm and the perfect size to fit in a man's hand. She stuffed the underwear into her purse along with the cloche and returned to Clark. Somehow he sensed that CC's breasts were unencumbered, and he slipped his hand into the opening of her dress front caressing her right breast and kneading the hard nipple while gently squeezing. CC enjoyed a man caressing her breasts, and when they broke from a kiss asked Clark to hold her other one. After a few moments, CC said, "I'm going to leave now. I'll be back in one week, and we'll continue getting to know each other. Please send Charles next Saturday to collect my belongings." She straightened the dress, kissed Clark on his mouth left the house and walked home.

Chapter 6

Daniel's House

CC was established as housekeeper and Daniel Clark's lover in short order. During the days she paid bills, arranged for repairs, ordered food, supervised the maid, cook, and laundress, and hired a new landscaper with whom she enjoyed conferring about the selection of flowers and shrubs in the neglected gardens. At night, usually after a dinner together, CC and Clark whose bedrooms were on the opposite sides of the house met in one another's rooms often spending the entire night together. Clark admitted that he had once seen CC working at another event in Cooperstown prior to the board meeting. He had inquired about her and discovered that CC had enjoyed a fine reputation among the wealthy families as one who could cook for large parties and supervise the setup and clean up as well. Strangely no one seemed to know anything about CC's personal life, which was good news to Clark. He had urged his cousin Stephen to ask for CC to help with the board meeting.

Daniel had visited the Orient after his wife's death. He been introduced to royal courtesans in Siam, and with them experienced the sexuality that he had always desired, but hadn't been able to enjoy. The courtesans taught Daniel the pleasures of prostate massage, mutual oral genital stimulation, and control for simultaneous climax. He was schooled to be patient and giving to his sexual partner and learned to enjoy that as much as the pleasure he received from her. Daniel returned home realizing that what he had learned and enjoyed so much would be impossible to achieve with a woman from the ranks of the widows and divorcees who were regularly introduced to him by his well-meaning friends and relatives. He knew that in 1929 few American women realized that they even possessed a clitoris and, if they did know, would not know its function. He embarked on a search for a physically, mentally and sexually exquisite woman, and had recognized that his search had to be wider than the Cooperstown area, but then he spotted CC running a dinner party for the medical board and their spouses. He was immediately attracted to her long legs; tight curvy body, exquisite face and light caramel colored skin especially her skin, which he longed to feel next to him. The women in his world were pale and appeared to be cold all of the time. He also realized that by enticing CC to live in his home, and for them to become lovers he was risking social ostracism by most of his friends, the Presbyterian clergy, and business associates. Although he also realized that at the same time the men would privately be envious. Clark could have lived in Manhattan along with other family members. In fact, he thought about living in the Dakota Apartments; a cooperative built in the 1880s by his great uncle Edward Clark. At the time the magnificent structure on West 72nd Street was considered to be too far north and as remote as the Dakota Territory hence the building's name. He chose to stay in Cooperstown, which was a manageable place, comfortable for him, and where he was known. He preferred to visit New York for the Broadway shows and nightclubs, Florida in the winter and his house in Northeast Harbor, Maine during the summer.

Late one evening, Daniel was in CC's bed. They had exhausted each other and were lying together CC's back to Daniel's front. They both enjoyed being that way because Daniel could fondle CC's breasts from behind her, and she could move her beautifully shaped firm rear against his penis. Often they fell asleep in that position and woke together resuming their love-making until the morning when they separated prior to the house staff's arrival. This night CC asked Daniel about Clarissa, Daniel's deceased wife. "Did you love her?" CC hadn't asked Daniel anything personal before, and he was surprised.

"I did in my fashion," Daniel answered. "Clarissa was pleasant to everyone. But she really was distant and reserved toward me and our children. I believe that's the reason they both moved away after college. Peter is in the motion picture business and lives in California, and Caroline stayed in Ann Arbor after graduating from the University and is raising her family in Michigan. After Clarissa's death, I hoped they would move back here, but neither one wanted to live again in a small town that's so remote. I want to visit them soon. It's something I should do more often. I've been to California only one time, and twice to Michigan when the girls were born." He felt odd talking about Clarissa while caressing another woman, but somehow CC always put him at ease. Some of the nights they lay together touching just hands or feet and not moving beyond those gentle caresses. Clark experienced even greater sexual satisfaction with CC than with the women in Siam, which he hadn't believed was possible. During the colder nights CC usually wore only dark blue soft cotton T-shirts purchased at Brooks Brothers men's clothiers in Manhattan that she loved feeling against her nipples. In spring she switched to cotton pajama bottoms and slept without a top.

At times Daniel couldn't believe his good fortune in discovering CC, and her willingness to share his home and bed with him. His dilemma with their arrangement was that they couldn't be seen in public together in Cooperstown except as employer and employee. He wouldn't subject CC to that so he continued to accept invitations for himself to social events as an eligible widower at dinner sitting next to the latest friend or relative of the hostess who wanted to marry again. He suffered through the evenings attempting to be polite, but eating little and saying less. His thoughts of CC waiting at home for him probably already in bed kept him aroused and disinterested in any conversations directed at him.

Daniel had read sections of Kraft-Ebing's work *Psychopathia Sexualis* (Sexual Psychopathy), lent to him by his doctor, since only physicians were permitted to purchase the disturbing study of human sexual behavior. While most of the Austrian psychiatrist's bold statements didn't interest him Daniel concluded that his feelings fit the definition of *paradoxia,* the experience of sexual excitement that occurs independent of the sex act, which thankfully was on-going since CC entered his life.

On the days when Daniel was away on business Charles drove CC to visit her only relative; Aunt Vanessa, her mother's younger sister who lived north of Cooperstown in a tidy house. Vanessa was a widow and a baby nurse well known in the area for her skill with newborn babies and in restoring order to homes after the blessed event. Her own two babies were all grown up and had moved away. If Vanessa was curious about CC being driven to her home and later called for by a chauffeur driving an expensive automobile, she didn't say anything. And she didn't question CC's generosity when an envelope stuffed with money was left whenever she visited. Vanessa recognized that CC was a beautiful woman and smart. If she was using her god given gifts to have a good life and was generous to her aunt, Vanessa wasn't going to complain.

Daniel and CC did create a unique social life for themselves beside the occasional lunch together on Saturdays at the Otesaga Hotel. Over the next two and a half years, Daniel brought CC to Albany, Boston, and New York City to see shows and musicals. In Manhattan, they stayed at the elegant Sherry Netherland Hotel in adjourning suites. CC shopped in Saks Fifth Avenue, Lord and Taylor and De Pinna while Daniel visited with Stephen Clark who lived on Sutton Place. New York was awash with illegal whiskey, speakeasies on every block and gorgeous women dancing, smoking and drinking alcohol in public.

The 1920s had uncovered sexuality in America. Sex was promoted in movies, magazines, and books openly for the first time, and it was all in New York. Daniel and CC loved every bit of it. They dined at Jack and Charley's 21 Club and drank first class Scotch whiskey out of tea cups. Then up to Harlem to dance to Cab Calloway's band at the Cotton Club. Owned by gangster and bootlegger Oney Madden who was serving a term in Sing Sing prison, the Cotton Club had a strict white patron's only policy, but the waiters, cooks, entertainers, and cigarette girls were all Negros. CC's presence was never questioned.

They also enjoyed the libertine excitement of the Central Park Casino where whiskey, music, and sexuality combined to create the hottest of New York's hot spots. The City's mayor "Gentleman" Jimmy Walker an elegant dandy led the nightly reveling that broke dozens of local and some federal laws. Walker while a family man was always accompanied by the beautiful Betty Compton a Ziegfeld Follies dancer who prided herself on wearing the skimpiest costumes in the most daring chorus line on a Broadway stage. In fact, it was known that after the Follies closed each night; members of the chorus could be found continuing to entertain and supplement their incomes in the bedrooms on the Casino's second floor. Daniel wondered how Walker was taken seriously as the mayor of America's largest city since he caroused all night and slept most of the days. Apparently, the citizens of the city had similar feelings because Walker was eventually indicted on corruption charges and he and Betty Compton fled to Paris where they lived as celebrity expatriates.

During the harsh Cooperstown winter, Daniel and CC boarded New York Central's Empire State Express train in Albany, which brought them to New York's Grand Central Station. Their luggage was transferred to the Atlantic Coastline Railroad that ran trains from Manhattan's Pennsylvania Station to Charleston, South Carolina and then on to Tampa, Florida. The Atlantic Coastline Railroad was assembled by Henry B. Plant in the 1890s and was a patchwork of small railroads that Plant had merged in order to provide regular rail service to Georgia, South Carolina, and western Florida, and connect to his steamships that sailed to Cuba from the Port of Tampa that Plant had built in order to encourage trade with Central America.

Henry Plant also built Florida's first resort the Aladdin Night's inspired Tampa Bay Hotel in 1891. Plant's railroad had been extended to Tampa, and he believed that a first class hotel served by a rail line would attract wealthy vacationers. As was usual, Plant was correct. His Tampa Bay Hotel was the world's largest at the time. Its main structure built in Moorish Revival style featuring a dozen steel covered minarets poking into the sky was a quarter mile in length and covered five acres. It was surrounded by over one hundred and fifty acres of lush tropical gardens along the Hillsboro River. The hotel contained five hundred guest rooms and parlor suites along with salons, ballrooms, a dining room, which served ten-course dinners, and a one thousand foot long veranda. A golf course, racetrack, and playing fields offered a total resort experience. Guests included American presidents and European royalty as well as wealthy industrialists, and their families and servants from Chicago, Detroit, St. Louis, Cincinnati, Pittsburgh, Boston and New York.

The hotel had been the headquarters for the American Army that invaded Cuba in 1898 setting off the Spanish-American war. Army officers under the command of General Shafter, using Cuban maps, laid out their plans for battles against the Spanish Army on tables set up on the long veranda, and then retired to the dining room for the fine cuisine. The war was the nation's first incursion into global politics and made America an international power through Spain's ceding Cuba, Puerto Rico and Guam to America as war repatriations, and giving up the Philippine Islands for a payment of $20 million. Americans remained in Cuba almost as an occupying force until 1903 leaving after Cuba agreed to lease a large part of the Guantanamo Province to the United States for its naval base to watch over the Caribbean.

Daniel and CC arrived at the elegant establishment for a two month escape from the Cooperstown winter. They were ensconced in separate parlor suites on the hotel's third floor in a wing that had minimal traffic, which suited them as they visited each other's rooms regularly. An elaborate brass elevator, the first one installed in a hotel in Florida, offered access to the two floors of guest rooms. Daniel and CC, however, preferred to use the circular stairs that was oddly almost hidden within the hotel's walls since it was appropriately mysterious as was their relationship to observers.

During the stay, they met Babe Ruth baseball's most famous and controversial player. He was also a hotel guest along with a coterie of friends. Ruth, who enjoyed his ability to attract beautiful women, was intrigued with CC who wore daring backless gowns that revealed that she was braless during the nightly formal dinners when even slender women wore elaborate foundation garments. Ruth openly flirted with CC because his wife Claire was far away. Daniel was more amused than angry. CC tried to avoid the Babe but he appeared whenever she walked by herself in the hotel's gardens or walked on the nearby bridge over the Hillsboro River to Tampa's downtown. She was polite and kept him at bay, and reported the encounters to Daniel who urged her to merely ignore Ruth as much as possible. Dressed as she was in the latest fashions, and with hairdressers and manicurists on call, CC sparkled as the belle of the hotel's dining room each evening. Daniel loved the stir CC created just by appearing there. He noticed the admiring looks from the men and even the women when he and CC danced to the twelve piece orchestra. Daniel was willing to share her visually because he knew that she was only his for the rest of the night.

The Tampa Bay Hotel's dining room was an immense square space with a round ceiling that projected into one of the building's minarets providing a room height of four stories. Near the top was a series of cut out squares each about four feet high and trimmed with dark red velvet drapes. During dinner, beautiful music played by musicians standing behind the openings was enjoyed by the diners. Below the musicians a circular mural featured painted red hibiscus, and above them, the round ceiling was colored sky blue with touches of clouds.

CC looked forward to dining in the evening in the elegant atmosphere enhanced by the starched white table cloths, sterling silverware and Rosenthal Moss Rose pattern china. The meals were elaborate and included fine Beluga caviar from Russia, French pate' foie gras, Yorkshire pudding and steamship rounds of standing rib roasts of prime beef carved for each guest, and served from huge silver warmers on rolling carts. Chefs wearing long white aprons and tall white hats carved the roasts to order and waiters in formal wear served the pre-heated dinner plates to the diners. Large baked potatoes, their skin hardened by the high temperature coal fired oven, were cut apart and fresh creamery butter inserted. Maison Veuve Clicquot Champagne shipped directly from Reims in France to Tampa was served throughout the meal along with other wines and American spirits.

Another of the Hotel's innovations was the salad course, which did not yet have its regular place in America's dining habits. The dinner salad consisted of crisp head lettuce, red onion, tomatoes and carrot shavings with a thousand Island dressing containing finely chopped green olives, peppers, pickles, onion, and hard boiled eggs bound together by Richard Hellman's mayonnaise sent from New York City. The crisp head lettuce arrived daily during the hotel's season. It was grown in Maine and carried by train to Tampa. The lettuce wilted if not kept cold so it was packed in ice, and became known at the Tampa Bay Hotel as iceberg lettuce.

For the hotel guests' entertainment, the management arranged for Babe Ruth's team The New York Yankees to play an exhibition baseball game against the Tampa Smokers of the Florida State League. Plant Field was a regulation size baseball diamond behind the hotel. Over three hundred chairs were set up for guests and refreshments were served in stands under large umbrellas. There was a great sense of festivity. Women carried parasols and the men wore straw boater hats. The teams arrived, and after some spitting and scratching, the Smokers, as the home team took the field.

The Babe struck out in the first inning and again in the third. At the top of the fifth inning, the score was 3 – 1 Yankees with two men on base. Ruth was on deck and spotted CC in the second row of chairs. He sauntered over to her with a bat on his shoulder and said, "CC this one is going all the way, and it's for you." CC smiled, and Ruth walked back for his turn in the batter's box. The first pitch was a ball. The second pitch to the Babe was hit for a home run. The ball was later found and the distance measured. It was the longest home run hit by Babe Ruth in his twenty-two seasons of major league baseball.

Chapter 7

Porgy and Bess

Gershwin sat down with Amy and Hank Plant. A waiter had brought ice in a silver bucket, crystal glasses, a bottle of pre-Prohibition 101 proof bourbon and a pitcher of water. They offered to pour for Gershwin, but he said, "I don't drink when I'm working."

Charles Rosenthal, the Plant's banker and friend of Gershwin, had believed that Hank Plant would consider providing financial backing for "Porgy and Bess" if Amy and he liked the story and music. "I want to play the entire score of "Porgy and Bess" for you and sing it as well as best as I can, but first you should know something about the place and the characters that DuBose Heyward created."

"DuBose's characters in his book "Porgy" are based on the Gullah people he met in Charleston and the islands. The Gullahs are Negros descended from slaves brought here to farm the rice fields. After the Civil War, they stayed around Charleston unlike so many other freed Negros who migrated North by railroad settling where the rail lines ended in New York, Chicago, St. Louis or Detroit. The Gullah people just stayed together and spoke their own distinct language, which DuBose found poetic. Dorothy Heyward is an accomplished playwright and adapted DuBose's book into a play that had a yearlong run on Broadway. I regret that I didn't see the stage production."

Dorothy would have been happily surprised to learn that Gershwin was impressed with her work because she believed that he didn't value her opinion.

He did but was put off by her guarded attitude toward him. Dorothy was a mid-westerner in spirit and personality. She was from rural Ohio and, even though she had been educated at Columbia University and Harvard, she still maintained a suspicion of people from the big cities especially anyone from New York. Playwrights were the outsiders in stage productions once the director took over. Writers worried about their creation in the manner of a parent for a child and weren't always consulted regarding the actual staging of their work. With that in mind, Dorothy was wary of Gershwin.

"Porgy and Bess" is a love story, but also one of betrayal and tragedy," Gershwin continued. "Perfect elements for opera and it's the first truly American work that compares with the great European operas. It will be accepted by Americans because of course the score is sung in English; a partially Gullah version, but English." Gershwin's passion for the production was evident as he went on to describe Catfish Row and its residents. "For the director, the Theater Guild has recruited the experienced Rouben Mamoulian, and we have the best performers of the Negro theater. John "Bubbles" Sublett as Sportin' Life, Ann Wiggins Brown from Julliard for the Bess role, Warren Coleman as Crown and Todd Duncan as Porgy. Each one fits their role perfectly." Gershwin went on, "It's also a good opportunity for Negro performers to step up from their traditional secondary roles in serious theater."

Listening to Gershwin's description of the production one could assume that it had come together easily, but that was far from what had really happened. Months of auditions and rewriting still had to take place. Gershwin had urged Heyward to come to New York to help stage the production when it was the time for that. Heyward promised to help, but Dorothy was always worried about their finances since the opera hadn't yet paid them anything. She was critical of Gershwin whom Heyward considered a genius, and he continued to be thrilled by his association with the composer. The cast will number sixty-five, which was an unusually high number of performers, but Gershwin and Heyward refused to cut even one role. They did cut some of the songs in the final days on Folly Island since the opera was running about four hours. In addition, the production even prior to its opening was criticized by the white press as not really an opera; referring to it as a "folk opera," which infuriated

Gershwin, and was disparaged by the Negro press as the work of two white men claiming to know about life among Negros in the South.

He didn't share the problems with the Plants who seemed fascinated with the production's origins. Gershwin rose and approached the piano again, this time with a thick book of hand written sheet music. Over the next two hours, he played the entire score of "Porgy and Bess" singing most of the parts and providing an explanation prior to playing each musical number. His playing was flawless and his beautiful music was dramatic and rich, transporting one to a secret place. "I assure you the cast will be brilliant singing their music so please don't think of me in their roles," he explained as he finished with the great Negro spiritual style song, *I'm On My Way*.

Amy and Hank Plant, to their credit, were still attentive and realized that they had witnessed a unique performance by America's greatest composer. Gershwin sat down with them and took a long drink of ice water. He didn't appear tired and actually was exhilarated. He smiled and said, "Well that's the music and the story. I probably didn't do it the justice it deserves, but what do you think about our opera?"

Amy spoke first. "Mr. Gershwin," she had a difficult time addressing him by his first name even though they were close in age, "I loved your music and I was carried away to the point that I actually felt I was there on Catfish Row. I was concerned for Bess. She's so innocent about Crown and the happy dust, and I felt sorry for poor Porgy. Am I correct?"

Gershwin smiled and was about to answer her, but Hank Plant spoke first. "George there's no doubt you are the most talented composer of our time, and Amy and I were treated to a performance we shall never forget." He hesitated his face showing pain, "I am aware that you have given me the opportunity to provide financial backing for the opera, and I appreciate that, but I must consider the business side before the artistic." He hesitated, looked at Amy who was frowning, and continued, "I do not believe anyone will pay to see an opera based on the lives of poor colored people."

Chapter 8

Maestro George Gershwin

Almost at noon two days later, a green Pearce Arrow motor car driven by a chauffeur, wearing the green Belleview Hotel staff uniform, parked on Ybor City's busy main street in front of the Excelsior. The driver got out and opened a door to discharge his passenger. A slender taller than average man with thinning brown hair wearing a tan light wool suit, white shirt with collar pin and blue tie emerged from the Pearce Arrow's back seat. He took in the surroundings his face expressionless, but clearly not pleased with what he saw. The chauffeur, busy removing several large pieces of luggage from the car's trunk allowed his passenger to acclimate himself to the Excelsior. Suddenly Harvey Sparks emerged from the hotel's front door and was surprised to see a man standing on the veranda next to a pile of Asprey of London luggage. "You must be Mr. Gershwin. It's a great pleasure Sir to welcome you to the Excelsior Hotel and Ybor City." Harvey attempted to say more but the visitor obviously deep into his thoughts just nodded, and walked into the hotel, took in the small lobby, spotted the upright piano, and sat down while Harvey and the chauffeur handled his Nile crocodile-skin luggage.

Gershwin had been severely disappointed with Hank Plant's reaction to "Porgy and Bess." He had not slept well that night wondering if Plant was correct about the value of the opera. Always so sure of himself, Gershwin had written his first hit song at seventeen. He wondered if this time he was mistaken.

Was his score too heavy, and the book too somber, and would white audiences pay to see a serious musical production about Negro life in the South? Their view of colored people had been shaped by minstrel shows and movies depicting Negros as inferior and childlike. Hollywood's first major production "The Birth of a Nation" starring Lilian Gish, and made by D.W. Griffith glorified the Ku Klux Klan members riding on white horses as the saviors of Southern gentry, and protectors of white women's virtue from the wild former slaves.

Griffith's movie was shown at the Woodrow Wilson White House and the president complimented the movie maker for the film's historical accuracy, which, of course, was far from the truth. The movie's plot had disturbed Gershwin a decade earlier as he was sympathetic to the reality Negros faced in America that their presence was disturbing to the majority of Americans. He remembered the Norman Studios "race movies" that depicted Negros in serious roles as adventurers, heroes, and others in comedies that didn't demean the actors. Gershwin had seen some of the movies shown in Harlem but wasn't sure how widely the films were distributed outside of Negro communities, since they were contrary to popular opinion. He wondered if "Porgy and Bess" would face the same controversy.

Gershwin publicly admitted that Negro composers and musicians had a great influence on his work. The great Lucky Roberts, a stride pianist, was the most important along with gifted composer James P. Johnson. He always shared credit for a successful composition with everyone who had a part in it.

Evaluating his work in this manner made Gershwin nervous. He was used to receiving positive reactions from audiences and critics. Finding financial backers for anything he wanted to undertake was never a problem. Perhaps Hank Plant didn't like opera or entertainment that featured Negros. The Plants were originally from Connecticut, and had lived on Manhattan's Fifth Avenue for two generations. Southern life was mysterious to northerners especially anyone who didn't have to venture far away from their luxurious surroundings and servants. He wondered if that was why Plant was willing to dismiss "Porgy and Bess" so quickly or if it was just a business decision because as Hank Plant had admitted many of the family's holdings were losing value, and were about to be closed or sold.

Rather than embarking on another musical project Gershwin realized that he really should be going back to New York to finish up "Porgy and Bess," which even with Ira's daily collaboration would take months to accomplish. But he had given Heyward his promise that they would begin a new musical together, and that's what he was going to do. Gershwin decided that he would spend no more than two weeks in Ybor City gathering ideas, perhaps writing some of the music, and then return to his other obligations. Once they agreed on the story Heyward could take it over and write the book and dialogue and place the songs that the Gershwin brothers would complete in their spare time. This would upset Ira at first, but he always came through for his brother.

Gershwin, after thinking about what music he had promised to compose and for whom, began to play the piano in the Excelsior Hotel's lobby. He played his own music for about a half hour. He started with *I'll build a Stairway to Paradise*, and continued with *Oh, Lady Be Good*, *I Got Rhythm*, *The Man I Love*, *It's Wonderful*, and finished with a rousing rendition of *Strike Up the Band*. He seemed oblivious of the surroundings that he was in a small hotel in West Florida, and he didn't know a single person. Gershwin was in a personal place where the music and emotions took over his mind and body. He played without considering notes, rests, meter or phrasing. Upon finishing the impromptu recital Gershwin appeared to wake up not knowing how he played or who was listening. He stood, and for the first time since arriving at the Excelsior smiled acknowledging the applause from Consuelo, Harvey, and other guests and hotel staff that had been attracted by the melodies. Consuelo approached him, her hand extended. "Welcome, Mr. Gershwin. That was beautiful. I've seen your shows on Broadway and I felt as if I were there again. I'm Consuelo Middleton Davis, and this is my hotel."

Gershwin took her hand lightly in his, and said, "Thank you, but the piano needs tuning," and walked over to the reception desk to register for an indefinite period.

Chapter 9

Cooperstown, NY 1932

The telephone rang at 11 pm an unusual occurrence in Daniel's home. He answered and heard the Bell System operator asking for Daniel Clark. She announced a person to person call from Ann Arbor, Michigan. Daniel was immediately wary about a call from Caroline late at night. He knew he was correct to be concerned as soon as his daughter began speaking while crying. "Oh Daddy, Timothy was killed in an accident in the plant this afternoon. I've been frantic and don't know what to do."

"Is anyone with you?"

"Just the housekeeper. She's taking care of the children, thank god."

"No one else?" asked Daniel.

"Oh, there were people from the company and the church with food as if I could eat anything. I'm trying to hold myself together. He left this morning, and will never come back."

"Caroline I will leave here in the morning and be there Wednesday. What about Tim's family?"

"I haven't even called them. I don't know how to tell them, but I will. Betsy Durant from college is coming to stay with me. She still lives in Grosse Point."

"I'll find out tonight when a train leaves Albany for Detroit. I'll be on the first one. It's faster than driving a car. I will take care of everything. I'm so sorry about Tim."

CC stood by not saying anything until Daniel hung up the telephone. He asked her to help him pack and to call Charles on the house intercom to tell him to get ready to drive to Albany's Union Station. Daniel knew that New York Central trains ran regularly from Albany to Buffalo, and he wanted to be there for the next one. He would switch to a Michigan Central train once in Buffalo and proceed to Detroit. CC packed two large leather valises carefully folding two dark wool suits appropriate for the mourning period and funeral. She also packed starched white shirts, neckties, socks, shoes, and underwear, but Daniel assured her that he would purchase anything else he needed at the J.L. Hudson's Department Store in downtown Detroit.

Charles brought the Packard under the portico and put the valises into the car's trunk. CC wanted to offer soothing words, but after a brief goodbye and quick kiss; Daniel left the house with a determined look on his face, and didn't look back. CC watched the car's lights until it was out of sight. Somehow she knew that her life had undergone a great change as had Daniel's.

Daniel arrived in Detroit in less than two days after leaving Cooperstown. He was met at Detroit's Union Station by an executive of the Singer Sewing Machine Company who put his car and driver at Daniel's disposal. Grateful for the hospitality, Daniel napped during the almost two hour ride to Ann Arbor. His son-in-law was an industrial engineer for the Cadillac division of General Motors. Tim was on an inspection visit to the Cadillac Works located in Detroit when a rolling crane broke free from its ceiling mounted track and crushed him to death.

Upon his arrival, the first words spoken to Daniel by his tearful mourning daughter were that she and her girls were moving to Cooperstown, and returning to the family home. Daniel assured Caroline that he would love for her and his granddaughters' ages three and five to come home. It was only later that first night alone in Caroline's guest room that Daniel thought about CC, and sadly he realized that their time together was about to end.

The next two weeks were filled with the dozens of details that follow an unexpected death. After the funeral at St. Andrew's Episcopal Church, the internment, the luncheon at the country club, and seeing out the last of the house guests an exhausted Caroline sat with her father in a corner of the living room. They sipped fine French Cognac brought across the Detroit River from Canada by an acceptable bootlegger. Caroline her eyes hollow and face pale thanked Daniel for taking over and directing everything. Daniel was surprised. "You're my daughter. Why wouldn't you expect that of me?"

"Because Daddy most of the fathers of my friends are so removed from their children. They hardly know each other. They would have paid the expenses but would have been more like visitors. I even saw you in the kitchen organizing the caterer."

"I do know how to do some things," said Daniel smiling, "Even though the Clark's have been blessed with means for a long time." He had been occupied all week with Caroline's move to Cooperstown. Daniel had decided that they would all travel by train and had made the arrangements for the booking of three Pullman roomettes. One for Caroline with Elizabeth and Josie, who being so young hadn't grasped the situation and were excited about a train trip, and another for himself and one for Coleen Beers the housekeeper and nanny to whom the girls were attached, and was coming to Cooperstown to live with them. New trunks were delivered from J.L. Hudson's, and the packing of clothing, toys, photographs, Caroline's oil paints and family mementos began. A Railway Express truck picked up the trunks for shipping on the rails and after about one week another truck would deliver them to Daniel's house. Timothy's brother, an attorney, agreed to handle the sale of the house and its contents, but not for a while as he was devastated by his younger brother's death.

Daniel had spoken with CC only one time since arriving in Michigan. He had described the funeral and the sorrow whenever a young person passes away, Caroline's strength, necessary because of her young daughters, and their plans to return to Cooperstown. CC hadn't asked about their relationship, but what was left unsaid was enough for CC to know that it was time to find another place to live.

Chapter 10

CC's Time

Another project that Daniel undertook while he was in Ann Arbor had come to a successful conclusion or so he wanted to believe. A telephone call he had received from Hank Plant, Henry Plant's grandson, and Morton Plant's son and heir, was reassuring. Daniel had gotten to know him during the time he and CC had stayed at the Tampa Bay Hotel over the last winter. The two men belonged to wealthy and powerful families so they easily connected even though Hank Plant was closer in age to CC.

On a mild day with bright sunlight reflecting off Tampa Bay, Daniel and CC toured Ybor City the famous cigar making district in north Tampa. They were being chauffeured around in a 1929 Hispano-Suiza H6 automobile manufactured in Barcelona, Spain for a distinguished clientele of titled Europeans, English nobles, and wealthy Americans. At the time, even with the international economic depression, Ybor City still housed about one hundred cigar factories each employing from ten to two hundred cigar rollers who turned what they did with bits of Cuban tobacco and large cigar leafs into an art form, creating boxes of hand rolled clear Havana cigars all appearing exactly alike in length, diameter and color. During the day, with men and women employed in the factories, and a thinning of the population due to the lessening of the demand for hand rolled cigars, the streets were not as crowded as they had been for decades. Daniel and CC could casually walk and take in the large buildings that housed the Cuban Club, L'Unione Italiana, El Centro Espanol, and other ethnic based organizations in their elegant brick buildings adorned with iron-work, balconies, and steeples.

A smaller white building caught CC's attention. The Excelsior Hotel was a two story structure on Seventh Avenue near 18th Street adjacent to the grand Italian Club. The pleasant appearing building was covered with white painted shingles and windows had green summer shutters set on an angle over them to keep the sun out during Tampa's long hot summers. CC got out of the car, walked up onto the hotel's veranda and entered the building curious about its size and ambiance. She noticed that everything was freshly painted inside and out, and that black ceiling fans turned steadily in the lobby, which housed neatly arranged wicker furniture with floral patterned yellow cushions. A reception desk that featured polished brass turned rods stretching from the elaborately carved counter to a wood structure below the ceiling gave the hotel's interior the solid appearance of a bank. A wide white staircase was the lobby's focal point. The man stationed behind the desk asked if he could help CC in a voice filled with concern since it was unusual for a woman by herself to check into a hotel.

"Oh no thank you. I'm admiring this place and wanted to see the inside. "

The hotel's obviously relieved receptionist informed CC that the hotel had twenty rooms all with their own wash rooms, all with ceiling fans. The build-ing was fireproof, since under the white shingles there was concrete, which also helped keep the hotel cool along with a giant roof top exhaust fan housed in a covered shed. "It was built just like the Tampa Bay Hotel across the river," the clerk proudly informed CC. "That's the hotel to see some time."

CC thanked him and returned to the Hispano-Suiza and Daniel. "It was so nice inside, and look at the lovely red flowers along the veranda. I could see myself running a place like that especially during the winter."

Daniel agreed with CC's assessment, and he also spotted the tidy cigar maker's cottage next to it with its front square of yard turned into an elaborate garden. At the time he wasn't sure why he had filed this impression in his mind, but later after Tim's death he was glad he did.

From Ann Arbor, he had telephoned Henry Bradley Plant. Although Plant resided on Fifth Avenue in New York City, he maintained an extensive list of businesses in West Florida and asked Plant to inquire about purchasing the hotel and cottage in Ybor City. Plant did and through his real estate holding company Bellevue-Biltmore Properties committed to the hotel's purchase. The hotel's proprietor was actually ready to sell, and retire, and the cottage's owner accepted what turned out to be about twice the asking price of similar cottages. Plant's attorney also spoke with Harvey Sparks, the hotel's front desk manager, who agreed to stay on and work for the new owner.

Daniel had conferred with his lawyer John Braddock of the White & Case law firm in New York City. Braddock understood Daniel's plan and began to implement it. He dispatched a bonded messenger to Tampa with certified checks for the purchase of the two properties on Seventh Avenue. Along with the checks was a power of attorney giving Plant's company the right to negotiate the purchase in the name of the Wilmington Sewing Machine Company, a Delaware corporation owned by Daniel Clark, and currently without liquid assets, but in good standing with the state. He also prepared a document for Daniel's signature funding the company with an infusion of fifty thousand dollars from a trust fund account and the acceptance of the two properties as assets of the corporation. Another document transferred 100% of the stock of the Wilmington Sewing Machine Company to Miss Carmella Chase c/o General Post Office, Cooperstown, NY.

❦

It took two steamer trunks borrowed from the trunk room in the attic of Daniel Clark's home to pack up most of CC's clothing acquired while living and traveling with Daniel. His generosity with her had no bounds, and when she was reluctant to purchase an expensive dress or gown or wrap Daniel would insist especially during the few times he accompanied CC to De Pinna, the elegant clothing emporium located on Fifth Avenue in Manhattan. They would be shown to a private space where CC and Daniel were served Chauvenet Red Cap Sparking Burgundy Champagne in tall tulip shaped Bacharach glasses while relaxing on silk covered divans. Lovely women tall and slender, similar in shape to CC modeled beautiful clothing for them. Dresses from Paris, coats from Italy and leather purses from England. CC would whisper to Daniel her opinion of the garments and the ones she liked were put aside and later delivered to her at the Sherry Netherland Hotel. Prices were never disclosed.

At some point during the clothes modeling; Leo De Pinna, son of the founder, and now the store's president would stop by to speak with Daniel and CC. Leo like his English father Alfred was a distinguished looking man with a gracious continental manner. CC enjoyed the conversations with Leo De Pinna and she absorbed some of his worldliness. They shared a love of the French Impressionists and sometimes talked for an hour while Daniel settled the bill and walked around the store seeking a surprise gift for CC. Later, at the Sherry Netherland, CC would model all of the purchased clothing as Daniel enjoyed watching her dress and undress. With the last item, CC didn't use underwear so when she finished the fashion show and removed the final dress she wore only black stockings.

Much later that night, and after a dinner delivered from the hotel's restaurant, CC told Daniel that he was too good to her, and that she hoped he was happy. He assured her that he was, and that it was the best time of his life. They stopped talking at this point because other couples might have gone on and made plans for their future together.

Daniel and CC spoke on the telephone two days before he was to leave Ann Arbor with his family. CC assured him that she understood his dilemma and would pack and leave without a trace. She was grateful for the almost three years they were together and for his affection and generosity. Daniel explained in detail what he had done in Ybor City for CC and that the hotel and cottage were waiting for her. CC realized that Daniel was sending her far away from Cooperstown and him so that the chance of her accidentally meeting his daughter was remote. She had always assumed that there were whispers and rumors regarding her and Daniel, but without a family around him, Daniel didn't care. CC had picked up the legal papers sent to the Post Office and began to understand that she owned property for the first time in her life, and the implications of operating a business. Daniel also told her that she could contact the Plant Steamship Line's Tampa office manager for help with the hotel if it was needed, and John Braddock in New York for legal advice. The current hotel front desk manager, a pleasant resourceful man had agreed to stay on to help get her started. An interest bearing account was set up in her name with the money from the Wilmington Sewing Machine Company in the Plant's Bowling Green Trust Company of New York. In fact, she was a major depositor. CC absorbed all of Daniel's explanation and wasn't afraid. She was finding the beginning of a new chapter of her life thrilling, and realized that her life had been pretty ordinary until Daniel had seen her, and moved people and events so that they could be together.

For the first time, CC thought about leaving Daniel's home, and their no longer sharing intimacies. Their relationship had been unusual, but probably not rare. CC knew Daniel cared for her, but he never said he loved her. She wanted to believe that if Tim had not been killed, and Daniel did not have to take responsibility for his daughter and granddaughters; their relationship might have eventually become public and acknowledged by his by asking to marry her. They probably would have had to live in a place more accepting of mixed race couples, although no one ever was sure about CC's ethnicity. Greenwich Village in New York was the only place that came to mind, especially with its painters, writers, and musicians, but there might be others. Daniel's Northeast Harbor house in Maine was so secluded that they could be there for months without anyone noticing them unless they were invited guests. In fact CC usually sun bathed nude on the second floor porch off the master bedroom without fear of anyone but Daniel seeing her.

Railway Express picked up the trunks the following day for shipment to Tampa. CC closed her account with the First National Bank of Cooperstown, and prepared to travel to New York City. She visited Aunt Vanessa and they had an emotional afternoon reminiscing about CC's mother who had died about ten years before. Vanessa said, "I have something for you." She held out her hand to CC, and gave her niece a ring on a gold chain. "I should have given this to you before, but I didn't know how you would react. You mamma used to wear the chain all the time with the ring dangling from it. It was the only thing she ever got from your father, except you."

"I remember," CC exclaimed. "There were times I wondered about the ring and chain. I assumed it was buried with her. So you saved it for me until now.

Thank you. Momma used to say the emerald was green like my eyes." After hugs, kisses, and tears Vanessa promised to come to Tampa someday, but CC knew her aunt didn't enjoy going very far from her home. The next day Charles drove her and some hand luggage to Albany's Union Station. He said he was sorry that she was leaving as he and CC had become friends, and often took tea together in the afternoons when Daniel was away and Charles wasn't polishing the Packard.

In New York City, CC took a taxi from Grand Central station to check in to the Pennsylvania Hotel on 33rd Street across from the magnificently designed Pennsylvania Station. In two days she would board the Atlantic Coast Line Pullman to Charleston, South Carolina, and from there the train to Tampa. It would be the first time travelling on her own in the South, and CC was aware it would be a different experience without Daniel smoothing the way. She probably would take meals in her train compartment to make it easier on the exclusively Negro Pullman staff that would have to respond to inquiries from the other passengers in regard to even a fair skin colored woman sharing their dining car. She made a visit to De Pinna to explain to Leo that she would be absent from New York for a while, but her promise to come back to see the new dress collection next year resulted in his giving CC a fine Italian gold heart and chain. He said good bye and watched until she left through the Fifth Avenue entrance wondering about her, and hoping he would see her again. The following morning CC was meeting John Braddock at the White & Case law firm on Park Avenue.

Braddock had some news for CC he wanted to deliver in person. He enjoyed seeing the beautiful light brown woman, and wondered how Daniel could have ended their relationship, but he understood family obligations. When CC was escorted to his office by a secretary Braddock greeted her formally, but they sat in the two wing chairs rather than at his desk.

CC was dressed in the latest fashion and the mid-calf length dress showed off her shapely legs. However, Braddock was all business and explained that the annual retainer paid to White & Case by Daniel covered whatever legal questions that might arise from CC's operation of the Excelsior Hotel in Ybor City or any personal legal issue. He also was pleased to inform CC that a loan made by Daniel to the Hertz Corporation of Chicago had been paid back to the

Wilmington Sewing Machine Company when Hertz was sold recently to the General Motors Corporation. The loan was in the amount of $200,000 and the accrued interest amounted to almost $30,000. Daniel had forgotten about the loan and that it had been made by his Delaware company that was now owned by CC. Her immediate reaction was to refuse to accept the money, but Braddock assured CC that Daniel had insisted that the money go to her.

Still not completely accepting that she was a wealthy woman, she filed that away to think about later when alone. CC asked Braddock to help her to change her name legally in order to divide the past from what was ahead. She believed a complete break with her life in Cooperstown, as a domestic, a hospital orderly mopping up blood and urine, and then the years as the exotic mistress of a wonderful man had to be made so she could disappear, and begin another life. She felt it unlikely that anyone she had known would ever venture into Ybor City due to its reputation as an amalgamation of races and ethnicities unlike any other place in America. Braddock assured CC that Daniel, Hank Plant and he were the only ones who knew about her new life, and also know her new name. She wondered what the future held. She would have a new identity, a history that suited her, and enough money to do whatever she desired. Her new name would set the parameters for every one of her future relationships. The name she chose was Consuelo Middleton Davis.

Chapter 11

Ybor City 1934

"My father worked for Mr. Ybor's company, Martinez Ybor & Co., manufacturers of *Flor De Martinez Ybor* and *El Principe de Gales* clear Havana cigars until 1925 when he passed away. I grew up in Ybor City. The Flynns were one of the few Anglo families that lived within the boundaries of the cigar making community. Even though I was a minority member in my school I never felt like an outsider because the population of Ybor City included all shades of skin color and even people who had unusual sexual preferences and different manners of dress. We were all tossed together in a busy and exciting place that was enlivened by the politics of Cuba, and free flowing money due to the seemingly endless demand for the cigars produced in our town."

Reported by Victoriano Manteiga editor of *La Gaceta* February 15, 1927 (Translated from the Spanish) In fact Ybor City is perhaps the most integrated place in America. Since 1905 the state of Florida has passed laws forbidding mixing of races in marriage, employment, schools, public transportation, hotels, and restaurants. The inhabitants of Ybor City laughed at the new laws because Cuban families contained black, white and brown people, and the cigar factories were a multi-racial rainbow. The Tampa Street Railroad, which ran from downtown Tampa to Ybor City was supposed to separate white and colored passengers, but gave up because of the mixed makeup of Cuban families that regularly used the rail line; as did the Seventh Avenue trolley that ran to Palmetto Beach south of Ybor City. Ybor City's stores and restaurants welcomed everyone, and groups of men of all shades talked sports, politics and union business at the Columbia Café. However, the mutual aid societies that began in Ybor City were defined by the ethnicity of their membership. The grand Cuban club opened in 1917 following the dedication, in 1914, of Centro Asturiano, and a new home for Centro Espanol in 1912 both for the Spanish cigar workers, and the L'Unione Italiana also opened in 1912. The buildings, made of red brick were decorated with iron filigree giving Seventh Avenue a New Orleans character. Each organization was actually founded in the late 1800s, but their early locations were either too small or were destroyed by fire. La Union Marti'- Maceo was a society for black Cubans, and Caballeros de Luz a fraternal organization welcomed all Cubans. The societies provided medical care by contracting with doctors who regularly held clinics in the club houses. Recreation, festivals, musicals, theater and vaudeville shows were also offered to the organization's members. Some of the societies have restaurants and swimming pools, and offer English and Spanish language classes and banking offices.

Reported by Ramon Valdespino in *La Traduccion* April 22, 1929 (Translated from the Spanish) Baseball is a favorite activity for the young men of Ybor City. Teams sponsored by the cigar factories played in the Cigar City League and their players represented different races because talent was the criteria for membership. Women employees of the factories played in a basketball league set up by the cigar companies. The employers attempted to bolster the worker's sense of loyalty to their company by encouraging team sports. They also permit a *Cafetero* to deliver hot coffee to the cigar rollers three times a day. An *el Cafetero* was granted an exclusive franchise for each cigar factory to provide the coffee on credit so that no time would be wasted collecting the fee and making change. The *Cafetero* gave out enameled metal cups, and filled them early in the morning, noon and mid- afternoon with fresh coffee. The cigar rollers paid their coffee bill on Saturdays.

"However all was not peaceful in our community," James Flynn continued. "Three years ago, in 1931, factory owners decided that the lectors were no longer allowed to read in the cigar factories. There had been bitter labor disputes accelerated by the factory owner's belief that the lectors were radicalizing the workers by reading Communist propaganda to them encouraging strikes and violence. That eliminated the beloved listening to readings of literature and newspapers while the cigar rollers worked, which was devastating to them, and an exodus from Ybor City to other places and other kinds of work began." It was a terrible idea that struck at the heart of Cuban culture," Flynn said. "Coupled with the elimination of lectors in the factories; many of the residents believed that the golden era of cigar making was ending due to mechanical advances in producing the smokes, and the public losing interest in buying expensive clear Havana cigars. We all found that hard to believe, but factories were closing." Something called the New Deal had begun and it tried to get some money to people and to get new businesses going. It was happening all over the country except in Ybor City where they still cling to life as it was happening in Cuba."

"I still work in Ybor City although I moved my family to Tampa's East Bay section near Hyde Park two years ago. My office is above the Centro Bank on Seventh Avenue. Besides being a lawyer I'm also a customs broker which pays better. That's an agent for receiving foreign goods here and shipping goods to foreign countries, especially Cuba, Central and South America. I do all of the paperwork required by the government and arrange for bills of lading to be paid by the bank so it's convenient that we're in the same building."

"Ybor City has changed recently. Machines to strip the tobacco leaves were introduced in the factories cutting the number of workers. Some factories are even trying out cigar rolling machines. Almost no one in Ybor City believes that a machine can roll a clear Havana cigar. However the demand for clear Havanas has been slowly dropping now that Prohibition is over, and thousands of speakeasies have closed that had sold the expensive cigars. Interestingly enough," observed Flynn, "I have seen that the movies, which we all love feature a new practice that of the stylish women and men smoking cigarettes almost all the time. The thin white tobacco filled paper tubes, and the smoke curling from them look invitingly romantic when used by leading ladies Betty Grable and Joan Crawford and their Lotharios. On the other hand, the actors portraying the villains: George Raft, James Cagney, and Edward G. Robinson smoke cigars."

"I graduated from Stetson Law School in Deland with an LLB degree and opened a law office, *James Flynn, Jr. Esq.,* but most of my clients needed assistance with imports and exports so I became a customs broker as well. It's handy sometimes to know the laws of Florida, but as far as the laws of other countries, especially those in Central America, I haven't figured them out. One good thing about being a lawyer was meeting Consuelo Middleton Davis. The bank manager referred her to me one day when she had a question he couldn't answer. I don't think I helped her, but we have been acquaintances ever since. So much in fact that my wife accused me of moving our family out of Ybor City so that I could see Consuelo more often on Seventh Avenue. She says that when someone mentions Consuelo I get this dreamy look and stop listening to her. I admit that it may be true, but Consuelo is just an image, a dream maybe a fantasy."

Chapter 12

Havana's Poet

Growing up in Cuba at the turn of the 20th Century, young men from wealthy families were expected to stay away from politics, join the family business, the priesthood, or the university. Arturo Dardo, whose wealthy family had built Cuba's second freight railroad in 1843 from Matanzas primarily for the shipping of sugar sacks to the Port of Havana Casablanca Rail Station, disliked trains, didn't believe in God and dropped out of the University of Havana.

Dardo was born in 1887 and had watched the Cuban cigar makers move from his country, first to Key West in Florida, and then to Tampa's Ybor City. He was intrigued by the cigar rollers' skill and speed as they selected the tobacco to make a clear Havana cigar; rolled it in a premium leaf, sealed the perfect tobacco tube, and quickly trimmed off the end with a special knife. He found it somehow poetic, even though he did not use tobacco, and wrote down his thoughts in the notebook that he always carried with him. Sometimes Dardo didn't realize that he had been writing poetry until he looked at the book much later.

When the Hershey Chocolate Company built its own electric rail line from Matanzas to Havana, in order to control their sugar supply for export to Pennsylvania, which was almost parallel to his family's railroad, Dardo's angry protest poem was called *Traicionado por El Chocolate*. (Betrayed by Chocolate) The Hershey train also included some passenger cars so it made several stops along its route. The Matanzas – Havana line owned by Dardo's family didn't stop along the way so it covered the sixty miles to Havana in half the time, which allowed it to remain profitable by running several trains a day. Hershey's train hauled sugar only for the company's own chocolate production. It added passenger cars to help pay the railroad's costs.

He had visited Ybor City several times, as had many Cubans, who regularly came to see relatives working in America. Dardo, however, visited to observe his countrymen and other cigar workers whom he believed were being exploited by the factory owners. He usually held court in the Columbia Café where he occupied a favorite table after the factories closed for the day. Dardo had read many books and pamphlets written by labor sympathizers and Socialist authors documenting the struggle of the working class, and how they were kept in their place by the owners of production. He came to believe that the ownership of business should not be controlled by individuals but shared by all who work with their hands.

He became a dedicated Socialist and found a comfortable place for his beliefs in a post-World War America that was unsure of itself and threatened by anarchists, Socialism, and Communism that were believed to be brought about by the foreign elements allowed into the country in spite of attempts by the government to limit immigration. Dardo, always seeking answers by flirting with danger, had secret meetings with Sicilian anarchists Pietro Scaglione and Luigi Lodato who by day worked in a cigar factory, and by night plotted the government's overthrow, but were really only helpless idealists.

In order to expand his knowledge of the worker's protests, Dardo traveled from Ybor City to New York City during the spring of 1934, and found fellow sympathizers among the union movement engulfing the northeastern United States. He met Norman Thomas, the Socialist party's perennial candidate for president of the United States, and was impressed by his intellect and passion, but felt Thomas was naïve, pleasant but weak. He flirted with Communism, but couldn't identify with the seemingly unbalanced eastern Europeans who controlled the movement, and who unlike the Socialists had little humor about themselves; always blaming someone or something for their failures rather than their lack of organization or unattractive demeanors. Dardo searched for a place to fit in, but he didn't join picket lines and refused to hand out pamphlets and avoided rallies. He preferred talking with individuals about social inequality or with small groups as long as his ideas were heard.

After being frustrated because he couldn't find a place where he was comfortable in the swirling mass of labor politics, he decided to return to Ybor City and finish the narrative poem he had been working on for some time. Dardo was skillfully recording the travails of the people who had left their homes in Cuba to work in the cigar factories of Tampa helping to produce what had become "America's addiction" the millions of cigars smoked yearly that Dardo actually considered an unpleasant habit.

Dardo's return to Ybor City was delayed because he was befriended by a seemingly like-minded American born Communist, Joe Jacobson, who brought Dardo to late night suppers in Ratner's dairy restaurant on Delancey Street on Manhattan's Lower East Side. Ratner's was a kosher restaurant serving dairy and fish dishes only, and best known for the baskets of hot onion rolls placed on every table by the fast moving, fast talking, and usually entertaining, waiters. He was introduced to another faction of young Communists who were first generation idealistic American Jews so Ratner's was a comfortable place for them. They didn't have money for a Ratner's meal expecting only to purchase a coffee and eat the free onion roles, but Dardo had plenty of money, which he generously shared with them. Urged by Dardo to order freely; plates of soft cheese filled blintzes covered with sour cream and cinnamon, and latkes with applesauce arrived at their table along with bowls of pea soup and cold borscht laced with sour cream.

Dardo enjoyed the strange food, even eating gefilte fish, a ground and orb shaped fish and herb dish from Eastern Europe boiled, and then served cold in a clear gelatin coating along with chopped horse radish sauce, a favorite at Ratner's. They talked, shouted and plotted until the restaurant closed for the night. Dardo after several nights at Ratner's over several weeks confided to Joe Jacobson that he was returning to Ybor City to be among his own people and their struggle for better wages and working conditions. He realized that he didn't have a place in New York, it was simply too big, and that the revolution was needed more for the Cuban cigar workers than the intellectuals. He left the city never knowing that Joe Jacobson was an agent of the Bureau of

Investigation a government agency that watched the activities of immigrants and Communists.

On his way back to Ybor City by train, Dardo reflected on his own life. As the scion of a wealthy Cuban family, he had the option to forego employment and fight for the rights of workers. He didn't see the irony that the labor of Cuban railroad workers and sugar cane cutters in Cuba's hot fields was making his leisurely life possible. He didn't feel guilty because he believed that at least some of the privileged people had to be sympathetic for workers to make gains in their struggle for better treatment.

While on the train going south Dardo poured over the selection of magazines he had purchased at Pennsylvania Station. He loved the American periodicals published weekly. His special interest was the advertisements for Springmaid sheets found in almost every issue. Colonel Elliot White Springs, a flamboyant businessman, dared to have ads created that featured drawings of comely women showing all of their legs and most of their busts. Dardo saved the advertisements that featured women with dark hair which, in his mind were the most erotic, especially the ones showing their underwear snugly in place or around their ankles. When his trip was over, the latest Springmaid ads would be added to the scrapbook he kept. Dardo didn't have family living in Ybor City so he regularly stayed at the Excelsior Hotel and looked forward to seeing the beautiful and fashionable Consuelo Middleton Davis.

Chapter 13

Along With the Rain

I t was a Monday Consuelo would later remember when asked about the guest who checked in on a rainy August morning. She was at the reception desk looking over the guest register and attempting to figure out if it had been wise to keep the hotel open during the summer when guests were few, but she had wanted to keep her staff together, so full salaries were paid, even though the hotel was only about one quarter occupied. A man was looking around the lobby before approaching the reception. His clothing and the two suitcases were soaked from the downpour outside.

"Good morning," Consuelo said, "I see the rain is still heavy. It's what happens here in Florida almost every day in the summer."

Consuelo attempted to attract his attention, but the stranger didn't look up from the newspaper he had picked up from a pile on the table next to the piano. It was *La Gaceta* published in Ybor City daily since 1922. When he did look at her he said, "Is this the only paper you have here? It's in Spanish."

"We do get the *Tampa Tribune* every day and also the *Havana Telegram*, but that one is a few days old by the time it gets here from Cuba."

The stranger's face showed disapproval, but he didn't say anything more about the newspapers. Instead, he looked at Consuelo for the first time. His eyes bore into her face, and he said, "I want to speak to the hotel's owner."

Consuelo not used to being ignored, especially by a man, took a breath and calmly said, "I'm the owner. I'm Consuelo Middleton Davis. Who are you?"

He didn't show a sign of surprise, but said after looking at her face carefully, "You're a colored woman. Some kind of high yella. I bet your grandmammy was a yard child somewhere in Mississippi or Alabama, and I've seen you before."

Consuelo held her temper and in a level voice told the stranger, "My people are from upstate New York and England; not that I care what you think about me. However, I am considering whether or not to have you and your wet luggage removed from my lobby because both are starting to stink."

The stranger seemed to be considering his options and was silent for a few moments, but obviously remembering the wet weather, he asked about a room with a private bath. Consuelo told him the daily and weekly rates and that her rooms had private baths. She turned the registration book around asking him to sign and to pay in advance since she didn't know him. "I'm well known in Washington," was his only protest.

Consuelo turned the register back to her, and read the neat script signature. John E. Hoover, Washington, DC. "I work for the government. I'm director of the Bureau of Investigation." He went on about his role in finding foreigners living in America who were disloyal to their adopted land, and the reports from loyal American cigar workers in New York and Pennsylvania about the radical and anarchist Cubans, Italians and other "spics" who use the cigar factories in Ybor City as their hiding place because of all the mixing of the races there made it hard to find them.

"I'm here on official government business so I don't expect you to tell anyone about that." Hoover wanted to impress Consuelo with his importance. Consuelo had been intimately acquainted with wealthy and powerful men. She had been pursued for her friendship and her sexuality by handsome dashing men, and by famous men. Hoover as far as she was concerned was a mosquito to be swatted before he caused damage. She estimated Hoover was five or six years older than her and two inches shorter. His complexion was ruddy, and his hair she observed when he took off his hat to dry his face was dark brown, thinning and twisted. He noticed her looking at him and replaced his hat.

Consuelo was amused by the blustering Hoover. "You may trust my discre-
tion John E.," sensing that using his first and middle names rather than calling
him Mr. Hoover would annoy him so she decided that he would be John E. for
as long as he stayed at the Excelsior. She casually mentioned that in the evening here in the lobby another hotel guest, one who was world famous, often
played and sang some of the music he composed. "He's George Gershwin who's
engaged in some research for a new musical production using Ybor City as its
backdrop."

Hoover about to lift up his two suitcases stopped and with a snarl said,
"That Jew piano player is here? We investigated him. His name is Gershovitz.
His father was from Russia; probably a Communist. Attorney General Palmer
wanted to deport all of them, but the Labor Department stopped him." Hoover
picked up his luggage and headed for the stairs to the second floor without looking back.

Hoover was known in Washington especially by the faction that was
attempting to deport foreigners who didn't look like real Americans. At twenty-
four years old Hoover had been a willing participant in the infamous Palmer
raids of 1920 organized by Attorney General A. Mitchell Palmer in response
to several destructive bombings by anarchists. The threat of more bombs being
detonated by anti-government groups was real, and of great concern to President
Woodrow Wilson. Palmer with Wilson's ascent tossed out the Constitution's
guarantee of the rights of people accused of crimes, and successfully deported
over five hundred suspects before the U.S. Department of Labor, which sur-
prisingly had jurisdiction in this area, stopped him before every foreigner in the
country was deported. Palmer called his ruthless group of federal agents the
Bureau of Investigation. Hoover who had recently completed his legal studies
at George Washington University enjoyed the opportunity to impress Palmer
with his remorseless hunt for suspects.

Eventually, Palmer had to resign in disgrace, but Hoover's reputation was
saved. Whether or not they were guilty, or just looked guilty, he worked hard
to gather any evidence that could be used to deport them. After two exhausting years of hunting down the many unfortunates who were easy to catch and
deport mostly because of their association with other suspects, the Palmer raids

ceased, and Hoover was rewarded for his zeal with an appointment as the director of the Bureau.

Hoover helped to promulgate America's "Red Scare" during the 1920s. He and other alarmists who were jockeying for power through the unelected government, Washington's bureaucracy knew that many uninformed Americans were afraid of a Bolshevik style revolution in their country and would agree to hand over government power to anyone who would fight that threat. However as the threat of revolution abated, the nation was experiencing an even greater crisis brought on by organized crime syndicates that had become rich and powerful during Prohibition.

Prohibition ended in 1933, but the intricate web of criminal activities it had spawned had become substantial organizations preying on legitimate businesses due to the legalization of alcohol sales once again, which had ended the criminal organization's greatest source of revenue. Hoover was urged to control and prosecute the criminal enterprise. Law enforcement leaders, members of Congress, and the governors of several states that had a significant presence of the national crime organization that had become known as the Mafia, the Combination, and La Cosa Nostra were becoming concerned and wanted action from the federal level. Hoover resisted all advice and steadfastly kept denying that the Mafia even existed in America. While In fact, the American Mafia had recently established a beachhead in Havana.

Confidential report dated December 20, 1933 by Max Kase editor of the *Havana Telegram* newspaper to publisher William Randolph Hearst. The Nacional De Cuba Hotel opened in Havana's El Vedado section high above the sea in December of 1930. While heralded by the Cuban government as its own flagship project to attract wealthy tourists to Cuba, the hotel, in fact, is owned by the National City Bank of New York, and the only part of the hotel that is Cuban is the flag that flies alone near its entrance. It was built by the American construction company Purdy and Henderson that had also built many of Havana's important buildings since their arrival to Cuba in 1909. The building was designed by McKim,

Mead and White, America's premiere architectural firm. The hotel's board of directors includes only one member with a Spanish name; Mr. Juan F. Rivera. Anti-government unrest that produced bombings and murders are rampant in Havana, and recently American racketeers were invited to operate the Nacional's gambling casino, and in reality, take control of the hotel's overall operations. No one at National City Bank objected, and now Meyer Lansky the power behind the national crime syndicate of the United States has arrived at the Nacional De Cuba Hotel to take charge. In fact, all of Cuba's gambling casinos in its luxury hotels, and Havana's famous Oriental Park Racetrack were taken over by the American gangsters because they know how to make them profitable. Lansky has brought experienced operators from his Saratoga Springs casinos, Ben Marden from the Riviera in Fort Lee, New Jersey and dealers and pit bosses from Miami's Colonial Inn. None of this activity was done secretly. In fact, some of my colleagues, the New York newspaper columnists, have hinted about it under their bylines."

Hoover's attention, however, remained on harassing the obviously foreign born who hadn't acculturated to American life, along with Negros speaking out for civil rights and he had agents chasing bank robbers, which generated headlines across the country for him and the Bureau. Whenever a famous criminal was caught or killed by federal agents; Hoover would show up just before the press and photographers. Newspaper reporters would interview him, and photographers would take his photo, and Hoover would be credited for the capture even though he was barely aware that the agents were in pursuit of the criminal they faced in the latest shootout.

Hoover led a charmed life in Washington. Attorneys general and presidents liked him and allowed him great latitude for his actions. Even the recently elected Franklin Roosevelt looked to Hoover for advice in controlling Communism across the nation. Hoover worked long hours and over weekends because he was unmarried and his much older siblings took care of their mother's needs.

Hoover didn't have friends or a life outside of the Bureau of Investigation until Clyde Tolson joined the organization. Tolson, like Hoover, had earned a law degree from George Washington University and had planned to practice law after a brief government career, but he was successful as a field agent leading daring raids that captured some well-known dangerous criminals. He quickly moved up in the Bureau and became the assistant director in 1930. Consuelo usually a good judge of people and their virtues or if they were dangerous, and without virtue; didn't understand the threat posed by John E. Hoover while he was staying at her hotel. One thought crossed her mind however when Hoover removed his hat for a moment; she thought she recognized him from some place in her past.

Chapter 14

By his third day in Ybor City Gershwin and Consuelo had gotten to know each other, and became friends. Through the banker Charles Rosenthal, Gershwin had known about Daniel Clark and his dazzling and sophisticated mistress and almost couldn't believe he was a guest in a hotel she owned. Gershwin told her about visiting the Bellevue to introduce the Plants to "Porgy and Bess" and his disappointment with Henry Plant's reaction. They talked late one night and Gershwin shared thoughts with Consuelo that had been closed up inside him for so long that even his psychoanalyst Dr. Zilboorg hadn't heard them. He admitted that Rose his mother was selfish and vain, but still even at his age and with his tremendous success sought her approval. She had insisted he provide an apartment with a river view for her in the same building as his penthouse. This disturbed him, but he didn't resist.

He lamented about growing up in a family that moved from one apartment to another several times a year while knowing that Rose's appearance, not a family in chaos, was her central concern. Beyond her constant shopping, for clothing to make her appear young, she allowed surgeons to stretch her facial skin in order to smooth out wrinkles and crow's feet. It worked, and Gershwin who had a first objected to the radical surgery was content that he could afford to pay for her vanity. He also admitted that he envied Ira's marriage to Lenore and the way she stood behind him supporting his work and decisions. But, while he appreciated his brother's good fortune, he also enjoyed the freedom of deciding where and when he wanted to be without conferring with anyone. When he realized just how much he had admitted to Consuelo he stopped and said, "You know you're better than my doctor. He says nothing to me, and that's how I answer him; with nothing."

Gershwin admitted that none of his brief affairs with women connected to show business were satisfying because they usually led to requests for parts in shows and reviews or movies. He reluctantly told Consuelo that there had been one long relationship with a woman he should have paid more attention to, and probably should have married. "Her name's Kay Swift. She's a lyricist and composer. We worked on some shows together and became involved. She was married and offered to get a divorce, but you can imagine how hard that's to do in New York." He stopped for a moment, "You remind me of Kay in some ways. Both smart and stylish."

Consuelo said, "I have to ask. What happened?"

"Kay was ready to get a Nevada divorce. She had to live six weeks in a Reno hotel to establish residency, go to the local court with mail addressed to yourself in Reno, and receive the divorce decree. Then come home and remarry although she has three young daughters. The girls were a real issue for me because I hated the idea of breaking up her family." Gershwin hesitated, "That wasn't a problem for Kay. She wanted to leave James Warburg although I thought he was a decent guy."

"You knew him that well?"

"I'm embarrassed to admit that we're still friends. I was a guest at Kay's and Jimmy's estate in Greenwich many times. Kay and I would ride their horses, and there was always a big party on the weekends. We would play the piano and sing all night. Even though James was a banker and a Warburg, one of the world's wealthiest families, he wrote lyrics for music Kay composed. I lived on their estate one summer when I was finishing "An American in Paris.""

Consuelo asked, "So it didn't happen?"

"No. Actually, Rose was vehemently opposed. She said it was because Kay wasn't Jewish. We were barely Jewish. I wasn't bar mitzvah, I think Ira was. And then one day I realized that Rose was jealous of Kay. Rose couldn't stand being compared to a young glamorous daughter-in-law so she had to destroy our relationship, and she did." Gershwin was quiet now, and then sadly said, "I may have made a terrible mistake, but also I was afraid. I liked Kay's children, especially Andrea, but they would have hated me for taking away their mother and leaving their father by himself." Gershwin's face showed his mixed up emotions. "Maybe Rose was right."

Kay's husband James Warburg was an exceptional man. Born to great wealth he nevertheless was a tireless worker in every aspect of his life. A bank president at thirty-one years old, he also traveled on diplomatic missions to Germany during the turbulent and dangerous times in Europe during the 1930s on behalf of the Roosevelt administration. James was Roosevelt's senior economic advisor, and even though they often differed on national fiscal issues especially leaving the Gold Standard; Roosevelt respected James, and conferred with him regularly. In fact James and Kay wrote and produced a successful Broadway musical "Fine and Dandy," but even that accomplishment didn't keep them together. When friends asked James if he was bothered by the close relationship between Kay and George Gershwin; he replied, "Oh that's Kay. She never could keep her legs together."

Gershwin's music was recognized everywhere in America, in Europe and the British Isles, and his work was staged in Russia. He collaborated with the world's leading musicians, conductors, lyricists, and performers, and he was lionized by all of them. Even with his fame he still had allowed his mother to dominate his life. Consuelo knew that Gershwin's devotion to music was the central force of his life, and because of the acceptance and recognition he had earned he would always work non-stop, and sacrifice the opportunities for a close relationship with a woman. It was obvious to Consuelo that he wasn't a good candidate for marriage because his wife wouldn't get the attention she deserved. Consuelo told Gershwin, "I wouldn't marry you even though you're handsome and the greatest musical talent in the world. You would never be mine even for a minute. You belong to everyone." Gershwin just smiled.

During another night of conversation in the living room of Consuelo's cottage, Gershwin speculated about what his life would be like if he didn't write so much music, and concentrated more on painting, golf and tennis. He was an accomplished portrait painter and a natural athlete. Of course, he couldn't just do that, but admitted he would like to have more time to do what, he wasn't sure. No music was in his blood and in every breath he took.

Then he was effusive in his praise for DuBose Heyward. Gershwin admired Heyward's expert use of the language, honed by his poetry and novels of an almost secret part of southern life. He considered "Porgy" Heyward's great story of Gullah life in the low country of South Carolina a masterful piece of writing that had supported the Negro based literature that led to the Harlem Renaissance. Gershwin wasn't certain that writers like James Weldon Johnson and Langston Hughes would agree, but he liked to promote other cultures, as did Heyward. Consuelo was deeply affected by Gershwin's unusually generous attitude toward the Negro race and wondered how he considered her, but she suspected her ethnicity didn't register with him.

Gershwin had explained to Consuelo that he and Heyward felt so much satisfaction in their collaboration on "Porgy and Bess" that they had talked about another partnership. They wanted to convey a lighter subject using a Caribbean or sub-tropical background, and he cautiously believed that Ybor City and Arturo Dardo's narrative poem just might be the place and atmosphere they were seeking. Heyward was planning to visit Cuba, and some other places to search for material for the new project, which would be more traditional Broadway type musical theater. Travelling to the Caribbean could be avoided if Dardo's poem was as inspiring as Gershwin believed.

Consuelo had asked James Flynn the customs broker who had grown up around the cigar factories to bring Gershwin to the Columbia Café and introduce him to cigar rollers and other Ybor City people. They had done that and Gershwin learned first-hand about the tabaqueros (cigar makers), the rezagadores (tobacco selectors), and the other skilled people required to produce fine clear Havana cigars. He was surprised about the many steps taken to make sure that every cigar of a brand was uniform in appearance and smoking character. The day before he had met Arturo Dardo briefly at the hotel, but Dardo hurried away to a meeting at the Cuban Club. Consuelo was certain that Dardo who was usually preoccupied didn't listen to her introduction, and missed Gershwin's name.

Consuelo had given Gershwin a bound copy of Dardo's forty page narrative poem recently published by an Ybor City print shop; *A Time in Ybor City* written in both English and Spanish. He had read it last night, and liked the cadence. It reminded him of The *Rime of the Ancient Mariner* as the poem's rhythm kept the reader engaged. Dardo's work painted a picture of the cigar workers as members of an under culture struggling for recognition and survival against the factory owners and the threat of mechanization. He touched on the introduction of women working alongside the men, and the flirting and sexual opportunities that now emerged that were missing before. Gershwin was impressed by the poem. He was especially attracted to the parts about the lectors and the cafeteros, and the women who peeled the cigar leafs who were called strippers, and thought about ways to feature their colorful jobs in musical numbers.

He planned to talk with Dardo about working with Heyward and him to expand the poem into a score and collaborating on a stage production set in a cigar factory. He enjoyed smoking clear Havana cigars, which made the project even more interesting. He liked being immersed in daily life of the characters portrayed on stage as he had with the Gullah people on the islands when he and Heyward visited their churches and participated in their music.

In February of 1932, over two years before, Gershwin vacationed in Havana with good friends Evert Jacobs, Emil Mosbacher, and Kay Swift. Their days were spent at Havana's Oriental Park Racetrack; dining in the exclusive Jockey Club, and gambling in the casino. Gershwin had become especially interested in the indigenous music of Cuba, and he spent every evening listening and enjoying the energetic bands and singers that put forth great rhythms and sounds almost non-stop.

He even purchased musical instruments that were typically Cuban and shipped them to New York. Gershwin's fascination with the sounds of Cuba ran so deeply that he couldn't allow the music from Havana's streets and bars and clubs to leave his mind until he had composed *Cuban Overture* immediately upon his return home. The work was premiered by the New York Philharmonic in an all Gershwin concert attended by almost 18,000 during the summer of that year in Lewiston Stadium on the campus of the City College of New York. Now he had a showcase for *Cuban Overture*, which would memorialize the work into the American culture as had his *Rhapsody in Blue* a decade before.

His plan was to open the newly conceived Gershwin-Heyward production with the beautiful sweeping *Cuban Overture* its melody reminiscent of Havana's colors and passions, but first he had to make Arturo Dardo believe that his work would be treated well on Broadway. The person to convince Dardo of anything since he was a difficult and self-centered individual was obviously Consuelo.

Gershwin had observed that she had the ability to make Dardo stop and focus just by asking him to do so. Consuelo was excited by Gershwin's plan for a new musical production set in Ybor City, and in fact, she had surprised him by offering to make a substantial investment in the show. The other investors would be the partners of Ladenburg Thalmann the Wall Street firm that handled Gershwin's finances. Gershwin thought about a backers' meeting involving the staid, conservative, German-Jewish bankers, members of Manhattan's ultra-exclusive Harmonie Club founded in 1865, and the gorgeous, curvy, emerald eyes and caramel skin Consuelo Middleton Davis. He laughed and looked forward to it happening.

Chapter 15

Hoover was also busy learning about Ybor City's inhabitants, but from an entirely different prospective than Gershwin's. Eager to find enemies of the government; early one morning Hoover arrived at the Tampa Police Department located on the corner of Florida Avenue and Jackson Street, in the city's central business section. He was seeking information. The officer who oversaw Ybor City's policing was Captain P.J. Cavanaugh originally from Boston, but who left New England's freezing winters after learning about western Florida's tropical climate.

Cavanaugh listened politely to Hoover's description of the guests of the Excelsior Hotel, and its colored proprietress likening it to the biblical Sodom and Gomorrah. "I'm certain Captain that there are many Florida laws broken at the hotel, and in other parts of Ybor City, and federal law was blatantly ignored regarding the sale of alcoholic beverages throughout the entire Prohibition era. They all drank that pineapple rot gut they call mamba. Everyone was making it at home. More important however are the dangerous foreigners who hide among the Cuban and Italian cigar rollers pretending to be ordinary factory workers. They're all radicals. It's in their blood. I'm going to talk to the factory owners, and tell them by allowing anarchists and Communists to work for them; they're just as guilty of sedition as the bomb throwers. They have to fire anyone who acts suspiciously. I'm collecting names."

Cavanaugh was an intelligent man, a graduate of Boston Latin High School in the same graduating class as financier Joseph P. Kennedy except Cavanaugh finished near the top and Kennedy near the bottom. He knew about the Palmer raids, and Hoover and the Bureau of Investigation to which the Tampa police sent its cards with the fingerprints of arrested suspects for inclusion in a national archive for the identification of criminals.

Now observing Hoover as the federal agent ranted on about threats to the nation; Cavanaugh wondered about the effectiveness of the Bureau with its four hundred agents scattered around the country having made a poor showing during the period known as "the lawless years." In regard to crimes related to Prohibition, bank robberies, kidnapping and murder there was no doubt that the Bureau had failed. Now the former bootleggers were taking over other kinds of businesses in a dozen large cities while Hoover steadfastly denied the existence of a national crime organization. Cavanaugh knew better. He had seen gangland killings carried out to take over territory first hand in Boston, Providence and Fall River, and then New Orleans, and now Tampa. "Mr. Hoover, you don't seriously believe that a few nuts are more dangerous than the organized criminal activity that has gotten powerful and very daring since the beginning of Prohibition?"

Barely hiding his scorn for Cavanaugh's opinion, Hoover responded, "Captain you are naive, which is understandable living in this back water town, and dealing with minor criminals. One of my plans is for the Bureau to educate police departments in the practice of the scientific collection of evidence. I personally have used the system of evidence collection and can say categorically that there are no connections between rival gangs in one city, and certainly none between cities. They don't like each other, and will never cooperate. The criminal mind is less intelligent and disorganized. They will never put together a plan that assigns territories and controls competition. They are crude and uneducated, and don't trust anyone especially fellow criminals."

Cavanaugh was also patient. He hoped that Hoover might still make some sense, but was becoming convinced that the federal agent was more used to stirring up and worsening problems than solving them. He stood up showing Hoover that their talk was over. Cavanaugh at 6'2" towered over Hoover even with the brown fedora perched on his head. Hoover made one last attempt to enlist Cavanaugh in the hunt for suspicious foreigners. "Captain I have to report to you that the state's miscegenation laws are ignored at the Excelsior Hotel. I am aware that Miss Davis, the hotel's owner, a Mulatto person has sexual relations with white men. She and her Jew piano player George Gershwin from New York are together long into the night in her lodgings. He has brought dark men and women to the hotel to sing together with white people and then they all go to Miss Davis' cottage and engage in I am certain, illegal acts."

Cavanaugh smiled slightly at Hoover hoping that the troubling man would leave soon. "Captain you're obviously not shocked by this kind of behavior. It must be this hot climate you live in, which has broken down your morals. I am also aware that Gershwin is writing music for a stage production that glorifies the Communist cigar workers at the expense of the factory owners written by some Cuban who also is staying in the hotel. It's seditious and must be stopped before he can put it on a stage in New York. It could become a rallying point for the Commies all over that city.

Cavanaugh his eyes narrowing said, "I'm beginning to think you have some personal problem with Miss Davis that goes beyond your authority, and I remind you that you're in Florida now and we don't like interference from federal people."

Hoover had become agitated. "Captain my authority exceeds any that you imagine you have. I have captured bank robbers and murderers all over this country without so much as a nod to local police. That's how I run my agency."

Holding on to his temper, Cavanaugh replied, "Good bye Mr. Hoover. I learned a lot from you today." Hoover left the police department, and Cavanaugh decided to telephone Consuelo whom he admired. When he was really fortunate he was her occasional lover.

Hoover left police headquarters unhappy and dissatisfied. He would have to take care of the Gershwin situation himself and soon. Now he could go back to Washington as he had been informed that the crisis in Congress had passed. He had been advised to disappear for a while during the current congressional snooping into his bureau's business. If he wasn't around Congress couldn't bother him, and would find other agencies to annoy. Hoover unlocked his LaSalle Coupe and drove back to Ybor City.

Chapter 16

A New Musical

Thanks to Consuelo's persuasiveness Dardo agreed to allow Gershwin, and Heyward who was waiting for a summons from Gershwin to come to Ybor City, to use the poem as the book for their new musical production. He wasn't really happy about it, but Consuelo assured him that his message would reach the widest possible audience. Dardo had not known of Gershwin's fame, and was suspicious that his work would be stolen from him, and his story mangled by allowing it to be turned into a stage production; especially of all things a musical. Gershwin who was almost always in an upbeat frame of mind was now dreading the association with Dardo who was usually in a dark mood about anything that came to his attention that day. Rose Gershwin would have called Dardo a "crepe hanger" referring to the practice of some European Jews of placing black crepe material around the front door of one's home to indicate that there was a death in the family.

For that reason Gershwin held off on asking Heyward to travel by train to Tampa until there was a written agreement between Dardo and them. Gershwin had decided to produce the show taking on the financial responsibilities connected with a Broadway production. Once the document that was being prepared by James Flynn was signed, and Dardo was paid an initial amount by Gershwin; a good faith payment in advance of royalties that were expected from the show and sheet music sales; they would begin to work.   Gershwin had outlined a libretto using Dardo's poem as a guide. He mailed copies of both to Heyward's home Dawn Hill in Henderson, North Carolina where the Heywards were now staying. Heyward telephoned the hotel and left a message for Gershwin that the material had arrived, and that he was studying both in order to create the show's book and actual roles for the story. He also said that he didn't feel the need to work in Tampa right now, but would come there eventually.

Gershwin had happily been anticipating another collaboration with Heyward. After completing "Porgy and Bess" he had given Heyward a photograph of himself at the piano with Heyward and Ira standing close by taken in Josephine Pinckney's home in Charleston. Pinckney a noted Southern novelist and poet often invited them for evening cocktails and tidbits, which passed for dinner among some of the city's elite who took their large meal at lunch. Gershwin had written on the picture the notes from their song *A Woman is a Sometimes Thing*, and the message, "Here's hoping our collaboration is an 'always' thing." Ira had written, "Being associated with you on 'Porgy and Bess' has been not only an honor but a pleasure."

Heyward felt the same way about the Gershwin brothers and was happy to be included in the heady world in which George and Ira traveled with ease. Even Dorothy, Heyward's protective wife had softened her attitude toward the Gershwins because they had treated DuBose with the respect he deserved. She wasn't happy however about her husband's plan to go to Tampa to work again with George Gershwin because she considered West Florida a mosquito infested swamp, and was concerned about DuBose's fragile health especially when he was away from home without her.

Nevertheless, Dorothy and DuBose had taken a grand tour by steamship in 1929 through the Mediterranean region that had culminated in Cairo. While in Egypt they rode camels among the pyramids and over to the Sphinx while clothed in traditional British style desert attire purchased at the safari outfitter Abercrombie and Fitch, in New York. In Jerusalem, which was part of Palestine a British Mandate, they found most of the religious sites distastefully commercial, and in his letters home DuBose wrote, "You either feel like laughing or being ashamed at the way the beautiful old legends are distorted and made to support a lot of dirty Jews and Arabs." He found that almost everything related to the religions had been made into commercial enterprises, and complained that the Christian sites were "providing a sense of high pressure sightseeing." In the mosques however he saw "a certain bare dignity and spaciousness that's a relief from the crowded and tinseled ornamentation of the churches."

He had shared those thoughts with George Gershwin during an evening together on Folly Island while they walked along the beach near the surf. Gershwin understood that Heyward didn't dislike people because of their ethnicity or religious belief. He enjoyed associating with people different from himself as he had proven with his affection for the Gullah people as evidenced in his writing. What he didn't care for were dishonest and deceitful people or those who were ostentatious and braggers. Heyward admittedly was most comfortable with those he considered of his same class who knew the expectations of polite society, but he also loved everyone associated with the theater from the actor playing a character with one line to the star.

In Heyward's next letter to Gershwin, he named the cast and their roles using Dardo's poem as inspiration and background. Gershwin was relieved to see that so much had been accomplished since time was running short. Ira telephoned daily pleading for him to return to New York to put the finishing touches on their opera, and to convince Heyward to be there as well. He was needed to work with the performers since even though they were all accomplished actors and vocalists; their training in theater had been in New York, and they had no knowledge about the Gullah. Heyward excited about the new show wrote to Gershwin.

August 2, 1934

Dear George,
    Greetings, and how are you finding Tampa? I have given some thought to the new project, and like what you have suggested as a plan for the production. My notes incorporating your musical ideas follow:

A Time in Ybor City a musical in two acts. From the first notes in the opening number "Cuban Overture" to the final notes of "Reprise," A Time in Ybor City contains 19 songs which demonstrate the location, enhance and define characters and produces a Cuban vibrancy. George from your authentic instrumentation; Tres Cubanos, Bata Drums, Cuban Laud and Maeimbula to the intricate rhythms of the Cuban-laced orchestration, one will be transported body and soul so much so by the music that the outside world is forgotten. While watching the show, <u>You are in Ybor City!</u>

The time is 1929, the place is the Havana cigar making capital Ybor City in northeast Tampa.

The production begins in Havana on a busy street at night with bright colors, loud music, dancers, excitement and two young women Dalia and Delores are plotting to go to Ybor City and earn lots of money as cigar rollers because they were taught the art by their grandfathers. The next day they travel by steamship from Havana to Ybor City with their cardboard suitcases against the wishes of both of their families. Once there and after contacting other Cubans for a place to stay; they find jobs in the Hoyo de Monterrey cigar factory not as cigar rollers, but as tobacco strippers. They are told that to work up to the higher paying position they had to be "nice" to the factory's manager. There are plots and sub plots to develop, intrigue and love affairs, managers against workers, threat of strikes, heroes and treachery. Through it all Dalia maintains her moral compass though she flirts with Jacinto the lector, and emerges as a union leader of the cigar workers, but after some temptations discovers Manuel who has quietly been in love with her all along, but was afraid to speak out. Dalia in her soliloquy bemoans the troubling prospects of the Cuban cigar world that has begun to change, and she questions the future of the handmade cigars because America is tiring of the high spending anything goes "Roaring 20s." (According to our friend Scott Fitzgerald) Always Cubans, and missing their families, Dalia and Manuel return to Cuba to marry.

The Cast:
Jacinto San Martin, the lector, a tall suave Cuban who is idolized by the cigar rollers in Hoyo De Monterrey cigar factory.

Dante Sanchez, the Spanish factory manager who answers to no one in Ybor City.

Dalia Gonzalez, a pretty young woman, and a skilled cigar roller who has a crush on Jacinto.

Lolita Rodriquez, the vamp flaunting herself and tempting the men working in the cigar factory.

Manuel Flores, a handsome young man, a cigar packer and shipper in love with Dalia.

Pablo Valdes, a slippery character and Dante's henchman.

Dolores Rios, Dalia's good friend.

The Strippers, a chorus line of beautiful women (strippers separated tobacco leaves from stems)

The Banders, a chorus line of young men (banders match up and put a dozen cigars together with a paper band)

Emilio Perez, el Cafetero (the coffee man)

Juan Diaz, a cigar roller
Teresa Sanchez, a cigar roller
Bernardo Garcia, a cigar roller
Gustavo Casellas, the gambler took a bet on anything.

Music:
"Cuban Overture"
   "Havana Nights" (Dalia and Delores)
   "Stroll Along With Me" (Manual)
   "Rumba Sequence" (Strippers and Banders)
   "Reading Shakespeare" (Jacinto)
   "Hot Coffee Three Times a day" (Emilio)
   "Busy Ybor City" (Juan, Teresa, Barnardo)
   "We are Cubans" (Ensemble)
   "Workers of the World" (Delores)
   "Strike, Strike" (Strippers and Banders)
   "Clear Havana Smokes" (Juan, Teresa, Bernardo)
   "Tamale (Hot for You)" (Lolita)
   "I Love You Dalia" (Manual)
   "Be lucky for me" (Gustavo)
   "Am I a Fool?" (Manual and Dalia)
   "I Believe in You" (Manual)
   "Dalia's Soliloquy" (Dalia)
   "We're Going Home" (Dalia, Delores, Manual, Strippers, and Banders)
   "Reprise" (Ensemble)
   George, I am ready to join you when you believe the time is right, and we can move forward on A Time in Ybor City.
   With my best wishes, and sincere regards to Ira,
   DuBose

Chapter 17

S omething was wrong. Books had been moved, papers shifted, and some desk drawers were slightly open. Someone had been in the bedroom closet and moved her dresses around. Ybor City people didn't lock up their homes following in the Cuban custom. Consuelo realized that her office had been searched. But why? Nothing in the office or her cottage had value to anyone but her. She knew that Harvey Sparks never entered her office except if she was there, and if she needed him they usually spoke in the lobby. Consuelo didn't trust John E. Hoover. He seemed slippery and she wouldn't have been surprised if he was snooping around her office, but her clothes closet?

Consuelo had noticed some differences in the contents of her cottage lately, but with George using the dining table to compose and then going to the hotel's lobby to play his work on the piano, she assumed he had moved some things around. Gershwin wouldn't do that as he liked his environment neat and planned out, and respected other people's places. He had been spending most of the evenings with Consuelo talking late into the night, and playing the new music after their suppers at the Columbia Restaurant, which had grown from a small café opened in 1903 to a block long Cuban restaurant. Gershwin had enjoyed Havana's restaurants when he visited there and liked the Columbia's familiarity. He and Consuelo drank sangria with brandy added as a complement to their arroz con pollo, sweet plantains, and salads with the Columbia's secret recipe dressing. They finished with sweet black Cuban coffee, pasteles, the pockets of fried dough filled with guava and cheese, and more brandy while listening to Cuban music played by enthusiastic bands and soulful singers. Amazingly both enjoyed as much food as they wished to consume without adding to their body weight.

Another favorite place for their dinners was the Las Novedades Restaurant located across and down the street from the Excelsior Hotel. It was famous for its garbanzo sopa a Spanish black bean soup, which along with excellent Segundo Bakery bread, and plates of lightly fried plantain strips dipped in mojo (garlic) sauce made a delicious and filling supper. They finished the meal with pineapple and coconut pasteles and Cuban coffee. During the midday, a Cafetero showed up at the Excelsior Hotel delivering coffee and Cuban sandwiches for the hotel's staff and anyone else who happened to be in the lobby at the time. Consuelo happily paid for the service of which Harvey Sparks kept close track making sure the charges were accurate when the weekly collection occurred on Saturdays.

Gershwin enjoyed fresh fruit especially the tropical fruits available at the Italian owned fruit and vegetable stands along Seventh Avenue in business during the morning. So Consuelo had Luisa one of the hotel chamber maids shop for pineapples, mangos, oranges, the newly introduced pink grapefruits and coconut, which she kept in the new GE Monitor Top Refrigerator the most important part of her cottage's kitchen because she didn't cook anything at all. After years of preparing food, and cleaning up afterward sometimes for large parties in Cooperstown Consuelo didn't want to cook or clean, and didn't even want the smell of food cooking in her home, and she was wealthy enough to pay others to do that for her. In fact her tendency to find suitable places to have meals away from home fit with the Cuban practice of daily taking small meals in the cafes that opened to the street and were scattered around the community. At times Consuelo was the lone woman in the café. She smiled at everyone who passed by and men out of respect tipped their hats to her.

At home in New York Gershwin would stop by the Fairway produce market on Broadway at 74th Street, a few blocks from his penthouse. Nathan, the store's owner, would rush over when he spotted his famous customer calling out, "Maestro, Maestro what can I get for you?" The fruit sold there was primarily apples and cherries from upstate New York, strawberries from New Jersey, and blueberries from Vermont during the summer, and bananas the only tropical fruit available, which have been imported into New York from Central America since the mid-1800s. When he was a boy growing up in the East New York section of Brooklyn produce mostly vegetables and apples were sold from pushcarts in the crowded streets. Fairway's fully packed store reminded him of those times. Perhaps there was a future musical production based on that experience. On the other hand most people growing up on the crowded streets of New York's immigrant neighborhoods would more than likely want to forget those times.

During the days Gershwin soaked up the Ybor City Cuban cigar making culture. Strolling along the avenues and stopping at the stores to talk with shop-keepers he purchased anything that caught his eye. He enjoyed shopping in new places, and sought out local artists' work. He also bought cigars from individual cigar rollers stationed in the nooks and alleys along Seventh Avenue. Gershwin connected with the Jewish merchants who had found their way to Ybor City after emigrating from Romania. Max Argintar owned a large general store and pawn shop that offered a great variety of goods. Gershwin would speak in his limited Yiddish to the members of the Argintar family who also spoke perfect Spanish and Italian in order to better serve their customers. He purchased straw colored shoes in Segal's shoe store, and discovered they actually had a pair of tennis shoes his size so he bought them as well.

The Jewish merchants and their stores were a popular and trusted part of the cigar making community and their fortunes coincided with the state of labor peace in the factories. There was an on-going tug of war between the cigar workers and the factory owners, much like the labor situation in New York's garment district. Gershwin's favorite Ybor City store was Steinberg's because it was like the busy clothing shops of his youth in Brooklyn. Whenever he spent time in a store talking to the owner or staff member he purposely bought something for himself or a gift to take back to New York for Ira and Lenore. He didn't buy anything for Rose his mother because she was hard to please and preferred picking out presents herself. He found hand worked gold bracelets, six in number, thin with intricate designs in Max Argintar's that he bought to thank Consuelo for her hospitality.

Consuelo thought about how much time she and Gershwin were spending together daily and often late into the night as well. They had only touched hands, their intimacy took the form of talking about their feelings and fears. At one point Consuelo was about to explain who she was or who she had been, but Gershwin stopped her before she told him about her early life and her time with Daniel. "Consuelo I have to leave in two or three days. I haven't been home for two months, and I'm becoming nervous about what's facing me with the opera and other commitments." Ira called and left messages for his brother almost every day. Paul Mueller called two or three times to tell his boss about his mail, and messages from friends and producers who wanted Gershwin's attention. "I'll start home Friday if I can take a train from here to Charleston and reserve a Pullman compartment to New York."

"George I'm going to miss you. I'm used to seeing you every day and hearing your music." She wasn't happy about his leaving as they had an easy relationship that defied definition. Despite his fame Gershwin was a pleasant humorous man. Consuelo had become attracted to his charm and presence and wondered if he was as uninhibited sexually as he was about everything else. She hoped to find out. "I enjoy our talking at night after you stop working. I hope we can be more than that. I had a passionate relationship with a great man that ended two years ago. I haven't thought about anyone else until now."

"I'm not disappearing; just going back to New York. You can take the train anytime you want to see me. In fact I want you to be at the opening of 'Porgy and Bess.' And you should meet your fellow backers of our new show. They're looking forward to meeting you."

"I can just imagine what they'll think when I walk into their board room. George, you're a devil, but I like that about you. I very much like it."

"Look I have to finish scoring 'Porgy and Bess' and that will take months. It's a complicated collection of music sung by soloists, duets, and choruses; played by a full orchestra, and it's running far too long. I have a lot to do. The Theater Guild wants to preview it in Boston next fall and then open on Broadway by the end of the year." He looked at Consuelo anxiously. "I'm really comfortable with you, but I can't think about that right now, but I want you, to come up for the opening or before then if I make good progress."

Consuelo always trying to be reasonable said, "Let's see what happens when you get back to work in New York. Remember you've been away for a long while so your army of admirers have missed you, and won't let you get bored. Shall I ask Harvey to arrange for a Pullman ticket for you?"

Gershwin's absence from New York wasn't unusual for him. He enjoyed traveling and in 1928 along with Ira and Lenore spent almost three months in Europe. They visited with the great stage star Gertrude Lawrence in England, worked on "An American in Paris" in Paris, and ate Sacher Torts at Café Sacher in Vienna listening to *Rhapsody in Blue* at almost every event they attended. They were in the company of the continent's most celebrated composers and musicians. George charmed everyone, and returned home buoyant and ready to work on an opera.

Gershwin walked into Consuelo's kitchen and opened the refrigerator. He took out a perfect Florida orange. "I'm going to miss you and the oranges, but I'll miss you more." It was as much as he could reveal of his feelings for Consuelo, and she understood what he didn't say.

Chapter 18

Heyward's letter received this morning provided some relief to Gershwin. He had told Heyward that they would work on the new production in Ybor City, and was about to write to him that plans had changed and he was going back to New York soon. In his letter Heyward had written that he now preferred they work on the show in New York as Dorothy and he would travel there in early October for the premiere of "Day Without End" Eugene O'Neill's play of Catholic boyhood that turns the suffering hero to Socialism, Communism and atheism before returning to the fold. It was opening on Broadway in the Henry Miller Theater produced by the Theater Guild. O'Neill was a friend of Dorothy from their days at Harvard's writers' program, and had invited them to the premiere. Heyward offered to secure a ticket for the performance for Gershwin. Gershwin in his return letter to Heyward would decline as he didn't enjoy O'Neill's work and didn't like O'Neill. He was fascinated with O'Neill's latest wife Carlotta Monterey however and had thought about fashioning one of the characters in "A Time in Ybor City" after her.

Gershwin had been working day and night composing the melodies for the songs Heyward had assigned to the characters and numbers performed by the choruses he created. He used the memories and imagery he had stored in his mind, and brought them to life in his score of *Havana Nights* using the music and tumult from the visit to Havana two years ago. It had a completely different beat from his *Cuban Rhapsody*. *Reading Shakespeare* was written in *grandioso* style signifying the haughty demeanor of the lector Jacinto San Martin, one of the show's featured roles. The songs style was big and regal in regard to orchestration and structure. Gershwin's favorite so far was the rousing *Hot Coffee Three Times a Day* an ensemble piece sung by the entire company. *We are Cubans* a fiery song that Dalia, Manuel and Delores take turns singing the solo passages, which then slowly builds by adding a voice to form a duet and finally all three singers combine into a powerful trio singing in a defiant manner as they assert their ethnic background remembering their days in Cuba.

For the song, *Busy Ybor City* Gershwin reproduced the sounds and sights found along Ybor City's Seventh Avenue during the times he talked with the store owners. The stirring energy of soaring violins and violas rise above the percolating rhythms of the orchestra's Cuban drums and guitars. However, he wasn't sure who would sing this number. *Tamale (Hot for You)* was Lolita's song message to all the males in the cigar factory. It featured trumpets, trombones and the woodwind section transmogrifying the sexual lyrics into hot Cubano jazz music.

He created the music for *Clear Havana Smokes* to be sung by the cigar rollers; while he puffed away on an Antonio Cespedes handmade cigar that "catered to the individual tastes of fastidious smokers." "*Clear Havana Smokes*" was written as a slick, prodding piece emoting both the cigar workers and the smokers. It utilized slow downward glissandos by the string section while the upper woodwinds play a contrary counterpoint melody in the upper register to the clarinets and oboe, and all the while the basses and bassoons play the deliberate, repetitive oblique counterpoint melody. He drew the musical notes and symbols neatly on the printed song sheets. His work was as precise as a draftsman, and the horizontal pages appeared to be graphic designs of an artist who also knew how music was written.

The last musical number he scored in Tampa was *Be Lucky for Me* for Gustavo the gambler performed while Lolita distracted the other dice players by changing out of her work clothes into a slinky red dress. The music highlighted a sexy melody featuring the alto sax moving up and down the register culminating in a high trill at the end of the piece bringing the melody to an abrupt but satisfying closure. Gershwin had ideas and written notes about the other pieces of music but believed he had composed enough to keep Heyward busy writing lyrics when they got together in New York in just over a month's time.

He was pleased that pieces of the show had come together and that Arturo Dardo had been available to share his ideas. To Gershwin's surprise, Dardo understood the show's development process that was loosely based on his narrative poem. Heyward was writing the show's book, which sorted out the story, cast, and dialogue, but they had agreed to follow Dardo's work as closely as possible. Dardo said he liked the music Gershwin had composed and had some ideas for lyrics.

Gershwin decided to invite Dardo to come to New York and work with Heyward and him. Dardo didn't feel comfortable there after his last visit because New York was dirty and dangerous, and men sold pencils and apples on street corners so he didn't accept Gershwin's overture at first. Then he learned that when in Mexico for almost a month the year before Gershwin had struck up a friendship with the controversial muralist Diego Rivera., Rivera was considered a Communist by the American government, but not enough of a Communist by the Soviet government, which had expelled him from Moscow while he was making a large wall mural. Dardo was rarely impressed with anyone, but Gershwin's knowing Diego Rivera created a bond with the composer, and he agreed to join Heyward and Gershwin in October in New York.

Gershwin saw the pieces of the Ybor City show coming together and felt that he could relax a bit and go full speed on "Porgy and Bess" once he returned to New York. Ira had suggested getting the production in shape by accepting Emil Mosbacher's invitation to use his Palm Beach house, and work undisturbed until they finish since George was already in Florida. A good idea, but he wanted to return to New York first.

By inviting Dardo to New York Gershwin was taking a chance that the superb relationship among Heyward, Ira and himself forged by their work on "Porgy and Bess" would be disturbed by the moody Cuban. Perhaps they could rehabilitate Dardo by introducing him to the Broadway theater world, and life in their slice of the city. Gershwin believed Dardo had talent. He liked his writing and perhaps with the right coaching, Dardo's ideas about society and inequality could be turned into plays suitable for the New York stage. He would seek Heyward's opinion regarding Dardo's potential as a playwright.

Chapter 19

Strangely the bulb in the ceiling fixture was out. The Excelsior Hotel's second floor back section was black as pitch as Luisa Vasquez used her pass key to enter Room 16 at 10 pm. Luisa was the chamber maid for the four rooms in the section, and also tidied up the lobby and Consuelo's cottage, and covered the front desk when Harvey Sparks was called away. Two other maids cleaned and changed the linen in the hotel's remaining sixteen rooms. Rooms 16 and 18 were considered the best accommodations because they overlooked the Port of Tampa about a mile away. They were slightly larger and more expensive than the others. Room 16 was occupied by Arturo Dardo and Room 18 by George Gershwin.

Luisa arrived daily to the hotel by eight in the morning and reported to Consuelo who either sent her to purchase fruit on Seventh Avenue or asked her to begin cleaning the office and cottage, which never were really in disorder. Occasionally George Gershwin slept in the cottage's guest room after working well past midnight into the early morning. On those days, Luisa wasn't allowed to clean up as Consuelo didn't want Gershwin's sleep disturbed. Although Seventh Avenue was a busy noisy street with cars and trolley's moving around all day, Gershwin slept through the commotion that surrounded the hotel. Luisa after completing her work in the cottage and the hotel left the Excelsior at four every day and walked to her family's home on Ninth Avenue near 12th Street across from the *La Flora* cigar factory. Her father Pedro had been a skilled cigar maker for *La Flora* a tabaqueros until his death two years ago. He began to cough and found it difficult to stop. He chewed sugar cane brought from Cuba, which helped at first, but after three months of coughing and chest pain he died.

Their home was almost an exact replica of Consuelo's cottage except it wasn't painted on the inside, and the furnishings were simple. It was clean and neat. Lisa lived there with her mother who operated a cigar bunch-making machine in the Martinez Ybor cigar factory, along with her younger brother who attended high school. The Vasquez family purchased the cottage from the Martinez Ybor company ten years before when Luisa was nine years old. The cost was $725 including the land it stood on. They had paid $10 every month until the debt was satisfied and now the cottage was theirs.

Luisa had stopped at the meat store on her way home, and was preparing dinner. Cuban rice and beans with pork and fried plantains. The pork was covered with mojo crillo, a tangy sauce of garlic, orange and lemon juices and spices, and grilled in an iron pan. Luisa was a good cook and realized that eventually she would leave Ybor City and find a place; probably in a large city where her cooking and other more important talents would be rewarded. She saved her extra earnings for the time when she would move out. After dinner with her family, Luisa walked back to Seventh Avenue to attend a meeting of Disciulas de Marti' a women's organization founded in the 1890s that met regularly at the Cuban Club. The meeting featured plans to aid families suffering from misfortune, and then an exchange of gossip, which was the evening's highlight. Afterward, Luisa returned to the Excelsior Hotel.

Upon entering Room 16 from the dark hallway using her pass key she turned on a floor lamp that cast a low circle of light. Luisa opened the closet door and selected one of the three dresses hanging there, and picked up the pair of black two-inch heel shoes with ankle straps. In a dresser drawer wrapped in white paper were a black silk slip, black Chantilly lace under pants and brassiere, and a black garter belt with several pairs of silk stockings. Luisa gently rubbed the silk underwear on her face enjoying the smoothness and wishing her entire body could be covered in silk.

Among the lingerie was a white Excelsior Hotel envelope. Luisa took it and stuck it securely in a pocket of her dress. She had about a half hour to change her clothes so she entered the bathroom and removed all of her clothing hanging up the dress and underwear on a hook behind the door. Luisa washed her face before going back to the dresser to find the Max Factor makeup kit brought from New York City. She applied mascara to her eye lashes and red gloss to her lips and nipples. Then she dressed. Luisa was slender, about five foot six inches tall with a figure that men observed with pleasure. She had large brown eyes, a straight nose, and a sensuous mouth made even more desirable by adding the lip gloss. Her black hair was cut shorter than most other young Cuban women in Ybor City, and tonight she combed it to one side. When she finished with the makeup and putting on the articles of clothing she looked in the mirror, satisfied with her reflection. Then Luisa relaxed in the easy chair next to the floor lamp her legs crossed to show off the silk stockings and stylish shoes.

She waited only ten minutes until a key inserted in the lock opened the door. Arturo Dardo came into the room. He smiled slightly observing Luisa in the dim lamp light. He said, "Consuelo how nice of you to come here."

Chapter 20

⸙

Return to New York

It was the time to pack up clothing and what he accumulated during his excursions along Seventh Avenue visiting the stores first for research, and then because he enjoyed shopping for handmade objects and gifts for the people in his life. Gershwin looked at the clothing and other things piled on the bed, chairs, and dresser and wondered how he going to bring all of it home with him the day after tomorrow when he would board the train in Tampa. In New York, Paul Mueller would have taken care of the packing and the shipping of his possessions, but now Gershwin was on his own.

Gershwin left his room on the hotel's second floor and walked down the grand staircase to the lobby. Harvey Sparks was on duty at the front desk. "Hello, Mr. Gershwin. I'll have your bill ready tomorrow or would you like me to mail it to your home?

"Oh no. I have bank checks with me. I prefer to pay before I leave. I'll need some assistance with my luggage and help with shipping home some things. I guess I'm going to need some sturdy cartons and a way to get them to a shipper."

Harvey replied, "Miss Consuelo has an extra steamer trunk that she asked me to dispose of. Why don't you use it and we can have it picked up by Railway Express. It's in the storage room. I'll have Julio the night man bring it to your room. He's in early today putting out the trash barrels."

"Thanks Harvey, I knew you'd have a solution." Gershwin made a mental note to leave a generous gratuity for all of the telephone messages taken accurately and meticulously from Ira, Heyward and Paul Mueller, and the other courtesies extended by the front desk manager. He returned to his packing promising to take along much less clothing on future trips.

It had gotten late and he had to dress for the dinner he and Consuelo were having at the Port Tampa Inn that sat on a pier a mile into the bay that led to the ocean. The entire port, the pier, the rail line and two hotels had been built in the 1890s by Henry Plant. The Port Tampa Inn had barely survived the reversal of fortune the port had undergone since the end of the Gilded Age and the current financial depression. Its sister hotel the St. Elmo had stood nearby, and had been closed and demolished about ten years before.

The Port Tampa Inn existed as a getaway for adventurous couples married, unmarried and sometimes married to others. The inn was open only on weekends, but its dining room still offered superior cuisine. The room was divided into alcoves that offered privacy to the diners and lights were kept low. Candles on the tables added to the romantic atmosphere. The menu featured fresh fish as the hotel overlooked water on all sides. One of the Inn's unconfirmed legends told about guests fishing from their hotel room windows and the kitchen preparing the catch for dinner.

Harvey Spark's brother Milton was the maître d' hotel of the Port Tampa Inn, and between them a special dinner was planned and prepared for Consuelo and Gershwin. Also that night a trio of musicians from New Orleans was playing jazz and popular music in a corner of the dining room. Gershwin and Consuelo heard the music as they arrived at the inn, and were escorted to their table.

Milton Sparks welcomed them and uncorked a complimentary bottle of Dom Perignon Champagne. He poured the wine, and assured Consuelo and Gershwin that a delicious meal would be served. After toasting each other, they settled in and listened to the trio play the beautiful *Stardust* by Hoagy Carmichael, and then some great New Orleans jazz selections featuring improvisation by the trumpet player, a burly Negro man with a wonderful friendly smile. He wasn't older than the other players, but they referred to him as "Pops."

Consuelo and Gershwin were treated to the trio's playing hot jazz, as well as cool jazz. The three men played as one. The trumpet player was fluid and connected to the other musicians as they all played through the changes with ease each knowing what the others were going to do without verbal or visual cues. The performance thrilled Gershwin who appreciated other talented musicians. Then the trio played three Carmichael songs in a row, and Gershwin identified them as *Washboard Blues, Rockin' Chair* and *Georgia on my Mind.* Consuelo was impressed. "Of course you know Hoagy Carmichael's music because you must know Hoagy Carmichael." She hesitated before continuing. "Is there anyone famous you don't know? Of course not. So what are you doing here with me?"

Gershwin just laughed, "I thought we were having dinner."

At that point their shrimp cocktails arrived at their table. Four large shrimp perfectly prepared were nestled on shaved ice around a glass cup filled with spicy and sweet red sauce for dipping. Warm crusty bread served with circles of sweet butter appeared in a long basket covered with a thick gingham cotton napkin. Along with the bread were corn muffins shaped like small ears of corn and a dark bread laced with herbs. The rest of the meal was as delicious. The Sparks brothers had made sure that it was all perfect.

After they kissed for the first time, Consuelo whispered, "I want you to stay with me tonight." Gershwin, happy with Consuelo's invitation, acknowledged that he would. They stayed sipping Napoleon brandy from warm snifters as long as the trio played. When they packed up their instruments Gershwin shook the hand of each musician complimenting their playing and tipping them lavishly. The trumpet player said, "Mr. Gershwin, your music inspires me." When Gershwin asked for his name, the musician replied, "Call me Louie."

A taxi brought Consuelo and Gershwin back to the Excelsior Hotel just after midnight. They expected the hotel to be dark except for some lobby lighting but were surprised when they approached the hotel and lights were on everywhere, and Harvey and Julio Rio the night desk clerk were on the veranda looking anxiously for them. Julio had called Harvey who came back to the hotel and was about to telephone his brother Milton at the Port Tampa Inn when Consuelo and Gershwin's taxi appeared. Harvey opened the taxi's rear door. "We have trouble Miss Consuelo. Please come inside." They followed Sparks into the building. Luisa the chambermaid wrapped in a blanket was sobbing uncontrollably. A woman, who Consuelo didn't recognize, was attempting to comfort her. Sparks pulled Consuelo into her office and in a low voice told her, "Arturo Dardo was killed here tonight in his room. Someone opened his door with a key and shot him."

Consuelo digested the news and then asked, "Why's Luisa upset? Did she know Arturo that well?"

Sparks hesitated. He was embarrassed about what he was going to say especially to a woman who was also his boss. "Dardo was in his bed with Luisa when he was killed. Somehow the killer's shots missed her."

Consuelo knew what she had to do. She opened the desk's middle draw and took out a white card with a hand written phone number on the back. She asked the telephone operator to connect her, and after a minute a man's voice said "Hello, P.J. Cavanaugh here."

"P.J. This is Consuelo. I'm so sorry to call at this hour, but there was a murder in my hotel. I just returned and found out about it from Harvey Sparks. One of my guests was shot in his room. What should I do? Again I'm sorry to call you at home."

"No, no you did the right thing. I'll come over. I'll call headquarters and some deputies will get there soon. If they get there ahead of me tell them I'm on my way." P.J. hung up the telephone, and told his wife sleeping next to him that he was going out to investigate a murder in Ybor City.

Chapter 21

Murder in Ybor City

At precisely 10:30 that evening Arturo Dardo had left the rally at the Sans Souci Theatre on Seventh Avenue. It was held to raise money for the establishment of a school to maintain the Cuban culture and Spanish as a language for children of Cuban families who had become Americanized. Parents were concerned that by living in Florida their children would lose their heritage. The rally's chief sponsor was De Maximo M. Diaz, proprietor of the Florida Drug Company, Ybor City's first pharmacy and a proponent of preserving Cuban culture. Some of the white Cubans had adopted the practice of discriminating against their countrymen who were dark skinned even after having worked together for decades in the cigar factories. English was the only acceptable language in the local schools, and Cuban children were forgetting how to speak Spanish. Dardo supported the movement, but now he hurried down Seventh Avenue to the Excelsior Hotel excited about what was waiting for him.

He unlocked Room 16's door wondering about the unlit hallway. As he entered the room; he was relieved to see a woman sitting in the chair, her beauty enhanced by the dim light. When he greeted her as if she was Consuelo; Luisa didn't answer. They had done this before, and Dardo had told her not to speak because even if she looked like Consuelo, Luisa didn't sound like her. "Allow me to get comfortable. It's been a busy day, and I would like to change my clothes." In the bathroom, he quickly undressed, washed and put on his blue robe. Back in the bedroom he stood in front of Luisa and said, "I'm comfortable now so you should be comfortable also." Luisa understood what he meant, and stood up while Dardo sat on the bed watching the woman who resembled Consuelo undress. Luisa faced Dardo, and reached behind herself unbuttoning the top of the dress. Then she slowly pulled the garment up over her head tossing it to Dardo. She removed the black silk slip by moving it off her shoulders allowing it to slide down her body to the floor.

Looking provocatively at Dardo, Luisa slowly unclipped her stockings turning her back to Dardo and then unhooking the garter belt, and tossing it to him. Now she sat back in the chair. Shoes were undone, and slowly the stockings covering her fine slender legs were removed. Luisa sat with her legs apart allowing Dardo to enjoy her near nakedness. She heard him say, "Consuelo please continue." Luisa thought Dardo's imagining her as Consuelo was eerie, but the four ten dollar bills in the envelope left for her made up for any doubts she might have. Luisa was paid forty dollars a week working at the Excelsior Hotel, and Dardo had been supplementing her income two times a week at forty dollars each time whenever he was a hotel guest.

She stood again thinking about the money, and smiling. Luisa turned around unhooked the black brassiere waiting a few seconds before turning back tossing the under garment and moving directly in front of Dardo. Her firm breasts were close to his face and Dardo noticed her rouged nipples, adding to his already aroused condition. He held her breasts carefully squeezing and then burying his face between them. His tongue touched the tips of her nipples before he began to suck on them. Luisa was becoming aroused from Dardo's attention to her breasts. It was something she craved and enjoyed and felt herself responding by the wetness between her legs. Dardo's robe was open, and Luisa took hold of his jutting penis and stroked it. Dardo lay back on the bed while Luisa stripped off the silk under pants exposing her dark pubic triangle. She straddled his legs using both hands on his penis bending over to kiss it on the tip.

Dardo moved up on the bed to sit against the headboard allowing Luisa to lay full length and take his penis into her mouth. This was Dardo's favorite position. He covered Luisa completely with the sheet as she continued stimulating him with her mouth, tongue and lips. Covered as she was, Dardo could indulge his fantasy and talk to her as if it were Consuelo lying naked between his legs. He was happy and excited imagining the most astonishing woman he had ever known undressing and offering her body to him. Dardo considered allowing himself to climax but didn't want the moment to end even for the short time it took him to be ready again for more sexual activity. He thought about the pleasure of pretending to enter different places in Consuelo's body the next time. He decided that while he was fortunate to have Luisa's help indulging in this fantasy he deserved nothing less than that.

His climax was building. He stretched his legs and toes. His eyes closed. The pressure on his genitals increased, and as he began to experience the great release; the door of the room flew open. A figure its head covered with a shawl stepped in from the dark hallway and shot Dardo three times in the chest. Hesitating for only a second; the figure left slamming the door closed, and walked quickly to the open window in the hallway leading to the iron stairs fire escape attached to the building. It took only a few seconds for Luisa to untangle from the covers; run to the bathroom to vomit, and begin screaming.

Chapter 22

Two deputies arrived and Consuelo, Harvey, and Julio accompanied them to the second floor. They prevented anyone from entering Room 16 but didn't really know what else to do until P.J. Cavanaugh arrived. Harvey Sparks noticed that the door to Room 18 Gershwin's room was partially open. Consuelo opened the door stepped inside and saw that even though the place was full of clothing because Gershwin had begun packing; the room had been ransacked. Suitcases had been turned over and emptied, and dresser draws pulled out and dropped on the floor. There was disorder everywhere. Obviously, someone was searching for something, but was it found?

She told the deputies about the situation in Room 18 and went down to the first floor to find Gershwin waiting in her office. Luisa was quiet now. The woman with her turned out to be her mother summoned by Julio Rio. Consuelo told Gershwin what she knew about the murder, and that his room had been vandalized. "You better take a look at it, and see what's missing." They went upstairs, and Gershwin began sifting through his possessions scattered everywhere.

"My crocodile briefcase is gone. It's leather with two straps." He sat down on the bed. I don't care about the briefcase, but it's packed with the score of "A Time in Ybor City." "It was the only copy. All my notes and Heyward's outline and his letters are gone. And I just realized that the bound copies of Dardo's poem were in a box here. I was bringing them to New York to give to backers, and they're not here." He grew pale for a moment. "Where's Harvey? I need to see him." They ran down to the lobby.

Sparks was standing on the hotel's veranda waiting for P.J. Cavanaugh who was driving from Seminole Heights in West Tampa a thirty-minute trip even with light traffic at this hour of the morning. "Harvey is the office safe all right?"

Sparks was surprised by Gershwin's question. "Sure Mr. Gershwin. Let's go see just to make sure."

They quickly walked behind the front desk. Sparks opened a wood cabinet that covered a cast iron Mosler safe, 58 inches tall by 37 inches wide. He knelt and spun the silver dial putting in the four number combination, pulled down the handle and the heavy door popped slightly open. Before he could stand up Gershwin pulled open the door and reached in to grab a small version of his Nile crocodile skin suitcases. As soon as he opened the snaps on the case he was obviously relieved. The complete original score of "Porgy and Bess" was where he had put it for safekeeping at Harvey's suggestion. "This is what someone was looking for in my room, but why?"

P.J Cavanaugh had arrived after picking up Wilford Hanna the Hillsborough County coroner. They went upstairs after some brief introductions. While the coroner remained upstairs, Cavanaugh spoke quietly with Consuelo. "This isn't the way I expected to see you again. What do you know about the victim?"

Cavanaugh and Consuelo had some history, not very much, but there had been some occasions they had been together. Consuelo didn't regret it, but wanted to forget about it. She told Cavanaugh what she knew about Dardo and that he was a regular guest at the hotel. Consuelo neglected to mention that Luisa was under the covers in Dardo's bed when he was killed. She had assured Consuelo that she hadn't seen anything, and didn't know anything was wrong until she heard the shots. Luisa was resting in Consuelo's cottage. Cavanaugh was serious when he asked Consuelo who was the woman with Dardo as they found women's clothing around the room and in the closet. Consuelo had warned Luisa that if questioned she should insist that Dardo had seduced her with a promise they would marry, and they had plans to return to Cuba. "P.J. the woman is Luisa Vasquez. She is one of my employees. I believe Arturo made promises to her about a future together. She's young and in love. Somehow she was spared." Cavanaugh asked where he could find Luisa. He wanted to talk with her right then before she forgot anything that might be helpful. "She's with her mother in my cottage. Luisa was hysterical when we found her."

Luisa and her mother sat on the couch holding hands. Consuelo had given clothing to Luisa who was naked under the blanket. Gershwin had poured brandy and urged the two women to sip the amber liquor to calm them. P.J. introduced himself saying, "Mr. Gershwin I would like to talk with you at some point just to get your ideas of the situation. I understand that you and the victim were writing a musical show." Cavanaugh had remembered the morning in his office with John Edgar Hoover, and his rage over the Gershwin-Dardo collaboration. He also remembered Hoover's comment about Consuelo and Gershwin, and now, seeing her for the first time in almost a year, he felt envious.

It was 3 am by the time Cavanaugh finished questioning Luisa, Gershwin, Harvey Sparks and Julio Rio. The coroner had finished his examination and determined that Dardo's life was ended by three bullets fired into his heart. He asked Harvey for the front desk telephone and called the Boza Mortuary that served the Cuban community in Ybor City and West Tampa. A hearse would be dispatched to pick up the remains. The Boza family had been morticians in Havana since 1856, and moved a branch of the family first to Keywest and later on to Tampa following the Cuban migration of cigar rollers to Florida. Coroner Hanna standing at the front desk filled out the Hillsborough County death certificate for Arturo Dardo of Havana, Cuba. Cause of death was listed as three gunshot wounds (homicide), and his age was 47. He had made an original and two copies using carbon paper. The copies were clear, and he signed each one. The coroner gave a copy to Harvey Sparks instructing him to give it to the morticians when they arrived to collect Dardo's body. He gave Cavanaugh the second copy and kept the original for the county clerk.

When Cavanaugh told Consuelo that he was going to the Segundo bakery on the side street across Seventh Avenue nearby the hotel. She asked, "Are you hungry?"

"No. I want to talk with the bakers. They start work after 11 every night because the store opens at 5am. I want to find out if anyone saw anything that could help us. The cigar factories start work at 6AM so Segundo has to be ready for them. Warm bread and coffee is what the cigar workers have for breakfast every day. Please come with me." They walked together to the brightly lit bakery. The good smell of fresh baked bread reached them a half block before. The bakery's large doorways were open to the street and they saw what appeared to be brightly lit confusion, but was actually a place where a thousand loaves of bread and many other bakery treats were produced every day. After checking with the bakery manager, Cavanaugh called out, and work ceased for a moment. He identified himself and Consuelo asking if the bakers had seen anyone near the Excelsior Hotel at about eleven o'clock. Two men raised their hands. Cavanaugh before asking the men to step outside to talk looked at the manager who nodded his assent. Jose' Rodriguez and Ramon Diaz were bakers who almost every night walked along 18th Street by the Excelsior Hotel to their work, which began at midnight. They saw someone climbing down the fire escape on the back of the building about 11:30. Cavanaugh asked them to describe what they saw. Jose' did the talking for the two of them at first. "It was strange. It looked like a woman with a shawl on her head that hid her face. I couldn't see what else she had on. It's dark back there. "

Ramon agreed, "Yep, it looked like a woman, but I'm not so sure." When Cavanaugh asked if the person carried anything Ramon replied, "A satchel and a small box that she picked up off the ground."

"Did you see where the person went after climbing down from the hotel?" Cavanaugh was excited now. This was a good lead in a murder case.

Both Jose' and Ramon agreed that the figure ran to a car parked about a half block away. "What kind of car? What color was it?" demanded Cavanaugh? Jose' thought the car was a black Cadillac coupe. Ramon's pick was a dark green LaSalle; no particular model. Grateful but frustrated; Cavanaugh thanked the bakers, and he and Consuelo began to walk back to the Excelsior.

At Seventh Avenue, they stopped and Consuelo told Cavanaugh how impressed she was with his prediction that someone from the bakery had seen something that could be important in solving Dardo's murder. He was elated and said, "I'm not one of those crackers with a badge. If I stayed in Boston, I probably would be the head of the Murder Squad by now, but I couldn't stand the cold anymore. I was sick all the time in the winter. You know I went to Boston Latin. I studied Shakespeare, Chaucer, the Romantics and read Flaubert in French."

"I know you're smart. I wouldn't have spent those times with you if you weren't, but that's in the past." She put her hand on his chest. "You're a great guy P.J., but you're married, and besides I'm leaving Ybor City soon forever." As surprised as P.J. was, Consuelo was even more surprised that she had said it out loud because it was not something she had thought much about, but now having expressed it she knew that it was time to make changes in her life. She ended the discussion quickly. "I don't want to talk about it. Nothing is settled."

As they reached the hotel Cavanaugh asked, "Where's John Hoover? He's next on my list."

"Oh, he checked out this afternoon. He said he was taking a train at three for Charleston. Harvey got a taxi for him. He'll change trains there this morning and catch a Pullman to Washington. Why do you want to see him? He's awfully disagreeable."

"Because I'll tell you a secret that the coroner and I agree on. Dardo was shot three times. The bullets entered his body within an inch of each other like hitting the bull's eye of a paper body target the kind lawmen practice on. Most everyone else practices by shooting tin cans off fence posts. I need to find Hoover."

Chapter 23

By mid-day Dardo's body had been removed, his possessions packed up and stored. The bloody mattress rolled up tied and brought to the city dump. At Consuelo's direction, the chamber maids mopped up with bleach dissolving the blood stains. Consuelo discovered three of her dresses in Dardo's room; she threw them out, but kept the underwear and makeup that she assumed was Luisa's.

Cavanaugh had given Consuelo the white envelope containing four ten dollar bills that he had found in the room. She said, "Oh Dardo paid his hotel bill at the end of the week. I guess he didn't have a chance before he was killed." When Luisa came to the hotel that afternoon Consuelo gave her the envelope and a bag containing the underwear and makeup. "I know this money was for you. I'm not judging you, but if you want to stay on you can't become involved with a guest again. I'm closing the hotel for a few weeks. Everyone will still be paid. You may come here Fridays and Harvey will give you your pay envelope. He'll let you know when we'll open again." Luisa hugged Consuelo, and hurried out of the building joining the throngs of people on Seventh Avenue who suddenly were interested in the Excelsior Hotel.

Consuelo's next task was to talk with Gershwin. Obviously, they had not spent the night together. Gershwin had fallen asleep still dressed in Consuelo's bedroom, but with Cavanaugh staying around until daylight she hadn't slept at all. Gershwin was leaving the next day, and she had planned a quiet supper in her cottage, but Dardo's murder changed everything. She found him in Room 18 putting clothes in a suitcase. He looked distraught. "George, what's going on? Consuelo hugged him their faces touching as she soothed him.

"It's my fault Arturo was killed. I talked him into the collaboration. Don't you see only our score and his poetry was stolen? Someone wanted to stop us, but who would go to such an extreme?" He held on to Consuelo who in spite of staying up all night looked lovely. "It was only a show, a musical. No one should die over it."

"George please don't blame yourself. You can't be blamed. Arturo must have made enemies that have nothing to do with your show." She hesitated, "I'm not supposed to say this, but John Edgar Hoover is a suspect. I don't know why he would murder Arturo, but the police are looking for him." They pushed some of the clothing away and sat on the bed holding on to each other afraid to let go and allow the world back into their lives.

Later in the cottage, they had drinks; Bacardi Cuban rum poured over ice cubes with pineapple juice. They drank to Dardo's memory. Neither was hungry, and the romantic dinner planned for Gershwin's last night was forgotten. Consuelo told Gershwin that she had closed the hotel at least until September, and that she was on her way to begin a new phase of her life, and she was going to leave Ybor City. She decided to tell him everything about herself, and how Ybor City a place with a culture so different from any she had known had become her temporary home. But first Consuelo wanted to help Gershwin pack up all of his belongings that were scattered about his hotel room.

She was about to go upstairs when Harvey Sparks called to her. "Miss Consuelo, Captain Cavanaugh is here to see you" Frustrated because her time alone with Gershwin was slipping away Consuelo met P.J. in the hotel lobby.

"I want to give you a progress report. I sent a telegram to the Charleston police department and the Atlantic Coast Line Railroad station in North Charleston where the train connection to Washington, DC is made. I asked them to look for John E. Hoover a United States Agent who is probably armed with a 35 caliber Smith & Wesson Government model pistol, which is what they issue to the Bureau of Investigation agents. I explained that he was a suspect in a murder investigation." Cavanaugh hesitated looking at Consuelo as if he was remembering their intimate times together.

His thoughts about her interrupted his report, but he forced himself to continue. "Charleston police and railroad police searched the train from Tampa. Hoover wasn't aboard. They checked the Pullman reservations from Charleston to Washington, and didn't find anything for Hoover. We've concluded that he wasn't on the train." He stopped talking. He looked into her green eyes and then at her smooth neck, and into her cleavage exposed in the Cuban style sun dress. "Look I have to get out of here. I can't think when you're around. I have another lead to check out so I'll be back in a couple of days." He left quickly, and Consuelo went upstairs to see what she could do for Gershwin before he left the next morning.

Gershwin was making a lackluster attempt to push clothing into suitcases and the trunk that Julio had delivered to the room. A usually meticulous dresser, Gershwin was careful about his clothing, but now he was cramming his fine shirts, suits ties and shoes into any space open in the suitcases and the trunk. Consuelo was surprised by his lack of interest in packing properly. "George what are you doing? Let me help you." She salvaged some light weight summer suits and folded them. Soon she had packed an entire suitcase with carefully folded clothing, which would survive the trip to New York.

Gershwin sat on the bed. "I have enough to get on the train. It's all in one suitcase. That's all I'm taking with me, and the small case in the safe downstairs of course." He appeared exhausted. "You can give all of this away to a charity. The clothing is mostly new. Someone might use it." He lay down with his head on a pillow, but kept watching Consuelo as she plucked pieces of clothing from the floor, folding each neatly and placing it in an open suitcase. "Come here. Please stop packing. I don't care about any of that stuff." Consuelo put down the English custom made shirt she was folding kicked off her shoes and joined Gershwin on his bed. They faced each other and pulled close together. Within minutes they were asleep.

Chapter 24

Consuelo was awake at 5am, and left Gershwin's room. She had remembered something she wanted to take care of before Gershwin left for his 11 o'clock train. Four days earlier Arturo Dardo had given her Gershwin's Leica 35 millimeter camera. Dardo had wanted to take photos of the life in Ybor City especially the after work night life as a reference for their show, and Gershwin had lent the camera to him. Now Consuelo recalled Dardo's agitated state when he handed her the camera, and said, "Consuelo put this away until George is ready to leave here. I'll explain the pictures to him, after he has the film developed, when I'm in New York." Consuelo wrapped the camera in brown paper, and deposited it in the office safe. Because it was covered with paper, Gershwin didn't notice the camera when he retrieved the "Porgy and Bess" score. She opened the safe and looked at the Leica wondering what was on the film, and whether or not she should tell P.J. about it. She closed the safe, and decided it could wait until George was safely back home.

Gershwin showed up at the cottage at 8:30. "I had a dream we fell asleep together last night." I'm ready to go home. I put all of my stuff in the suitcases and your trunk. Can you have it sent Railway Express collect?"

"Yes sure, Harvey will take care of that. And it wasn't a dream. We did sleep together, but that's all we did." They hugged, and Consuelo said, "Don't forget your camera. Arturo gave it to me a few days ago. He was worried about something; maybe some of the pictures he took with it so I put in the safe."

"Thanks I almost forgot about the Leica. It's funny, but it was given to me by Gregory Zilboorg, my psychoanalyst. He also taught me how to develop film. He has a darkroom in his house. I like working with the chemicals and making prints."

"George you're so surprising. Your doctor doesn't ask you anything about yourself, but teaches you how to develop pictures. I read about analysis. It seems it's only for wealthy intellectuals bored with their lives."

"Gershwin laughed at Consuelo's assertion. "You're probably right, and it's probably worthless. Come to think of it, about half of Kay Swift's Warburg family goes to Zilboorg. In fact, he's at the parties at the Greenwich estate in the summer. Gregory is a charlatan, but we keep him around for his amusement value. He's the court jester." He thought for a moment. "Consuelo, analysis is just something to do for some people with too much time and money who like to talk about themselves. Maybe that's why I did it."

"I'll get the camera and your small bag from the safe." Consuelo stood and left the cottage while Gershwin poured himself a large glass of fresh orange juice in Consuelo's kitchen. She returned and handed the camera to Gershwin.

"You know I gave the same model Leica to Kay's daughter Andrea for a birthday gift. I also taught her to develop film at Zilboorg's. The Warburg townhouses are across the street from his place."

"You live a life in New York that's unknown to everyone else. Do all of you do everything together?" Consuelo realized that Gershwin, Kay Swift, the Warburg's, their psychiatrist and how many others socialize and practically live together without the matter of a love affair between the wife of a prominent family member and a famous composer having an effect on their friendship. "George I'm impressed how accepting your friends are about you and Kay. Maybe because I'm just a girl from a small town I'm not used to people knowing everything about me. In fact I had an almost three year love affair that was kept secret."

"Yes, but I can guess who you were with because there's a name and an address in Cooperstown, New York stenciled on the trunk you gave me." What he didn't say was that he had heard about Consuelo and Daniel Clark before ever coming to Ybor City. "I better get to the station in case the train's early. They kissed goodbye passionately, and Gershwin walked back to the hotel lobby. Harvey Sparks had a taxi waiting. Consuelo remained in her cottage. Gershwin had promised to telephone after he arrived home. She hoped he would.

The next afternoon, P.J. Cavanaugh stopped at the Excelsior. He was happy he had an excuse to visit Consuelo even it is was official police business. Consuelo was in her office at her desk looking for the pass key attached to a square piece of wood that had been kept in the middle drawer. She hadn't used it but believed she should have access to all the hotel's rooms. Strangely it was missing. She looked up and Cavanaugh was standing in front of her. "P.J. you're quiet. I didn't hear you come in. I've been searching for my pass key. It's not here."

Cavanaugh shook his head. "That could be how the intruder opened up Dardo's and Gershwin's rooms. Do you lock up this place at night?"

"Not always. It's Cuban to leave doors unlocked. We haven't had a problem until now."

Cavanaugh sighed. "There's always the first time. Look I have something important to tell you about our man Hoover." He sat in the chair next to Consuelo's desk and took a small notebook from his jacket pocket and thumbed through the pages until he found what he was looking for. "All right here goes. I didn't try to stop Hoover after I found out he wasn't on the train. I really didn't know if it was him in back of the hotel the night of the murder. I had either a black Cadillac or a green LaSalle as the car possibly used by the murderer. They're made by the same company, but there are differences. I didn't want cops in five states stopping Cadillacs and LaSalle's, which are everywhere because I don't know for sure which way Hoover was going." He stood and removed his suit jacket. "It's too hot in here. Can we get out of the sun light?"

Consuelo also stood up. "Let's go to the lobby. The ceiling fans move the air around better than the small ones. I'll get some ice water." She went to her cottage and emptied all four of the small freezer compartment's ice trays into a ceramic pitcher and added cold water from a large rectangular refrigerator bottle. She returned to the hotel lobby with the pitcher and two glasses.

Cavanaugh gratefully drank the cold water and continued his story. "I decided to telephone Washington, and try to talk to Hoover directly. My call to the Bureau was answered by a Helen Gandy who said she was Hoover's secretary and assistant. She also said Hoover was in conference and couldn't be disturbed. I asked when John E. Hoover had returned to Washington, and here it gets interesting. Miss Gandy said he hadn't been away." He took another long drink, and Consuelo refilled his water glass. "I said, he was just in Tampa, Florida, and she said she didn't recall him ever going to Tampa, and he never referred to himself as John E. Hoover, but rather J. Edgar Hoover. I asked her to describe him, and her description wasn't far from what I remember when Hoover came to my office."

Consuelo asked, "Do you think our Hoover was an imposter, someone following Arturo?"

"I honestly don't know. I also asked Miss Gandy if she knew what kind of automobile Hoover owned. She said a Chrysler Airflow color tan. I also asked her if Hoover carried a firearm. Her answer was, 'Why would he? He's an executive not a cowboy. He wouldn't know how to use a gun. He's not mechanically inclined.' I asked her when I could talk directly to Hoover. She said I had to talk with someone named John Mohr who was the head guy after Hoover and Clyde Tolson. I said all right, and then I'm talking with another secretary. This one a Miss Church was just as friendly."

"Poor P.J. detective work isn't as much fun as I thought."

"Yeah well it has its moments. The next thing I know this John Mohr is on the telephone. I'm getting worried about the telephone bill, but I have to stay on. I ask Mohr when Hoover got back. He says 'I didn't know he was away from here.' Did you actually see him over the last week I ask? He says, 'Of course I see him every day; why are you asking?' I try the John E. name on him, and he says, 'who?' I saw no need to say anything else. They have Hoover bottled up in Washington. Even if we found more evidence the Washington police won't arrest him for us. I'm sure about that."

Cavanaugh reluctantly left, and Consuelo decided she would write a letter to Aunt Vanessa in Cooperstown. She would tell her only relative that she would visit soon. For the first time that she could remember she was lonely.

Somehow without much thought, she had made the decision to leave Ybor City soon. Consuelo was tired of the heat, the crowded streets, the strikes, the smell of tobacco leaves, and worse the cigar smoke. She resented the overwhelming Cuban machismo culture that surrounded her outside her hotel, and she was bored hearing about the latest crisis on the island they all left and loved, but didn't want to return to. She was exhausted from the recent events in her life. Dardo's murder, and knowing George Gershwin for two weeks.

Chapter 25

Consuelo had thought she wouldn't hear from Gershwin, but he surprised her by telephoning three weeks after returning home. It had taken that long to catch up with his commitments and appointments. He told her that he had stopped using Gregory Zilboorg as his analyst realizing that the doctor was dangerously incompetent, but Kay Swift was now heavily involved in a professional relationship with him. He admitted he was seeing Kay again, but asked Consuelo to be in New York on November 21 for the opening of the new Cole Porter show "Anything Goes" starring Ethel Merman and William Gaxton. "Kay will be living in Reno temporarily to establish Nevada residency beginning October 12 in order to file for a divorce from James," Gershwin explained.

"Kay's getting divorced? Does that mean you and Kay are getting married?"

"No, no it's not for that reason. She wants to end the marriage."

Gershwin's treating Kay's plan to divorce James so lightly surprised Consuelo. "Are you asking me to be your date for the show," Consuelo asked Gershwin?

"Why yes," Gershwin responded, "And for the party later at Sardis. I promise you'll meet some great people. I'll book a suite for you at the Plaza."

"Let me think about that. I'm planning to visit my aunt in Cooperstown before winter so it may work out for me. Have you told DuBose Heyward about Arturo's murder?"

"I did that as soon as I got home. Has there been any progress with the investigation? I noticed that the police captain didn't take his eyes away from you.

Not that I blame him. You're absolutely beautiful. Are you sure you don't sing and dance? I would love to write a show for you?"

"Thank you George, but that's not what I'm good at." Leaving Gershwin to imagine what she was good at. "There's some new information about Arturo's death, but I don't know what it all means."

"Please consider coming here in November. I miss you and our lost opportunities. I'll telephone again soon. Goodbye, my dearest." After hanging up the telephone, Consuelo sat still for a while thinking about her situation. If anything Gershwin's telephone call had made up her mind about leaving Ybor City, but his invitation had confused her. Kay was away so he needed a date for the Cole Porter show opening, but he could find dozens of women in New York who would be thrilled to go with him. Consuelo wondered if she meant more to him than his showing up with a presentable woman or if Kay read about the show's opening and George was mentioned along with a companion maybe it was better he was with someone she didn't know. If it was a woman Kay knew she possibly wouldn't care for that. He had made it clear to Consuelo that he was unhappy about missing out on the physical relationship they should have had, especially since they were emotionally joined together. She had assumed they would be lovers soon after meeting Gershwin. Planning for romance at the elegant Plaza Hotel in New York was just what Consuelo needed right now.

Consuelo evaluated her situation. She didn't have close friends in Ybor City, and in fact had no one at all she felt close to. All her adult life she had been alone, and had done much more than just survived. She was thirty four, and her face and body could compete with women ten years younger. Men always watched her, and even women too. Consuelo looked around for Harvey Sparks, and found him checking the towels and bed linen in the two storage closets on the second floor. "Harvey let's talk. I have some thoughts I want to share with you. Come to the cottage when you finish up."

He was surprised since almost all business between them was conducted at the front desk or in the lobby. Harvey had been in Consuelo's cottage only on a couple of occasions to bring the mail or packages that had been delivered for her. He locked the linen closets and wondering what the boss had on her mind followed her across the lobby and through the office to the cottage. Without any preamble, Consuelo said, "Harvey I'm leaving Ybor City as soon as it's practical. In any case before the end of the year."

Sparks was stunned. "Miss Consuelo I'm surprised. Where are you going?"

"First to New York, and then I'm not sure. But I wanted to talk with you about the hotel. If you want to own it, I want to work that out for you. I appreciate how much you've helped me. I know this is really sudden, but I need to know if you're interested."

"Sure I'd love to own the place. I always wanted to, but I don't have much money. My brother Milton could go in with me, but he has less than I do. I'm sorry I guess someone else will have to buy it."

"No, wait a minute," Consuelo protested. "I'm not asking for any money right now. I want to deed the hotel to you, and you can pay me from the profits. We both know the hotel is profitable most of the year. I really should have closed up this summer, but something made me keep it open, which wasn't a great idea. We can work out a value and payments, but don't worry I expect you to pay yourself first."

"Miss Consuelo I appreciate what you just offered me. I want to talk to my brother, and I'm getting married. Her name is Clemencia Reyes. I was going to tell you about her. We haven't picked the date yet, but I hope you'll be there. I have to tell her about this opportunity." Sparks was guarded in his responses as if he really couldn't believe what was happening. "Can I ask how much the hotel is worth, and is your cottage for sale?"

Consuelo thought for a minute. "I don't know how much it's worth because I really don't know how much was paid to the former owner, and come to think of it, I'll include the cottage as part of the deal. I'm leaving here, and not coming back. Consider the cottage my wedding present to you and Clemencia."

Sparks was stunned. "I don't know what to say, but yes, let's say we have an agreement." He knew he should seize the opportunity. "I know Milton and Clemencia will be happy."

"All right then I'll ask James Flynn to write up a contract. We'll make it as simple as possible. I want to turn over the hotel to you before I leave for New York in a few weeks." They shook hands and Sparks thanked Consuelo for her generosity. What he didn't realize was the relief she felt. Knowing that her tie to Ybor City was undone, her banishment was over.

Chapter 26

Manhattan November, 1934

On this train trip Consuelo didn't feel intimidated so she sat in the Club Car for most of the day sipping Bourbon whiskey with ginger ale. She relaxed in a comfortable reclining seat near a big window and watched the states go by. Consuelo brought along a book to read by a new author called John O'Hara; the novel, *Appointment in Samarra,* was his first published work, but she didn't read very much of it. She boarded the Richmond, Fredericksburg and Potomac Railroad's Champion passenger train in St. Petersburg, Florida south of Tampa at 9am on November 15, and expected to arrive at her destination the following afternoon. The Champion made stops in Jacksonville, Florida; Richmond, Virginia; Washington, DC; Potomac, Maryland; Wilmington, Delaware; Philadelphia and Trenton terminating at Grand Central Station in Manhattan. Consuelo traveled with her three matching pieces of Alfred Askew maple brown leather luggage. All of her immediate clothing needs were in the three valises. Whatever she left at the Excelsior was packed in a trunk, which Harvey would send to Consuelo once she found her next place to stay. The train arrived in New York City at 3:13 in the afternoon. A Red Cap took charge of the luggage and led Consuelo to the taxi stand on 42nd Street.

A short ride in the Checker cab brought Consuelo to the French chateau style Plaza Hotel across from Central Park designed by the same architect as the Dakota Apartments. She had lunched in the Plaza's Palm Court with Daniel when they had stayed in the nearby Sherry Netherland Hotel four years ago. Now she was alone and about to register for a stay until November 23. The white marble lobby sparkled and Consuelo's heels clicked along the wide corridor followed by a bellman carrying her luggage. Her suite on the fourteenth floor was ready, and she was informed by the desk clerk that Mr. George Gershwin had made the reservation, and would settle her bill. The clerk picked out the proper brass Plaza Hotel key, and an assistant manager escorted Consuelo to her suite and opened windows and turned on lamps. Two vases filled with cut flowers complimented the Champagne cooling in an ice bucket on the coffee table in the suite's living room. The luggage arrived and was placed in the French accented bedroom on stands eliminating the need for Consuelo to actually move anything. She sauntered around the high ceilinged rooms stopping at one of the wide windows to look at Central Park stretched out below. Obviously, when George Gershwin reserved a suite at the Plaza the best accommodations were provided. He had said he would telephone Consuelo and come to the hotel later so she knew she had time to rest. The train trip had been tiring, and she hadn't slept well in the Pullman compartment. Consuelo stripped off her clothing, donned a blue cotton T-shirt and got into the queen size bed. Within minutes she was asleep.

She was in the midst of a confusing dream when the telephone on the nightstand began ringing. She sat up trying to remember just where she was and was it day or night. It was Gershwin telephoning, and it was 7 pm. She had slept for almost three hours. "George I'm not dressed so please don't rush over to the hotel. I want to look my best for you."

"I'm sure you look beautiful. And I'm calling from the lobby on the house phone. I'll see you in a few minutes," and hung up the telephone.

Consuelo wasn't completely awake. She wasn't sure what to do so she hopped out of bed trying to think of what to wear when she heard the knock on the door. Still wearing only the T-shirt she opened the suite's door and pulled Gershwin into the room. Somehow during their intensive embrace and deep kisses, the T-shirt found its way over Consuelo's head and ended up on the floor. Within the next moments, Consuelo was back in her bed and Gershwin was quickly undressing before joining her. He turned off the lamp after closing the curtains, and they were entwined then joined, and in a little while happily depleted. "Gershwin had a wide smile. "I knew it would be wonderful. I'm so glad I surprised you so you didn't have time to get dressed."

"I wanted to be all dressed up when I saw you, but this was much better." She got out of bed to use the bathroom. Upon returning she saw Gershwin was watching so she pirouetted before joining him in bed again.

"You are gorgeous," he said, and reached for her again with even more intensity than before. Consuelo decided that it was too early in their physical relationship to introduce Gershwin to the exotic sexuality she and Daniel had enjoyed. Gershwin was a passionate but conservative lover believing it was his role to always lead. Consuelo could achieve an orgasm in almost any position so their having sex in the usual missionary style practiced by almost all American couples was satisfactory for her, but after a while she planned to introduce him to even greater pleasures. Dinner was forgotten about that night, and after a Room Service delivered breakfast the next morning; Gershwin left to go back to work with Ira and Heyward still revising their opera that was scheduled to open in the fall. He was going to Philadelphia the next day to talk with a theater owner about the staging for the first performances of the "Porgy and Bess tour." He planned to return Tuesday and they agreed to have dinner together, and actually get to a restaurant.

"You better wait in the lobby for me," Consuelo announced, "Otherwise I don't know what will happen if you show up here after four days away. Remember we have all night."

Consuelo had telephoned Leo De Pinna before leaving Tampa. The Fifth Avenue merchant was pleased to hear from her, and offered to have a selection of gowns for her consideration suitable for a Cole Porter opening night on Broadway, and the obligatory Sardis party later. De Pinna's was a few blocks from the Plaza Hotel so Consuelo walked along Fifth Avenue admiring the store windows and the busy New Yorkers rushing by. It was all vastly different from the slow pace of life in Ybor City. The day was bright and cool, and she was reminded of the good times with Daniel when they were in the city. Consuelo always felt invigorated by Manhattan's fast life and fast thinking people. At De Pinna's, Leo was hovering around the main entrance waiting for her. They embraced and Leo kissed each side of her face in the European manner. They talked for a while like old friends catching up. Leo asked her about the Cole Porter show's opening night, and Consuelo casually mentioned that she was going to accompany George Gershwin. De Pinna was stunned. "Really? I'm impressed. He has colossal talent. May I ask if Kay Swift is out of the picture?"

"I don't know," Consuelo confessed. "Kay's in Reno getting divorced, and George needed a date for the opening." De Pinna just shook his head.

De Pinna led Consuelo to a private area on the store's second floor. The location and ambiance was different from the place Consuelo and Daniel had sat to observe the fashion shows staged exclusively for them, but pleasant enough. He introduced Consuelo calling her Miss CC to an attractive redheaded woman. "This is Melony Levant, our chief buyer. Melony has selected gowns perfect for your height and lovely figure, which will make you the center of everyone's attention." He smiled at Consuelo. "Please excuse me for a little while."

Melony took over, and asked Consuelo to be seated. An assistant brought out the first gown on a silk covered hanger. Melony described the garment. "This one is from Worth of Paris. It has a beaded top; quite shear and a gathered black lace skirt that accents your height and stops short enough to show off your legs." Consuelo liked it so the gown was hung up while the assistant went to fetch another. Melony continued the narration. "The sapphire blue and black velvet gown is by Edward Molyneux. It features a plunging neckline, which you can wear with confidence." That one was also held on the side.

More gowns were shown, but Consuelo wasn't impressed with any of them. Melony thought for a moment and said, "Wait let's look at the gold lame and the blue silk." This time the assistant appeared modeling the gold lame chiffon gown. Consuelo just shook her head. When the blue silk velvet gown, knee length in front, with a daring plunging back appeared floating across the room carried on a hanger Consuelo fell in love with it. Melony was ecstatic. "Yes I agree it's you, and with it you must wear a necklace that goes all the way down your back Myrna Loy style. You'll be smashing let's try it on."

Next they looked at coats and, after trying on more than a dozen, Consuelo chose a floor length black cashmere wool adorned with a fox collar, and finally a Lilly Dache black wool cloche hat with a blue feather completed the ensemble.

Feeling as if she had accomplished something important over the more than two hours spent on selecting an outfit for her opening night date with George Gershwin; Consuelo paid for her choices by writing a check from her account with the Bowling Green Trust Company of New York. Melony promised the clothes would be delivered to the Plaza in the afternoon. Consuelo said good-bye to Leo De Pinna and walked a few more blocks south on Fifth Avenue to a Schraffts restaurant that catered primarily to women shoppers during lunch time.

After eating some bland food featuring lettuce and watercress, which she welcomed after a steady diet of rice, beans, pork and empanadas Consuelo feeling energetic walked to the New York Public Library at 42nd Street. She was seeking the society pages of New York's newspapers for their photos of Kay Swift.

Chapter 27

⁂

The Cotton Club

On Tuesday they were together again, but this time Gershwin waited for Consuelo in the Oak Bar off the Plaza's lobby. He was enjoying a Scotch whiskey on ice, and a Cuestra-Rey clear Havana cigar when she appeared. Consuelo wore the Worth gown purchased at the last moment from De Pinna's, and she caused a stir when she sat on a bar stool next to Gershwin. As Melony had described, the gown's top was sheer and featured a plunging neckline, which meant that Consuelo's unencumbered breasts were also featured. Gershwin was happy to see her and the attention she received. The business in Philadelphia had been successful. Theater owners out of town were always more cooperative than the Shubert organization that owned most of Broadway's theaters.

Dinner that night was at Café des Artistes on 67th Street across from Central Park. The understated elegant restaurant was a landmark for the city's theater and art world. The full wall murals made it unique. The Café was also enjoyed by wealthy New Yorkers living along Central Park West. Arriving at the Café they were welcomed by the host who had saved a quiet table in a corner so that Gershwin wouldn't be bothered by anyone. If the truth be told Gershwin enjoyed being recognized, and if a piano were there he would gladly play his music.

They selected G.H. Mumms Cordon Rouge Champagne to accompany the oysters Rockefeller ordered for their appetizers. When the cold wine bottle was opened with a discrete pop, and placed in the ice bucket after two glasses were poured Consuelo happily exclaimed, "I feel so decadent sipping cold Champagne in this lovely restaurant with the most famous bachelor in New York. And I love it." When the oysters arrived baked with a sautéed green vegetable mixture garnished with shavings of parmesan cheese they were quickly consumed. Playwright Clifford Odets appeared at their table on his way out of the Café to say hello to Gershwin but was distracted by Consuelo and her plunging neckline. When he left them they giggled like youngsters about his frankly admiring her breasts, which made Consuelo happy. She had found several photos of Kay Swift in the New York newspapers, and there wasn't any doubt that Kay was flat chested.

A narrow rolling table was wheeled close to them with copper chafing dishes heated from below by small flames. On an oak board were four prime petite filet mignon steaks. The captain with a flourish turned up the heat of one chafing dish and dropped a scoop of butter into the pan followed by shallots, minced fresh garlic, thinly sliced mushrooms, chopped green onions, Dijon mustard, beef stock and a generous splash of cognac. After a time, while a waiter heated two large dinner plates on the second chafing dish, the steaks were slipped into the mixture along with a measure of heavy cream and more cognac. Ground black pepper and some parsley as a garnish completed the Café des Artiste's famous Steak Diane. Alumette potatoes and Blue Lake green beans complimented the entree, which was perfectly cooked and delicious. They passed up desserts, but drank coffee and finished the Cordon Rouge.

During their dinner, Gershwin suddenly said, "There's something I have to tell you." Consuelo looked at him but didn't say anything. "Do you remember keeping my camera in your office safe?" Consuelo just nodded. Not knowing what to expect. "Well, I had forgotten that Arturo had used it to take some pictures in Ybor City. He thought they would be useful in making sets for the show. Two weeks ago I needed a break from revising and polishing "Porgy and Bess" so I went over to Gregory Zilboorg's place to use his dark room, and developed the film. Much to my surprise, there were about a dozen photos of men dressed up in women's clothing. Some had makeup and wigs and some were smoking cigars. It was very strange. But the strangest part is that I recognized one of the men. I'm sure it's John Hoover."

Consuelo gasped, "Maybe that's why Arturo was killed. It wasn't "Porgy and Bess" that someone was looking for it was your camera."

"Perhaps. I showed the photos to Gregory and he identified the men as practicing transvestism what he considers a harmless fetish, which according to him, may in fact improve their sex lives with women. However it's not something a government official would want known about himself. I've wondered if I should send the pictures to your friend the Tampa police captain."

Over coffee, Consuelo told Gershwin about the telephone call P.J. made to Washington trying to determine if in fact John E. was J. Edgar and had he been in Tampa. "P.J. isn't continuing the investigation. He told me that before I left Ybor City. There's no proof Hoover was involved. Poor Arturo's killer will never be found. At least Arturo was pretty happy just before he was murdered." Luisa had provided the details of her last time in Arturo's bed, which Consuelo now told to Gershwin.

The doorman at Café des Artistes hailed a taxi, and Consuelo and George sped off to Harlem. They were headed to the Cotton Club at 142nd Street on Lenox Avenue Harlem's main boulevard. Cab Calloway the great band leader and entertainer had moved on from appearing regularly at the Cotton Club. He and his band toured major cities and made a score of movies in Hollywood. The Club had engaged Harold Arlen, a prolific composer, credited with successful Broadway shows and movie scores. Music critics and *Billboard* magazine compared his work to Gershwin's, especially his greatest hit song, *Stormy Weather*. He and Gershwin were good friends with similar family backgrounds. They didn't feel they were competitors. Arlen's signature sound was a combination of blues and jazz, which caused great Negro composers and performers notably Count Basie and Duke Ellington to regard him as one of their peers.

Arlen composed the music for the "Cotton Club Parade 1934" starring Adelaide Hall a talented and popular Negro songstress. Miss Hall was a sensation and the show had been running for eight months by the time Consuelo and Gershwin were going to see it. While heading for Harlem Gershwin admitted that he didn't like the racist overtones of the past Cotton Club shows. Since working with DuBose Heyward on "Porgy and Bess," Gershwin had become more sensitive to the divide between the races. Once enjoying Al Jolson's prancing around in blackface, he now considered it cheap and demeaning. Consuelo said, "I'm proud of you George. It's comforting to hear what you just said. I've seen shows at the Cotton Club, and they were pretty much all good music, but I really hated some of the other material. Of course, we liked the chorus line of "tan, tall and terrific" beauties wearing tiny costumes. That was all about sex, which everyone is really interested in seeing."

They arrived at the Cotton Club in time for the 11 o'clock show. Charlie Bower the greeter had them whisked to a front row table. "Consuelo laughed and said, "They love you in this city. Will you ever get treated as a regular person?"

"I hope not," retorted Gershwin. "It's fun to be recognized. My mother always said I was a ham calling attention to myself, but that's show business. We all like being in the spotlight." The club was jammed that night with big spenders who didn't mind the $3.00 cover charge per person added to the check; the priciest in the city.

After their Bacardi cocktails were served, and they settled in, the lights dimmed and an attractive woman wearing a long white dress with a slit on the side that exposed her shapely legs as she walked across the stage began singing *I love a Parade*. She was Adelaide Hall and during the fast and well executed show; she sang some of the best of Harold Arlen's music including *Let's Fall in Love* and *As Long as I Live*.

The famous chorus line of gorgeous light brown young women all the same height dressed in skimpy silver costumes high kicked to the music of the Mills Blue Rhythm Band. As the band's sound grew to a crescendo an exquisite young Negro woman appeared on stage and sang the Harold Arlen and Ted Koehler songs, *Here Goes* and the sultry *What Can You Say in a Love Song?"* The vocalist was Lena Horne, age sixteen, whose introduction at the Cotton Club had alerted Hollywood talent scouts, and at the end of her contract in Harlem would be on her way to Los Angeles. The audience was entranced by the young songstress whose delicate face and feline manner made her appear mature and sophisticated. When the show ended Adelaide Hall who had spotted Gershwin and Consuelo joined them at their table. Gershwin embraced her and introduced Consuelo as his "soul mate." Consuelo was startled, but went along with it. "We loved the show," said Gershwin. "Your voice is better than ever, I didn't think anyone could improve on perfection."

Adelaide was thrilled by Gershwin's comment. "Coming from you," she said, "makes me believe that. Thank you. It means a lot to me."

Gershwin was smiling when he said, "I had only one problem with your show." And before Adelaide's face showed her disappointment, Gershwin said, "Adelaide, you didn't sing *Stormy Weather.*"

"Let me fix that." Adelaide rose and walked over to the band playing for the couples on the dance floor. After a brief conversation with leader Lucky Millinder, the band concluded their playing, and Adeline took the microphone and told the audience that she had a request to sing *Stormy Weather.* The entire club applauded and when she said the request was from Mr. George Gershwin, and a spotlight swept over him; the place erupted in cheers and clapping. *Stormy Weather* was never sung with more feeling, and would never be more appreciated by an audience.

Later when they were in bed in Consuelo's suite she asked, "Soul mate?"

"I didn't know how to introduce you. I had thought about saying you were my friend from Florida, but I wanted Adelaide to realize we slept together." Consuelo didn't ask Gershwin what he meant by that because he was busy following one of her suggestions that expanded their sexual practices, which he had quickly mastered like everything else he set his mind to do.

Chapter 28

Ybor City 1935

James Flynn posted a registered letter to the New York investment firm Ladenburg Thalmann containing a check for deposit to the investment account of Consuelo Middleton Davis. Not known to Flynn was Consuelo's substantial investment in the newly formed Consolidated Edison Company of New York. The privately financed public utility was a conglomerate of electric, natural gas, and steam companies created to provide heat and light all over New York City. It was believed by the people at Ladenburg Thalmann who had provided the initial financing for the consolidation that investing in the new enterprise would prove to be highly profitable in the future because there was every indication that New York's population was growing, and recovering from the Great Depression, and that there wouldn't be any competitors providing the same services. It was the first time Consuelo had invested, and she was nervous about it since results of the crash of 1929 were still felt years later. Flynn's check was the first payment from Harvey Sparks toward his purchase of the Excelsior Hotel.

"I was surprised when Consuelo asked me to draw up a contract of sale for her hotel. She was always a mystery to me, and no doubt to everyone else around here. I didn't really believe her story about coming down here from Virginia. She doesn't have that smooth accent you hear there, but everything else about her was surely right. Before Consuelo could sell the hotel I had to search the titles for the Excelsior and her cottage to find out who legally owned them. Imagine my surprise when after searching the records in the base ment of the Tampa courthouse I found deeds for both buildings that showed they were owned by the Wilmington Sewing Machine Company a corpora- tion in Delaware. Another surprise was the amounts paid for the buildings by Bellevue-Biltmore Properties a company owned by the Plant family. How were they involved? Anyway Bellevue-Biltmore after paying $32,000 for the hotel, about $5000 too much in my opinion, and $2900 for the cottage about three times more than its worth, transferred the hotel and cottage to the company in Delaware, which after writing to Delaware's secretary of state I learned was owned by someone called Camilla Chase of Cooperstown, New York."

"I confronted Consuelo about all of this and she laughed, and told me that she changed her name from Camilla Chase. She gave me the order from the New York court that legally changed her name to Consuelo Middleton Davis. It was as if she wanted to disappear from her old life. Another surprise was the law firm White and Case that handled her name change. They are one of the biggest and most expensive bunch of lawyers in New York. And still another surprise for me was the lawyer who filed the deeds on behalf of the Wilmington Sewing Machine Company was Spessard Holland, only the most important lawyer in West Florida, and a member of the Florida Senate. He personally, I found out from Harvey, spoke to him about staying on to work for Consuelo."

Flynn wondered about the beautiful woman with all the right connections, and what was she doing living in Ybor City? He realized that even after four years of a casual relationship and some legal business he really didn't know much about her. She didn't seem to care about the hotel's selling price. When he suggested $27,000 as a starting point Consuelo agreed immediately, and Harvey happily concurred. Flynn wrote the contract of sale eliminating a down payment, and prepared a 3% interest mortgage that Consuelo and Harvey accepted and signed. The cottage sold for one dollar, and Flynn filed the documents freeing Consuelo to leave in time to accompany George Gershwin to Cole Porter's show's opening.

Chapter 29

A Night on Broadway

It was Thursday the opening night and Consuelo was at her appointment at Elizabeth Arden's Red Door Salon on Fifth Avenue. The young women fashioning her hair, nails and applying green goo to her face were convinced she was an actress or someone they all recognized. "On no," Consuelo protested, "I just want to look good for my big date tonight." Then she laughed and said, I really do have to look great because I'm meeting Cole Porter, Ira Gershwin, Josephine Baker and Ethel Merman at Sardis for an opening night party." The Elizabeth Arden staff was used to celebrities, but weren't sure about Consuelo's claim of being a part of the Broadway elite. Their faces must have shown their doubts because Consuelo said, "I'm not in show business, but my date is. He's George Gershwin." She didn't think they were convinced, but Consuelo didn't care. She was looking forward to the evening's show and party and later talking with George about their being together. Were they really together or was she just his date of the week?

The big cone shaped dryer placed over Consuelo's hair kept out all of the noises swirling around her, and she closed her eyes, half napping. Her thoughts drifted to the Cotton Club, and the glorious and slightly tipsy nights when she and Daniel danced to Cab Calloway's band and watched the scantily clad light brown chorus girls perform their routines in the city's highest paying night club. Suddenly another thought that must have been buried in her mind appeared, and Consuelo remembered where she had seen John E. Hoover before the rainy morning in Ybor City. She had recognized Hoover and a taller light haired man at the Cotton Club almost four years ago sitting together at a small table half way across the room. She noticed them because it was unusual for two men to be there without women companions. If it was Hoover; why was he patronizing a place owned by the infamous gangster Owney Madden? Her thoughts were interrupted by the beautician who was ready to do the comb out, and cleanse the green pore tightening mask from her face.

After a light supper at the Oak Room, in the company of George's sister Frances and her husband violinist Leopold Godowsky Jr., they arrived at the theater a half hour early for the 8:30 curtain. Coats were taken for checking, and Consuelo was introduced to Lenore and Ira, Emil and Gertrude Mosbacher, publisher Bennett Cerf, lyrist Yip Harburg, and Todd Duncan, Ann Brown and William Coleman three of the leading players in "Porgy and Bess attending the opening at Gershwin's invitation. Lenore pulled her aside saying, "So you're the beauty from Florida that George is smitten with?"

"Well thank you, and yes I'm from Florida, and I'm happy to know George is smitten with me. He doesn't say a lot about that."

Lenore responded, "Oh I know. He's been with Kay Swift for years even though she's married, and they go everywhere together, and he doesn't say a word about her. Did you know Kay was in Reno getting divorced? I'm afraid when she comes back here she'll try to make him marry her."

Consuelo's concern was obvious. "I don't know what I can do about that. George is the most self-contained person I have ever known. He goes through life doing whatever he wants to do, and people let him do it. In fact they encourage him."

Lenore laughed and said, "You do know my brother-in-law. He's unique, and all of us have spoiled him, but if I looked like you; I'd get him to do whatever I want."

Chimes announcing the ten minutes to curtain were sounded, and before Consuelo could say anymore, Lenore said, "We'll talk later at Sardis."

Consuelo felt good about Lenore's easy conversation with her. *Daily News* photographers had taken photos of the fashionable group around George

Gershwin, and then concentrated on Consuelo and Gershwin by themselves. When Consuelo's necklace that cascaded down her bare back was noticed all of the photographers in the lobby rushed over to photograph the exquisite woman wearing the high fashion revealing gown. Gershwin was pleased, and asked if the pictures would be picked up by the AP or UPI, and seen around the country. A photographer from the *World-Telegram* answered. "Gee Mr. Gershwin we really hope so. You never know what the photo editors will use, but the shots of your lady friend I bet will be seen in California." That seemed to please Gershwin, and Consuelo wondered if he hoped the Reno newspapers would print their pictures.

"Anything Goes" was a happy romp aboard an ocean liner bound for England. It featured high society comic antics with a counter point provided by Ethel Merman's character Reno Sweeney a former evangelist turned night club singer. Consuelo thought the story was mindless, but Cole Porter's music was the show's saving grace. It featured the songs: *You're the Top, I get a Kick out of You,* and *It's Delovely.* Porter's clever lyrics and catchy melodies showed the breadth and range of his writing from the toe tapping *Anything Goes* to the wonderfully jazz-infused, *You'd be So Easy to Love.* Porter had written the show's score over weekends the prior summer in Newport, Rhode Island. He was the permanent house guest of Theresa Fair Oelrichs and her husband Hermann in Rosecliff their forty room summer cottage by the sea. Designed by Stanford White, Rosecliff was modeled after the Grand Trianon in Versailles, and the mansion's furnishings, European art, exquisite chandeliers and gold trimmed dinnerware for over a hundred guests made it one of the most expensive residences assembled in America during the Gilded Age.

Consuelo found it great fun to be surrounded by the best dressed and most suave people in Manhattan. She had done this before with Daniel, and felt at ease especially after the attention lavished on her by Gershwin's friends who all seemed relieved he was with someone other than Kay Swift. After a Champagne fueled intermission the second act filled with Cole Porter's music proceeded to a grand finale that brought the entire cast to the stage singing. There were many curtain calls with bows to the appreciative audience. Flowers were delivered to the stage, and Merman holding two bouquets made sure she was alone on stage for the final bows. Since it was opening night, Cole Porter, director Howard Lindsey, writer Russel Crouse, and Vinton Freedley the producer appeared on the stage to take bows as well. They knew their show was a hit and were exceedingly happy. No one in the audience applauded longer or louder than George Gershwin.

Taxis brought the opening night celebrants to Vincent Sardi's restaurant on west 44th Street. They were welcomed by Sardi personally and led upstairs to the private dining area where copious trays of sandwiches, bowls of shrimp with spicy cocktail sauce, and platters of blini filled with caviar awaited them. The walls of the Broadway institution were covered with the framed caricatures of show businesses most famous performers, writers, composers, dancers and directors. Consuelo spotted George's without him having to point it out.

Two bartenders were busy mixing cocktails and also pouring straight rye, bourbon and gin. Consuelo was handed an Old Fashioned on the rocks containing a bright red cherry and an orange slice by a man who eyed her up and down before introducing himself as an executive in the Shubert organization, which had offices upstairs in the Sardi's building. Lenore chased him away saying, "Are you lost Lawrence, the bar is that way?" Lenore proceeded to introduce Consuelo to Howard Lindsey, Russel Crouse and, saving the best for last, Cole Porter.

He kissed Consuelo's hand as she told him how much she enjoyed his music. "I'm flattered considering you're escorted by a real genius. I hope you and George will come to my apartment later for the after party affair. More music, more delectable food, more of everything." Consuelo was about to respond, but suddenly Ethel Merman and William Gaxton burst into the room, and bowed to enthusiastic applause. After moving throughout the room chatting with the cream of Broadway's talent and the best and famous of New York's fashion, publishing and banking worlds, they found Ira and Lenore, George and Consuelo and their sister Frances and her husband at a corner table. Lenore introduced Consuelo to Merman and Gaxton. Merman muttered "oh yes" and moved on to engage George and Ira in a critique of the show.

Gaxton, however, seemed stunned by Consuelo or her backless, shear top and leg exposing gown. He began whispering something about his desperate need to meet her for lunch tomorrow when they heard, "Oh Bill this is where you've gone to. I've been looking all over for you. The show is wonderful." It was Madeline Gaxton, the long suffering wife the only one who didn't know about Gaxton's long string of affairs.

With only a little urging Ethel Merman and William Gaxton agreed to an impromptu performance accompanied by Cole Porter. Sardi's waiters rolled out a spinet piano and the performance began. After a selection of his own music sung by Merman and Gaxton, Porter played, *Someone to Watch over Me* and *Fascinating Rhythm* two of the Gershwin brothers most memorable songs. Upon finishing, Porter stood and invited everyone at the party to his place for an after party gathering once the reviews were out. He resided in the San Remo an opulent apartment building situated between 74th and 75th Streets on Central Park West considered Manhattan's smartest place to live. Porter's ten room apartment shared the 24th floor of the south tower with only one other apartment.

When Consuelo told Lenore that she hoped they would go along with all who cheered when Porter extended his invitation, she was surprised by her reaction. "Ira and I aren't going, and I'm sure George won't bring you there. Cole's parties turn into orgies I'm told, and not just men with women; it's anyone with everyone. There's also lots of cocaine around there. I think that treacherous quack Zilboorg gives out prescriptions for it."

"Well, all right," said Consuelo. "I'll keep quiet about that. It's funny, Cole Porter looks so innocent."

Lenore smiled ruefully. "Well, he's not. He was a rich boy from Indiana who picked up some bad habits at Yale and Harvard. That's what I like about Ira and George, Harold Arlen and Jerome Kern; they learned their bad habits at home." As if on cue a waiter rushed into the dining room carrying copies of the morning editions of the *New York Times,* the *Herald-Tribune* and the *World-Telegram.* Lenore said, "Uh oh, the moment of truth."

The six copies of the *Times* were almost torn to shreds in the quest to read theater critic Brooks Atkinson's review of "Anything Goes." Vinton Freedley as producer read it aloud. "It looks like we have a hit. Atkinson liked it. He says, 'Cole Porter has written a dashing score with impish lyrics,' and the rest of the review is just as favorable." Even the dour Richard Watts writing in the

Herald-Tribune gave the show a positive, but cautious review writing, "Lots of fun, but no magic." The reviewer for the *World-Telegram* who liked light and frothy entertainment was also complimentary. And finally, a friend of Howard Lindsey called the restaurant to report that Dorothy Kilgallen in her *Journal-American* café society column *The Voice of Broadway* had written, "High society hijinks and misbehaving at the Alvin Theater was great fun to watch and its set to Cole Porter's music." As was the tradition, after reading the reviews the party broke up with some going to Cole Porters and others to El Morocco or the Stork Club. Taxis took the Gershwin group, without Ira and Lenore who decided to go home, to El Morocco on East 54th Street.

Their party included Frances Gershwin Godowsky and her husband Leopold, a classical violinist and chemist who co-invented color photography film. Charles and Mary Rosenthal had come along. They knew the Henry Plants and Daniel Clark. Consuelo had attempted to avoid them all evening and was now sitting at the same nightclub table with them. Orchestra conductor Leo Reisman accompanied by a lovely French woman, and Gershwin friends, Ann Ronell, Yip Harburg and Lou and Emily Paley rounded out the party.

El Morocco's owner John Perona came to the table of twelve to greet Gershwin and his friends. Overhead were sparkling white palm trees, and the banquettes were upholstered in the club's famous blue and white zebra stripes. A Latin band played mambos and rumbas to which Consuelo and Gershwin danced; to the appreciation of everyone who recognized him. When they returned to their table Kitty Carlisle and husband composer Moss Hart were sitting in their seats. They attempted to rise, but Gershwin wouldn't hear of it. He dragged Consuelo away to meet the former Ziegfeld Follies dancer Paulette Goddard whom he had spotted while they were dancing. Goddard was being considered for the leads in Broadway shows and by Charlie Chaplin for his movies.

Goddard was with three men whom she introduced quickly as Tony, Bart, and Eddy, but was obviously thrilled that Gershwin had remembered her from auditions. They chattered about "Anything Goes" until the house band that alternated with the Latin band began playing Gershwin's *I got Rhythm.* While they danced, Consuelo observed. "Paulette is unusually pretty. Is that why she's with three men?"

"I don't know, but I'd like to consider her for a leading part in a show. She's also talented. Can sing and dance very well, but she made a big mistake walking out on Ziegfeld when she was under contract to star in his latest revue. She took the lead in another show that ran three weeks. It had opened in Atlantic City, which was their first mistake."

Champagne, cognac, dancing and socializing with Manhattan's Café Society ended close to 4 am. The Gershwin party had left them over an hour before, and Consuelo was relieved that she hadn't had to speak with the Rosenthals. They decided to walk the five blocks north and three west to the Plaza Hotel. The walk cleared their heads, and they talked about the evening's events. "What about Ethel Merman," Consuelo asked? "She ignored me when Lenore tried to introduce us. By the way, I love Lenore."

"Yes, Lenore is loveable. I have always said Ira was a lucky man." Gershwin went on. "Merman is another story. I'm not impressed with her belting out songs that no one else wants to sing. She's not graceful and demands attention. Her great fear is that people will mistakenly think she's Jewish, but Cole likes her."

By the time they got to the hotel the sun was making its way up the eastern sky. Consuelo had removed her shoes, which she carried complaining that her feet hurt from looking good in the three-inch wedge heels on her silver and blue pumps. They were upstairs and passed out in minutes after reaching the suite, Gershwin remembering to hang the Do Not Disturb sign on the door.

Sometime around 10 the next morning Consuelo woke up and saw Gershwin still dressed in pants and shirt lying on her bed. She had taken off her gown and stockings and slept in a blue T-shirt, which was off now as Consuelo intended to shower. After washing her face and brushing her teeth she pulled Gershwin's pants off and hung them up along with his suit jacket and coat. He stirred a bit then turned over to sleep again. Later on when his eyes opened and being used to having Paul Mueller catering to his needs Gershwin blurted out, "I must be a mess. I need a razor, I need to shower, and I need clean clothes."

Consuelo laughed at him. "Yes sir, anything else sir?" She wondered how he was going to leave the Plaza Hotel in the daytime unshaven, in a rumpled suit and a shirt that had been slept in. Then she had an idea. "George go shower and clean up while I have your suit pressed, and I buy some haberdashery for you in the men's store next to the 58th Street entrance." She put her long coat on with sensible shoes, took her wallet and Gershwin's suit kissed him and left saying, "I'll be back in twenty minutes."

Consuelo took the suit to the concierge in the lobby who promised to have it pressed and delivered in about two hours. Next Consuelo left the hotel's 58th Street entrance and entered J. Guild Men's Emporium where she happily bought George underwear, socks, a fine shirt with matching tie and a safety razor. She returned to the Plaza and was back in the suite in the promised time. George had showered and had a towel wrapped around his waist. He gratefully took the packages from Consuelo asking if she was going to take off her coat. "I will, but I'm naked. I thought that was the fastest way to get everything done for you."

"Good so am I. Let's get back in bed and do what we were too tired to do early this morning."

"Um, lover aren't you going to shave your face? The way you've kissed me lately my thighs will be chaffed." That thought made the coat and towel fly off their bodies and they landed in bed. They enjoyed each other for the rest of the afternoon, and at one point Consuelo said, "We need food. I'm ordering room service because we're in no condition to be seen anywhere." She picked up the telephone, dialed 29, and asked the person on the other end for supper suggestions. After ordering what was recommended Consuelo fell back into bed wrapping herself around Gershwin.

An hour later two waiters rolled in carts with covered plates white linen and lots of silverware. Consuelo wearing her silk robe signed the bill added a tip and urged them out of her living room. Gershwin had dressed and wearing his new shirt, freshly pressed suit pants and socks lifted up the plate covers and began sampling the array of food.

"This is good. I'm so hungry. You really do get my blood going. I admit that I had heard a little about you before we met, and you were described as dazzling, and that's what you are.

Consuelo wondered about that but didn't say anything. Suddenly she wasn't hungry. "George that's the first time you mentioned anything about my past. I'd like to tell you about my life before Ybor City. We haven't talked very much lately. It's been busy, but nice. I had a lovely time this week. Look, I'm going to Cooperstown Saturday to have Thanksgiving with my aunt and her family. I haven't seen them for a long time. Gershwin didn't say anything. It was as if he wasn't ready to have this conversation. Consuelo continued, "I'll be back for Christmas with you."

Gershwin took a deep breath. "Consuelo I can't see you Christmas." He looked down and closed his eyes. "Kay is coming home December 18, and we have a date for Christmas Eve."

Consuelo felt numb. Had she completely misunderstood everything between herself and Gershwin? "George, don't I mean anything to you?"

"Of course you do, but I need Kay's work on Porgy and Bess.' She's a classically educated composer and she'll create the arrangements that I can't do. I told you about her. We've worked together for a long time."

"And been lovers."

"Yes, but we were never exclusive."

Consuelo had regained her balance. "George when you said you heard about me. What did you hear? That I was an easy lay? That you could have sex with me in a fancy hotel until your flat chested girlfriend comes home?

"Consuelo you just don't understand. I can't change what I am to be with you. I don't want to be tied to anyone. That's why it works with Kay and me. She doesn't care about attachments. It's the reason she divorced Jimmy and gave up custody of her daughters."

"How can you accept that? She's a monster even if she knows how to write music. I don't want us to end this way. I can't let you just go. Please stay tonight. We'll talk til we figure it out."

"I can't stay. My radio program is on CBS tomorrow, and I have to prepare. I work with the people at the radio station all day, but tomorrow night we can be together. Can we do that?

She hesitated but said, "Yes, of course. Will you telephone and tell me when I'm going to see you?"

Gershwin had knotted his tie and was putting on his shoes, suit jacket and overcoat. "Consuelo I never thought we'd be at this point, but we are, and now I have to figure out what to do about you since you're important to me really important. I can be here by nine tomorrow night." They hugged, kissed and he left.

The next morning found Consuelo walking through Central Park. She spent most of the previous night going over the conversation she and George had before he left her. Not knowing what to do she decided to return to the Plaza to telephone Lenore. Ira answered on the first ring. He thanked Consuelo again for the two boxes of his favorite Montecristo Havana cigars she had brought him from Ybor City. Then Lenore was on, and happy to hear from Consuelo. "Lenore I'm leaving tomorrow to go to Cooperstown and have Thanksgiving with my aunt. I wanted to thank you for being so gracious to me. You made me feel welcome."

"I was happy to. You're a very nice person, and I hope to see you again soon. Please tell me how I can reach you after you leave here."

"Yes, I will. I'm not sure where I'll be. I had hoped to come back for Christmas, but that's probably not a good idea right now. I'm not going back to Florida. I'll telephone once I'm settled. Well, goodbye and thanks, Lenore." Consuelo hung up the telephone and began packing. She was taking the train to Albany at nine the next morning so she'd leave the Plaza about an hour before. She wondered if George would stay with her tonight or would he be too tired from his day getting ready, and performing for the radio program.

At 8:30 Consuelo, wearing a silk dress that hugged her curves, and whirled around her legs when she walked, looked at her reflection in the suite's full-length mirror. I look good, she told herself, and then the telephone rang. It was George saying that he was involved in some new contractual possibilities with CBS, and the people there wanted to talk tonight. He was sorry, but it would be too late when he finished with dinner with the CBS people to come to the Plaza. He would try to see her before Christmas, and she should tell him where she would be. Consuelo didn't say anything except goodbye when Gershwin was obviously ready to end the call.

On the New York Central train to Albany the next morning, Consuelo tried to decide what to do. She was hurt but wondered why she hadn't felt this way when Daniel made it clear she had to leave his home and his life after three years. Maybe she hadn't really considered who George was. That he's an important and famous person who she had allowed herself to believe was like other people, but he's not.

Had she been fooling herself into believing that she and Gershwin had a future together? Consuelo had taken some Plaza Hotel stationary with her, and she began to write a letter to Gershwin. She reminded him and herself of a conversation they had late one night in her cottage. She had said that she knew that he would never belong to one woman because music was his first love, and he belonged to everyone. That was true then and still true, but maybe she had forgotten what she said that night. She went on to write down that it hadn't been fair of her to assume they would spend Christmas together as now she recognized he had obligations that had existed long before meeting her, and they were perfectly reasonable, and she apologized for the things she had said about Kay.

She also wrote about understanding that when the network executives at CBS wanted to talk with him regarding more work in radio, and because it made sense to do it just after his program ended last night; he had to seize the opportunity. Without her realizing it, the letter had covered three pages in her neat handwriting and ended with her saying that she had acted impulsively, and she hoped he would forgive her. Consuelo began to feel a lot better and began to think about the possibility they would soon see each other again. George did say he would try before Christmas, and she would return to New York or meet him any place he chose.

By putting her thoughts down on paper, Consuelo felt a sense of relief for the first time since Gershwin had left her suite the day before yesterday. Alone in the train seat, she closed her eyes and allowed the train's steady rhythm to sooth her into a light sleep. In the seat in front of her, two women bound for Poughkeepsie wearing elaborate hats talked about their busy lives exchanging stories and gossiping. The woman in the aisle seat asked the other if she had listened to the "Music by Gershwin" radio show last night. Startled by hearing the question Consuelo was now fully awake, and she wanted to hear their opinion of the show she had forgotten to listen to and their opinion of George. The woman sitting directly in front of Consuelo said, "I did listen. It's always good even when he plays other composer's music. But last night was special. He had a singer on the show he said was going to be famous. I remember her name. It was Paulette Goddard." Consuelo sadly and carefully tore up the three-page letter allowing the scraps to fall by her feet.

Chapter 30

Cooperstown 1935

Thanksgiving and Christmas passed and suddenly 1934 was over, and a new year began that held guarded hope for the nation. Prohibition had ended, and the Works Progress Administration was set to put hundreds of thousands of Americans back to work immediately. The Social Security Act would provide the first unemployment insurance and the beginning of pensions for the workers in factories and retail stores. The New Deal had begun to establish a "social safety net" for the working class; the first time in the nation's history. The federal government actively engaged in regulating banks, investment companies, food and drug manufacturers and interstate commerce. The protection and innovations developed for Americans by the Roosevelt "Brain Trust" and Democrats in Congress were regularly fought against in the courts by the Republicans who considered the measures that helped an unemployed and hungry population as creeping Socialism.

Consuelo had spent the holidays with her aunt's family. Thanksgiving was a pleasant quiet time with Vanessa and some of her friends. For Christmas, son Samuel, a postman in Springfield, Massachusetts took the train to Albany with his family. He and his wife Maddie had two girls ages 5 and 7. They met up with Samuel's sister Tonya, a Practical Nurse employed by Albany Memorial Hospital, and boarded a bus to Cooperstown a two-hour ride. They were happy to see their cousin CC after almost seven years. Christmas dinner was a joyous time with

Vanessa giving thanks between every course for the family being together for a holiday celebration. Consuelo discretely paid for the groceries and invited Samuel and Harriet to stay at the Prince Harold hotel in town where she had moved in more or less permanently. They willingly accepted as soon as Tonya offered to watch over the little girls while their parents spent a few nights in a hotel.

Vanessa had purchased a new 1932 Ford Model B Roadster with money her niece had given her before leaving for Ybor City. The car a V-8 cost $490, and when she applied for a driving license at Cooperstown's town hall and county seat building she was informed that she was the first Negro in the county to be granted a license to drive. She proudly reported to her children and Consuelo that she had started a business to supplement the baby nursing, which had dropped off lately. Now she brought parcels from place to place in and around Cooperstown providing delivery the same day at a cost of twenty-five cents for envelopes and small packages and fifty cents for boxes. Her best customers were the county government, law firms, the Bank and the Clark Family Office. When Consuelo saw the Ford and heard about Vanessa's ability to drive wherever she cared to go; she knew she had to have an automobile.

Consuelo was staying at the Prince Harold Inn on Cooperstown's Pioneer Street one block from Main Street. A place she knew from growing up in Cooperstown but hadn't actually ever entered the building. The Inn was built in 1802 of red brick and wide oak timbers and was gradually expanded into a thirteen room hotel with a pub below street level that was open weekends in the evenings. The furniture was old fashioned and the bed uncomfortable, but it was clean and the staff was pleasant. Coffee and sweet rolls were put out every morning in the small lobby, and in the winter the fireplace warmed the reception area. After the Christmas holiday, Consuelo carefully examined the old building looking into as many empty rooms as she could and spoke with the staff about their jobs. She realized that she was evaluating the Inn's business potential and abruptly stopped what she was doing. I must be crazy Consuelo told herself. I just rid myself of a hotel in a small town.

She had learned from the Village Library staff that, of all things, a museum of baseball was in the planning stage, and would open the following year in an empty building on Main Street. The plan was to attract baseball fans to

Cooperstown during the spring, summer, and fall when the town's weather was most pleasant, and the trees and flowers were at the height of their blooms. The Clark family was behind the baseball museum project as a way to keep the Otesaga Hotel full for at least half of the year.

The Prince Harold Inn was usually closed over the winter, but this year surveyors and engineers working for New York State's road department had reserved six rooms for the entire winter while planning the new roads NY 28 and NY 167 that would make Cooperstown more accessible to drivers of the "marvelous motor cars" that were appearing everywhere, and had changed the travel habits of Americans practically overnight.

"Miss Arnoff," Consuelo called out to the Inn's manager Madeline Arnoff who was behind the front desk this morning. "Can we talk? I have some questions about this property, and perhaps you're the person with the answers."

"Of course Miss Davis. Let's have coffee by the fire. I'll try to answer you."

They got comfortable in the warm living room-like lobby pouring coffee for themselves and sitting in easy chairs. Consuelo began by explaining who she is and why she was in Cooperstown. "I grew up near Fort Henry about ten miles from here. I'm part Cayuga, Negro, and half English, and I've been away from here for several years. My aunt, my late mother's sister lives just outside of town, and I'm visiting her, and her grown children. Also, you should know that I'm wealthy; really wealthy."

Miss Arnoff smiled and wondered where this conversation was going and why she was being told private matters by this beautiful woman who seemed a little desperate today, unlike the cool image she had projected since the beginning of her stay at the inn.

"I need a place to be more or less my permanent address. I need someone to take phone messages for me and receive my mail and packages while I'm away. Also, I want to reserve two rooms for at least six months; maybe more. One will be my office and the other, and it must be larger my living quarters." Consuelo had compiled a list of whom she would contact with her new address. Lawyers John Bradford and James Flynn, Harvey Sparks who would send her the clothing filled trunk and other luggage. Bankers at Ladenburg Thalmann, the Bowling Green Trust Company and her Tampa bank, The Plaza Hotel where she left two valises of clothing acquired during her stay in New York, and left there because she had believed she would be returning for Christmas, the State of Delaware for matters concerning her ownership of the Wilmington Sewing Machine Company, Lenore Gershwin and a few others that included George Gershwin. "And," Consuelo continued, "I'll buy new furniture, lamps, pictures, and rugs for the rooms and have a private telephone installed. I'll go to Myers department store in Albany for everything I'll need."

Marilyn Arnoff said. "I'll have to telephone the Morse's in Maryland. They own the inn. Let me understand. You will purchase the furniture for an office and your rooms, and arrange a telephone for yourself. There won't be any cost to the inn. Am I correct? And may we keep the furniture when you move out?"

"Yes, that's about it. I'll pay for everything and when you tell me the cost of renting the rooms; I'll pay six months in advance. I want to do this soon so please telephone the owners today. I'd like to go to Albany tomorrow or the next day if my aunt's available to drive there." Consuelo turned away and was about to leave the room, but stopped and said, "Miss Arnoff please try to resolve this for me. I need a place to stay near where I was brought up, and I have to ask you to promise me you won't tell anyone in this town I'm here."

"I'll keep your secret," Marilyn Arnoff answered suspiciously. "You're not in any trouble are you like Bonnie Parker?" Arnoff was referring to the notorious Bonnie and Clyde bank robbers and killers who had died in a shootout with police the previous May.

Consuelo didn't know if she should be amused or insulted. "I can assure you I'm completely law abiding. I need to stay out of sight for a while because of a love affair that ended some time ago, but the emotions are still fresh. I plan to leave here for a while probably in two weeks. So I want to have my living quarters all set so I have something permanent in my life."

Arnoff was impressed. "Oh, that sounds tantalizing. I'll phone the Morse's right now." She left Consuelo and entered the small office behind the front desk. Arnoff wondered if Consuelo was truthful, but if she paid six months' rent in advance what possible harm could there be. She made a person to person telephone call to Hiram Morse in Towson, Maryland, but no one answered. The operator said she would try the call again in an hour.

Chapter 31

The previous week Consuelo had accompanied Aunt Vanessa on her appointment with a doctor. The neat red brick building across from Bassett Hospital had four doctors' shingles hanging near the street. Vanessa's doctor, the only woman physician at the hospital was Dr. Barbara Collins. Her office on the first floor attracted female patients from a wide area around Cooperstown who preferred having a woman poking around their bodies for a medical examination. While waiting in the office for Vanessa to be called, Consuelo idly picked up one of the doctor's business cards and was surprised to read: Barbara Collins-Clark, M.D. General Medicine. She showed the card to Vanessa who shrugged and said, "I hadn't noticed. The sign outside was there for a couple of years."

When Vanessa was called to see the doctor Consuelo went with her since the visit was the discussion of the chest X-rays made last week. Dr. Collins-Clark was a pleasant woman estimated by Consuelo to be in her mid-forties. Consuelo watched the doctor carefully as she explained the results of the examination, X-rays and blood tests to Vanessa. Even covered by a white lab coat, the doctor exhibited an attractive figure. She urged Vanessa to cease smoking cigarettes as spots on her lungs were clearly shown in the X-rays. "I'm not sure what they indicate, but I believe and someday I hope my profession will believe that smoking is dangerous to our health and may be fatal." When Vanessa reacted with surprise, the doctor continued. "I know the advertisements even show doctors smoking Camels, and everyone having a grand time smoking cigarettes, but lung disease is rising, and I bet if anyone took the time to study the relationship between lung diseases and smoking there would be a high correlation of smokers and lung patients. So, Vanessa, it's time to stop and allow your lungs to heal."

At the time, lung patients were sometimes sent to a hospital in Denver where the treatment consisted of breathing the pure Colorado air for a year or so. When Vanessa asked Dr. Collins-Clark about that the doctor said, "I believe our air here in the mountains is just as clean as Denver's. I suggest you spend as much time outdoors as you can especially on cold clear days. Then come back in six months for another chest X-ray, and we'll see what's going on." She stopped, and said, "I'm afraid I won't be here then. My husband and I are moving to New York. In fact when he returns from a business trip to South Africa and Rhodesia he'll stay in New York for a while to get our apartment ready for us."

Consuelo interrupted asking, "Are you part of the noted Clark family?"

The doctor smiled and nodded. "Yes, I'm married to Daniel Clark for a little less than a year. We met when I began to practice in Cooperstown and since he's a hospital board member I was introduced to him at a hospital staff gathering. He's a widower. His daughter who also suffered a loss was living with him along with her two young daughters, but they moved to Manhattan for study at the Art Students League. She's a fine painter."

Consuelo, raging inside just smiled unable to speak. The doctor even surprising herself with her candor said, "Daniel misses his family, and loves New York City. He told me about the exciting times he had there during Prohibition accompanied by a mysterious woman so beautiful that she caused a stir wherever they went."

Vanessa asked, "Well Doctor who should I come to see? I like you and I like going to a woman doctor."

Dr. Collins-Clark seemed embarrassed, and said, "I'm truly sorry, but I'll suggest another doctor, and give your medical records to him. I'm sure you'll be well cared for. I like living here, but my husband wants to leave Cooperstown. We're selling our house. He now wants a completely new life in New York. We'll live in the Dakota Apartments, which was built by the Clarks a long time ago. It's an unusual place with big apartments. In fact Lillian Gish the film star is a neighbor."

Vanessa and Consuelo said goodbye to the doctor who promised to provide the name of a suitable new physician for Vanessa. They walked to Vanessa's Ford. Consuelo was silent while Vanessa chatted about how nice Dr. Collins-Clark was, and that she'll miss her. While Consuelo brooded, Vanessa said, "So she married your lover. You'll just have to get over it." When Consuelo's face showed surprise, Vanessa said, "I knew you and Daniel Clark were lovers. You didn't expect him to marry you, did you?" Consuelo didn't answer her aunt. She covered her face with her hands and sobbed until they reached the Prince Harold Inn.

Chapter 32

The Prince Harold Inn

Furniture and carpets, lamps and a desk with chair began to arrive at the Prince Harold Inn. The Inn's owners were happy to accommodate Consuelo especially since she paid for a six-month stay in advance. She had opened an account in the First National Bank of Cooperstown transferring the interest earned for the last three years from her bank account in Manhattan. Consuelo paid for all of her purchases at the Myers Department Store in Albany and tried to buy some things for Vanessa, but she only wanted the new type electric toaster.

Her office and two room suite turned out to be pleasant rooms especially because the windows afforded views of the snow covered mountains and tall evergreens. Consuelo didn't mind the winter cold as long as there were days that the sun shone and the snow sparkled. She often dined with Vanessa, and Cousin Tonya began coming home on the weekends she didn't work in the hospital so the three woman ventured away from Cooperstown to nearby towns Cobleskill, Oneonta, Gloversville and Rotterdam in search of places to have meals. Consuelo was used to the array of restaurants in Ybor City and of course, Manhattan had them everywhere, but country dining was limited so they returned often to the same places for simple hearty meals.

She spent more time with Marilyn Arnoff who lived in her own cottage adjacent to the Inn. The Inn's pub open on weekends attracted a good crowd looking for something to do during the long winter. When she wasn't with

Vanessa, she spent weekend evenings in the pub with Marilyn enjoying cocktails invented during the Prohibition era.

Consuelo had to leave Cooperstown before Daniel Clark returned from South Africa. She couldn't risk running into him. Clark's generosity had been predicated on her leaving Cooperstown forever to avoid his being embarrassed. Since she learned that Daniel and his wife were moving to New York City, Consuelo believed it was fair for her to return from exile in Florida to a place and climate she understood and in which she was comfortable, and re-establish herself. Therefore with her living quarters established, as well as her address, Consuelo made a plan that would take her away from Cooperstown for the rest of the winter. She made several telephone calls on her new private line, and reserved passage on the Pan American Clipper, which flew from Curtis H. Wright marine air terminal in Queens, New York to Dinner Key, Florida and finally to the Pearl of the Antilles, Havana, Cuba.

George Gershwin had spoken so lovingly about the elegant city by the Caribbean Sea and, after being surrounded by Cubans for almost three years who missed their Havana, Consuelo felt as if she knew the city and would find it inviting. She would begin the trip in six days.

Having sent a letter to every name on her list; Consuelo wasn't surprised when Railway Express delivered a trunk and a large wood crate that turned out to hold two valises. She was surprised however when a letter from the Tampa Police Department was delivered the day before leaving for Havana.

Tampa Police Department
Florida Avenue and Jackson Street
Tel. 1234

February 15, 1936

Dear Consuelo,
I wanted to write to tell you about the resolution of the Arturo Dardo murder case. About three weeks ago a man named Lancy Burwhistle was arrested in West Tampa for killing two Cuban men outside of a saloon. Lancy had an argument with

one of the men at the bar, and after that man left he came back with a friend. Lancy went outside and the men drew knives and yelled to him when they were about 20 feet away. Lancy shot both men in their hearts. Two perfect shots. He was arrested right away, and when I heard about it I asked Lancy if he knew Arturo Dardo. Lancy said he did, and called Dardo, that communist who liked the women. He met Dardo at Madame Zoraidas a fancy house in West Tampa that has women who will indulge in just about anything the customer wants to do. Dardo was a regular, and Lancy worked there keeping things quiet if a patron got out of hand. Well, it seems that both Dardo and Lancy had the same favorite girl. According to Lancy, Dardo was rough on her, and Lancy being the gentleman he is decided to teach him a lesson so he came to your hotel he says on the night Dardo was shot and saw the killer run down the hall and climb down the fire escape. Lancy said he hid in the dark, and in the confusion just walked down the stairs and out the front door. The thing is the mortician dug out the bullets from Dardo's chest and they were from a Colt 45 Navy Model which is like the gun Lancy used to kill the two Cubans. We also found shell casings that matched a Colt 45. We've charged Lancy with 3 murders and he is going to trial soon. I guess that solves the Dardo murder I'm happy to say. Harvey gave me your address in Cooperstown. I thought you would like to know who killed Arturo Dardo.

Sincerely yours,
P.J. Cavanaugh

Chapter 33

⬤⬤⬤⬤

Havana March 1936

After two days of exhausting travel, Consuelo found herself in the ship terminal of Old Havana directly across from the main squares. The Pan American Clipper was berthed there conveniently for visitors staying at hotels in the city's center. She had written to the Sevilla-Biltmore Hotel to reserve a suite for an open-ended visit. She mentioned George Gershwin had recommended the hotel, and her fib was rewarded by a telegram assuring her that any friend of Mr. Gershwin was welcome at the hotel.

A taxi brought her to Havana's Vieja section and her hotel; barely a block from the magnificent Presidential Palace. The Sevilla-Biltmore was built in 1908 in Moorish style and had been expanded in the 1920s. It had an impressive facade and would have fit comfortably among the architecture of Barcelona or Paris. Consuelo's suite on the ninth floor featured tall windows and a clear view of the Malecon Havana's fabled five mile stretch of wide sidewalk along the seawall. She made a promise to herself that she would walk the Malecon's entire distance at least once a week. Consuelo was hungry from the long flight. She hadn't eaten on the airplane as she was nervous during her first flight. She ordered a Bacardi cocktail, a sandwich and sweet plantains from the room service menu, and quickly showered. She wanted to see the Havana so loved by North Americans and so longed for by the Ybor City Cubans.

With map in hand, Consuelo began her tour of Old Havana at Plaza de la Catedral. The Baroque style church dominating the plaza was built in 1727 by the Jesuits who ran afoul of the King of Spain. The Jesuits were expelled from Cuba, and the Franciscans completed the church in 1777. Consuelo entered the massive structure whose interior was mostly unadorned except at the front of the church. This surprised her as she remembered the color bookplates of elaborate European churches from the art history classes she took in Albany. Sitting in the last pew far away from the mass that was in progress in the front of the church, Consuelo asked herself, what am I doing here? It's cool and restful, but there has to be more. I feel nothing toward what goes on here. I've lived for the moment for so long that I forgot there's a future. I really loved Daniel and tried to believe that it wouldn't just end, but it did. I liked Gershwin a lot, but he's not lovable. He's a genius so he gets to do what he wants.

Back in the sunshine, Consuelo swept the unhappy thoughts from her mind and concentrated on studying the elaborate buildings that bordered the city's four squares. Several of the stateliest Baroque style buildings had been the homes of wealthy families whose fortunes were made in the slave trade that continued in Cuba until 1867. She was bothered by thoughts of families; parents, children even grandchildren living sumptuous lives due to the hard labor of abducted Africans working until they died without hope or dreams.

Frustrated by thoughts of injustice, Consuelo walked to the largest square the Plaza de Armas that had been neglected for a long time, and now wisely was being renovated by the government. Money had poured into Cuba during the Prohibition era, and the enlightenment of sexuality during the 1920s, which was again being suppressed in America by religion and laws. Cuba had no prohibitions on sexual activities. In fact, it was known as a wild tropical playground in certain circles of wealthy easterners who willingly made the journey to Havana for liaisons with Cuban "mulatas" known to be skilled and compliant temptresses. The most prized and most expensive Havana cigars were those guaranteed to have been rolled on the thigh of a beautiful Cuban woman.

Feeling tired from walking in the sun, Consuelo stopped at the bar in the portico of the Hotel Santa Isabel on Calle Obispo. She lounged in a comfortable cushioned chair after ordering a tall Bacardi with pineapple juice, and lots of ice. The drink was brought by a pleasant waiter who also left a small glass bucket of extra ice. Consuelo had purchased her first pair of sunglasses, which were almost required for North Americans visiting Cuba. The glasses made her feel mysterious, and she could watch people without their knowing she was interested. After finishing a second Bacardi, Consuelo left the bar and found a taxi to take her to the hotel. She felt satisfied with the day in Havana; seeing the city's heart and learning its history. Tomorrow she planned to visit one of Gershwin's favorite places the Oriental Park Racetrack.

The next morning Consuelo conferred with the hotel's concierge regarding her plan to spend the day at the racetrack. Rafael Castro, the concierge, was happy to assist the beautiful American woman who already had gained a favorable reputation among the hotel's staff as a good tipper. He suggested that perhaps Miss Davis would be better served if she hired a car and driver for her stay in Havana. Rafael could recommend a dependable and honest man who owned a Studebaker Phaeton motor car, and would also look after the Senorita's safety. Consuelo liked the idea of having her own car and driver. Daniel Clark never drove. He had Charles to take him wherever he had to go. "All right Rafael, I'll talk with your driver. When can we do that?

"Right away Senorita. He is outside waiting. I will get him." Minutes later Rafael returned with a middle-aged man wearing a black suit, a white shirt open at the neck and eye glasses. Rafael introduced him to Consuelo saying, "Senorita Davis, please meet Carlos Rubio." They smiled at each other, and the introductions continued. "The Senorita is from America and is in need of a trusted driver to take her around the city. Carlos is a good driver and, in his youth was a champion middleweight boxer, and now he is a grandfather He has driven our hotel guests for many years." Consuelo thanked Rafael and asked Carlos to sit down with her on the chairs in a corner of the lobby. After speaking with Carlos in Spanish and English, and asking about his availability and the charge for his time and use of his automobile, which turned out to be reasonable, Consuelo felt comfortable enough to ask Carlos to devote the following week to her beginning with the racetrack in Mariano today. He happily agreed and said he would wait for her by his car.

"Let's agree on a time and place to meet up later today," Consuelo said as the soft top Phaeton motor car carefully driven by Carlos Rubio glided onto the park-like grounds surrounding Cuba's only racetrack. American horse owners brought their race horses here during the winter months because attendance and the betting handle was always high, and winning purses were larger than the tracks in the southern part of the United States.

Carlos said, "I'll wait for you, Senorita Davis. Whenever you want to leave will be all right. I work for you so the car will be in front of the Jockey Club. My cousin is the doorman there so I can park. I may make a few bets while I'm waiting for you." He got out of the car and opened the rear door for Consuelo.

She entered the Jockey Club and bought a ticket for a seat in the covered section across from the finish line. The racetrack and grandstand were surrounded by tall palm trees along broad boulevards. Cars were parked everywhere, and the general admission areas were filled with racing fans, almost exclusively men and almost all wore straw skimmers on their heads. Well dressed women occupied the reserved seats in the shade. Some held parasols and all wore large straw hats festooned with silk scarves. They were served by waiters busily bringing drinks from the Jockey Club's bars. There were betting windows in the club reserved for the seat holders so they could avoid standing in line to place their bets.

Consuelo studied the program selecting a horse based solely on its name. She picked "George's Music" as an obvious choice confident that she would be rewarded by placing ten dollar bets "across the board" to win, place and show. The mile and a quarter race started fast and was over in less than two minutes. "George's Music" ran last. Consuelo said to herself; well that says something. She hadn't any better luck the next two races, and was growing bored and restless. George was here with his friends, Evert and Emil and Kay Swift so they had a good time she enviously thought. Why am I alone she asked herself?

After ordering a Bacardi cocktail from a waiter passing by she heard someone say, "Excuse me I believe this is yours." The voice came from a man dressed in a tan suit, cream colored shirt, and yellow tie. His shoes were expensive; likely from London. He handed Consuelo her French purse. "It was left by the betting window. I was next in line, and frankly was so distracted by you I didn't notice your purse until you left there." His smile showed even teeth, his hair was black, eyes blue and all in all, he was an attractive man. He had been distracted by Consuelo. She assumed it was in a good way.

"Well thank you. I hadn't missed it yet, and would be lost without it." She hesitated, but said, "I'm Consuelo Middleton Davis, and you are...?"

He answered immediately as if he were afraid of being dismissed by this splendid woman. "I am, my name is Willie Levinson;" he was able to say while attempting to look only into beautiful green eyes, and away from the breasts and legs making up the most stunning woman he had ever seen. "I'm from New York. I'm here on business. I'm a lawyer." He seemed relieved to get that all out and was happy when Consuelo invited him to sit down, and have a drink with her.

"I'm from New York as well, but North near Albany, actually Cooperstown." Consuelo was happy that she could call Cooperstown home again. "I had been living in West Florida, but I'm back to where I grew up." She continued. "I'm on vacation to get away from the cold winter that I haven't experienced for several years."

Levinson said, "Cooperstown, do you know the Clarks?"

Consuelo hesitated before saying, "Everyone in Cooperstown knows the Clarks or at least knows of them." She was concerned that someone new could associate her with Daniel. "Do you know them?"

Oh no, I represented the owners of a small industrial sewing machine company in the Bronx section of New York. The company was sold to the Singer Sewing Machine Company. I dealt with their lawyer. I didn't meet anyone from the Clark family. Unlike the lawyers I'm working with right now, Clark's attorney John Braddock was a gentleman. A high-class guy."

Consuelo couldn't resist asking, "Do you mean John Braddock of White and Case?"

Levinson was surprised and it showed on his face. "Yes, you know him?"

"John's my lawyer," Consuelo said with a big smile.

Levinson said, "I see," but clearly he did not. He asked, "Are you married? Are you here with someone?"

"No to both questions. I've always taken care of myself. You're going to see more women making decisions for themselves."

Levinson smiled ruefully," My ex-wife made her own decisions. She's a modern woman and was secretary to the vice president of the Pennsylvania Railroad. She and her boss traveled a lot together on business in his private railroad car, and they fell in love. We're divorced two years. She admitted to infidelity so she didn't have to go to Reno, and she married him."

"I'm sorry. You seem like a nice person. I'm sure it hurt."

"Yeah it did, but I got over it. To be frank, I haven't spoken about any of it especially to a woman until just now. Will you have dinner with me? There are supposed to be some good restaurants in Havana, and I'll have an excuse to get away from the other lawyers staying at the Nacional. I'll get a taxi at the hotel, and pick you up wherever you're staying."

"That would be nice. I'd like the company. Let's say at 8, and I'll pick you up. I have a car and driver. In fact let's leave here now, and have a drink somewhere, and I'll drop you off at the Nacional until later."

Levinson was surprised and intrigued. This woman was full of surprises. He didn't know independent women, expect maybe his ex-wife, and he didn't run into them often. He had attended law school at Columbia. The school was all male; students and faculty, and had its own library so he rarely saw the Barnard College co-eds who were reputed to share Columbia's campus. His background was working class New York. His mother was Irish Catholic born in Cork and immigrated while a young girl. He inherited his good looks from her. The Black Irish dark hair and bright blue eyes. His father was born somewhere in Eastern Europe. He wasn't sure as his parents didn't accompany him to America.

Levinson's parents met in night school and fell in love. They still live in the family apartment on the Grand Concourse in the Bronx where Willie and his younger sister Amelia known as Molly grew up. Molly was a graduate of Hunter College one of the most influential colleges for women in America. He told most of this to Consuelo as they were driven by Carlos to the center of the city, and a rooftop bar.

During the following week, Consuelo and Willie Levinson spent every evening together frequenting Havana's best restaurants and night clubs with a nightly late hour visit to the Club Zombie reputed to be the city's hottest club. The music never stopped, and the dancers were beautiful almost nude Latin women wearing only G strings with a patch the size of a playing card over their pubic area. Consuelo wondered why they even bothered with the small cloth rectangle. Levinson wondered how the patch stayed on the dancer's bodies. They had become lovers their third night together, and spent late afternoons in bed in her hotel suite usually before going out for their evening rounds in Havana. Consuelo reasoned that they would be tired later on after a night of great food, tropical alcohol and late night leering at beautiful naked bodies so sex in the early evening was advisable and more enjoyable. Then, Levinson would return to the Nacional, and Consuelo would go to bed alone. Levinson agreed with any preference Consuelo had regarding sex. He had never been so happy.

Consuelo also was happy. Levinson was a considerate lover, passionate, and he was clear about the great depth of feeling he had for Consuelo. It was obvious that he was crazy about her. When his work in Havana was finished, and before he left for New York and his other clients, he proposed marriage to Consuelo.

Levinson had represented the Hanover Bank of New York. The bank was owed about $1 million from the sale of the Cuyamel Fruit Company to the United Fruit Company the most powerful American corporation operating in Latin America. The closing of the deal was held in Havana as a neutral place between Guatemala the center of United Fruit's operations and New Orleans home of Sam Zemurray's Cuyamel Fruit Company. Levinson's client, the bank, wasn't involved in the negotiations. His job was to collect a check from Zemurray when the sale closed. United Fruit was represented by two Sullivan and Cromwell lawyers from New York John Foster Dulles and his brother Allen. Levinson didn't like the Dulles brothers, and hoped he wouldn't hear of them again. Zemurray's attorney was from New Orleans, a graduate of Tulane's law school. If you planned to practice law under the old Napoleonic Codes in Louisiana; you had to be a Tulane trained lawyer. He didn't like the Dulles brothers either.

Last night had been the best one of his life. Levinson really believed it. His proposal to Consuelo wasn't a result of their fantastic sexual pairing. Oh, some of it was he admitted to himself, but he knew he loved her even though he realized that he had been the one talking about himself for the last five days. She hadn't said much about who she was, and he found it a little curious. Consuelo was content to listen.

She planned to stay in Havana for several weeks to make sure when she returned to Cooperstown Daniel and his wife were gone. Her reaction to Levinson's proposal of marriage was to ask him to wait a little while before she answered his offer. She suggested that he return to his life and law practice in New York for two or three weeks and, after thinking about their future together, return to Havana if he still wanted to marry her, and she would give him her answer. Levinson saw the wisdom in her suggestion however he planned to come back with a diamond ring from Tiffany's, but first he wanted to tell his parents and Molly about Consuelo. He knew they would urge caution because his first marriage had become a disaster. He was thirty-nine; four years older than Consuelo. That much he knew about her. She hadn't been married, but he was certain there were stories in her past that she might not want to reveal to him.

Levinson telephoned his parents as soon as he got home to his apartment in Tudor City off of 43rd Street and Second Avenue. He said he had some good news and would come up to the Bronx for dinner the following evening. His next call was to Molly. His sister was his best friend. She was two years younger, was married to Joshua a doctor, lived in the suburb of Scarsdale and had three children ages 7, 9 and 13 who Levinson doted over. Adele, his first wife, didn't want children. She wanted a Manhattan lifestyle having never recovered from discovering alcohol, sex and dancing during the Roaring 20s. Now she and her new husband lived in Bala Cynwyd, Pennsylvania. Molly was pleased but cautious about her brother's new relationship that could result in a marriage. "I'm impressed with her name. She sounds like a socialite. Was she a debutante from the right schools and country clubs where we can't go?"

Levinson laughed at that because he hadn't thought to mention that Consuelo was a colored woman. "She's not a debutante," he explained to Molly, "She's part Indian. A tribe from upstate New York, Cayuga I think, and Negro, and her father was English a writer, but she never knew him. The point is she's gorgeous, brilliant, nice to everyone, and I'm guessing rich."

"Oh boy," said Molly, "You better sign her up quick. I'm going with you to see mom and dad tomorrow night. I want to see how it works out. I hope Josh can mind the kids"

"I'm glad you'll be there with me. Just don't say anything before I get there."

"Don't worry. Now tell me more about the fantastic Miss Davis."

Chapter 34

Havana March 1936

Consuelo was back at the Oriental Park Racetrack not to bet on the horses but as an observer. She had decided to use her time in Havana more productively than just a vacation. It occurred to her, that what was missing in Havana was a book to guide visitors around the charming colonial city, and she would write it. It was a Friday, and the racetrack was busy with Americans beginning long weekends in the place where almost anything goes. She was sitting at a table in the Jockey Club's dining room reading over the entries made the day before in her notebook.

Over the last few days, Carlos Rubio had accompanied Consuelo on a tour of Havana's four main squares. He pointed out the places where the famous and infamous had lived since the city's founding four centuries ago. They also stopped by several of the small European style hotels on the side streets leading to the squares, and Consuelo made notes on the number of guest rooms and services offered by each hotel. Carlos told her about the hotel's reputation and matters of safety and friendliness of the staff. She planned to spend a full day tomorrow at the Nacional making notes about the Caribbean's best-known new hotel. Even though Willie Levinson had stayed there, Consuelo hadn't entered the massive structure that was usually fully booked with American tourists and businessmen.

She looked up from her notes, and standing by her table, each with a big smile, were Gershwin's close friends Emil Mosbacher and Yip Harburg. They had met Consuelo at Cole Porter's show's opening the previous November and, because both men, and their wives had asked her to stay in touch with them, Consuelo had written to them providing her address in Cooperstown. "Consuelo, I'm so happy to see you. What are you doing here," Mosbacher asked?

"Oh, Emil, Yip please sit down. I was about to order lunch." They took the empty chairs, and Harburg apologized for not responding to her letter. "That's all right, I know you've been busy. I read about you working in Hollywood. Luella Parson's column is even printed in the *Albany Times-Union,*" said Consuelo referring to the nationally syndicated newspaper woman specializing in Hollywood gossip. They ordered lunch, and made plans to have dinner together later.

Mosbacher took her hand in both of his and said, "I wanted to say how bad I felt when you and George parted. Please understand that sometimes he doesn't do or say what's expected. He is, after all, a virtuoso with a rare brilliance." Holding on to Consuelo's hand, Mosbacher asked if she was here with anyone.

"Emil I'm happy to tell you, and you and Yip are the first to know, I met a wonderful man here in Havana. He's from New York, and he asked me to marry him. When he returns next week, I'll accept his proposal." Mosbacher smiled, and let her hand go. He seemed disappointed.

"I'm happy for you. If I or Gertrude can help in any way, please call on us," said Mosbacher. He and Harburg were two of the people closest to Gershwin. They couldn't have been more different from each other. Mosbacher was a stock and bond trader who was fortunate enough to have divested all of his holdings in the markets prior to the 1929 stock market crash. He invested his fortune in the emerging fields of oil and natural gas and became richer. He was a patrician of German Jewish descent and was accepted into the world of Protestant bankers and yachtsmen as an equal. He was an officer of the Knickerbocker Yacht Club on the Harlem River. Harburg, on the other hand, grew up in a family of poor immigrants from Russia, meeting Gershwin in grade school and remaining friends. His parents spoke only Yiddish, and he tried to earn a living in business, but the crash of 1929 left him bankrupt. He began writing lyrics for songs, and in 1932 with composer Vernon Duke wrote *April in Paris,* a classic piece of American music, and a financial success. Now Harburg was in great demand to work on film musicals and Broadway shows.

"And I have a new project that began just a week ago. I looked for a guide-book to places that a visitor should see in Havana, and I couldn't find one so I'm writing one. I made notes about the buildings in Old Havana that can be entered to see the gardens and atriums hidden from the street, and I'm gathering infor-mation about hotels, restaurants, and bars. Next, I'll research the night spots."

Yip Harburg said, "Consuelo I volunteer to go with you on that part, but I'm serious; you have a great idea. I think it's a book that's needed, because in three trips here I've only seen the racetrack and the Garden of Eden Concert." Harburg was referring to a nightly musical revue produced by the impresario Victor de Correa that featured beautiful Cuban women dancers.

Mosbacher always the businessman said, "I suggest you talk with our friend Bennett Cerf when you return to New York. You may have met Bennett at Cole Porter's opening night party." Consuelo did remember meeting Cerf. Mosbacher continued, "Bennett and a partner began a publishing firm almost ten years ago, and called it *Random House* because they publish random books. You see most publishers stick with one kind of book; fiction or history or some specialty. Bennett could be interested in your book especially with so many of us going to Havana even with Prohibition ending."

"I'll ask you for an introduction. I expect to leave here before April." Consuelo, Harburg, and Mosbacher spent the next three days driven around Havana by Carlos Rubio to Cuba's capital building modeled after the U.S. Capitol, the Presidential Palace, Gran Teatro, basilicas, Prados, fountains and gardens. They also inspected rooftop cafes, hotel bars and restaurants hidden in old neighbor-hoods. The men were tired at the end of the days, but happy to have seen sights missed by most of the Americans visiting Havana.

A week later, Levinson almost driven mad by the separation from Consuelo returned to her along with a four carat diamond mounted in the newly stylish Tiffany setting. This time Consuelo booked a room for him in her hotel. They spent the first day in her suite mostly in her bed congratulating themselves on finding each other. They decided to marry sometime in September. Levinson's family was happy for him and anxious to meet the woman that loved their son and brother. Consuelo asked him, "Are you sure you told them everything about me. My background?"

Levinson laughed, "Your background? I don't even know your background. Maybe we should talk more about our lives, and what we had done before we met last month. I really don't care, but if you want to tell me anything you can. Except for my being married one time my life's been pretty ordinary."

Consuelo didn't know how much she wanted to say so she told Levinson about growing up in Cooperstown, and going to New York State Teachers College for two years. She also talked about working at the hospital in Cooperstown, but neglected to mention her affair with Daniel Clark. When Levinson asked in what capacity John Braddock acted as her attorney; she said, "I own the Wilmington Sewing Machine Company. It's registered in Delaware, and John handles my occasional legal work. I also owned a hotel in Tampa, Florida that John helped me acquire."

Levinson was surprised. "The sewing machine company. What does it do?

"It isn't an active company." James Flynn had said it was a holding company so she said, "It's a holding company. It holds various assets of mine, including a building leased to DuPont."

Levinson said, "Oh I see," even though he didn't. "It doesn't matter. Let's make some wedding plans." He suggested a civil ceremony, a judge. He knew several judges and was certain one would agree to officiate at their wedding. He had thought it all out and had spoken in length with Molly who was excited about helping with the plans. In fact, she suggested they ask Oscar Tucci, the owner of Delmonico's, who was a patient of her husband Josh if they could have the wedding at his famous restaurant on Beaver Street in the Wall Street area.

Consuelo readily agreed to Delmonico's and a judge. She didn't really care about the kind of ceremony or the luncheon details, but they seemed to be important to the Levinsons. Since she was about to be a bride however, Consuelo had to begin thinking about her dress, guests to invite and most important where they would live together. "Willie have you thought about where we'll live," she asked over dinner one evening at El Tocororo a Havana restaurant frequented by racehorse owners and the American yachting crowd? "I can't stay in your apartment. It was Adele's home."

"Levinson agreed. "Where do you want to live? I'll go anyplace you're happy." They had decided that Manhattan would be best as it was the place most accepting of racially mixed couples perhaps with the exception of Paris. He realized that they would have problems moving into some Manhattan apartment buildings, and didn't want their marriage to begin on an unhappy note. Look I can find out about buildings such as the San Remo, the Eldorado and the Dakota. I believe they're cooperatives and the apartments are owned by the tenants. I don't know if that's good or bad as far as we're concerned."

Consuelo found this funny. New York, the largest city in the country and she knew people in two of the three buildings Levinson mentioned. "We can't live in the Dakota. I'll explain, but not now." She gave him her best smile, and Levinson would have agreed to anything Consuelo wanted. "I do know someone who lives in the San Remo," Consuelo continued, I can ask about the building's race policy." Levinson thought that it would be difficult to ask about race, and told Consuelo. She replied, "Oh he understands those things. He's in show business and works with all kinds of people. He's Cole Porter, and I can telephone him when I get back to New York."

"Cole Porter? He's one of my favorite composers. You know Cole Porter? If his new show is still running when you and I are in New York we should see it. How do you know him?"

Consuelo began to giggle like a young girl. She had lost her usual control, and was laughing helplessly. Alarmed Levinson offered her a glass of water, and asked if he could help her. "No, no I'm all right. It's just that I was at the opening night of "Anything Goes," and spoke with Cole for a while. He's a good friend of my date that evening."

Levinson carefully asked, "Who was your date?"

Consuelo looking beautiful, desirable yet warm and approachable turned on her magic smile, and said to her future husband, "How late does this place stay open? Now I have to tell you my entire story, and it *will* take a while. For starters my date that night was George Gershwin."

Chapter 35

Greenwich Village, New York City

After the middle of April, Consuelo returned to Cooperstown to catch up on her life that had been interrupted by her stay in Havana. She had stopped in New York for a week to meet Willie Levinson's family. They were gracious and welcoming to her, and Consuelo felt comfortable with them. She hadn't much experience with family having been on her own since her mother died. Levinson explained that his parents were Socialist leaning people, and open to everyone. Molly and Consuelo easily connected, and Consuelo happily turned over the making of wedding arrangements to her future sister-in-law. Now it was May, and she had returned again to New York. While still in Havana, Consuelo told Levinson everything about her life from the time her mother had passed, and she had to make her own way.

Vanessa had her own children to raise, but tried unsuccessfully to get Consuelo to live with them in her tiny house. Consuelo from her teen years was in demand as a helper and then as a dinner organizer taking care of serving meals and the big cleanups after the guests had gone. She was well paid. She was a careful and competent worker, but she was also so good looking that her presence decorated the party.

She had lots of stories about her work in the hospital, and how Daniel Clark noticed her and arranged to meet her. Consuelo was honest about their relationship only leaving out the sexual techniques Daniel learned in Siam and his subsequent tutoring of her. Consuelo told Levinson that she and Clark spent many happy times in New York during Prohibition going to the Cotton Club, Jack and Charley's and the Central Park Casino where they met Mayor Jimmy Walker and his girlfriend from the Ziegfeld Follies. Their trips to the Tampa Bay Hotel, Babe Ruth's homer for her and times in North East Harbor were wistfully related to Levinson who listened intently without interrupting.

He knew his fiancée had a past. Everyone did, but not like Consuelo's, and he wasn't quite ready for the next phase of her story. "You mean to tell me Daniel Clark bought a hotel for you, and a house, and gave you his sewing machine company in Delaware?"

"Oh that's not the whole story," Consuelo admitted, "there was also the big Hertz loan paid back to my company, and my investments in electricity and oil have taken off because of the advice I regularly receive. It was at my hotel in Ybor City where I got to know George Gershwin, and we right away understood each other. We had some good times together, but I couldn't compete with his longtime lover Kay Swift. She's divorced now so I guess George will marry her. It's what he's always wanted. He was the most amazing man I ever met," Consuelo hesitated, "Until I met you. I really mean that Willie. I love you. I never said that to anyone, but you."

⸻ ✸ ⸻

They were sitting across from each other in one of the high booths in Chumley's bar room at 87 Barrow Street. It was a Greenwich Village restaurant that operated as a speakeasy throughout Prohibition without a sign or anything else to indicate that one of the city's busiest saloons was pouring whiskey day and night. Customers knew where it was, and told their friends. Consuelo had returned to New York to order a wedding gown at De Pinna and to help Levinson look for a place for them to live. Levinson agreed that the Village was New York's most accepting neighborhood, and that they wouldn't be noticed in that racially and sexually open small section of Manhattan.

It was Saturday and, after walking around the charming narrow streets most with green leafed shade trees, Consuelo and Levinson stopped for lunch at

Chumley's a place he knew from law school days. They were having steak sand-wiches garnished with salted French fries sprinkled with malt vinegar. About an hour earlier they had passed a federal style row house with a For Sale sign in its front window at 29 Grove Street a few blocks from where they were sitting. Levinson wrote down the telephone number and, after arriving at Chumley's, asked the bartender for the phone. He called the building's owner who agreed to meet them in two hours. Levinson left a quarter on the bar.

They had time for a leisurely lunch and talked about wedding plans, which Molly had been organizing, and had asked them for the invitation list. Consuelo decided it was time to write down the names for Molly who had arranged for Goldsmith Brothers the Wall Street stationers to print, address, and mail the invitations to the wedding and reception at Delmonico's. Levinson got a piece of paper from the waiter, and Consuelo went to work compiling her list. First was Vanessa, and her children and grandchildren. Marilyn Arnoff who Consuelo had gotten to know better recently, was added to the list. Then James and Elizabeth Flynn and Harvey Sparks and his wife from Ybor City, John Braddock and wife, Emil and Gertrude Mosbacher, Yip and Edelaine Harburg, Leo De Pinna, Lenore and Ira Gershwin with whom she kept in touch, and finally George Gershwin. Levinson read over the list and said, "Do you think the Gershwins will come to our wedding and the Mosbachers?"

Consuelo replied, "I know Emil will be there because he's going to give me away. I was going to tell you, but it slipped my mind. I'm worried about our finding a place to live outside of Harlem. I don't want to live there. I don't feel I belong, and I'm sure you don't want to live there either."

Levinson was used to living in the middle of Manhattan. He liked being near Broadway, the big Loews movie palaces, and all of the restaurants, and even the museums. He could walk to his law office in the Chanin Building on 42nd Street and Lexington Avenue. He said, "Look, wherever we decide to live will be all right for me. I want you to be happy there and happy with me. It's a big city. We'll find a nice place to live. Let's go look at the Grove Street house."

The house was a 19th Century three story red brick in the Queen Ann revival style that had been recently lived in by the owner Thomas Tucker and his family. The interior was clean, and appeared freshly painted. A twin house

shared a common wall, and the rest of the street had similar homes in different styles. Consuelo liked it immediately and looked around for signs of water
either from leaking pipes or poorly fitting windows, and didn't find any problems. Having owned the Excelsior Hotel she knew what to look at. Electricity
and water worked where it was supposed to, and the newly introduced gas heat
was hooked up and working according to the owner. Levinson hadn't ever lived
in a house so he didn't know what to look for beyond all of the rooms and spaces
they were acquiring. He and Consuelo conferred for a few minutes agreeing
that the house while larger than what they needed was on a nice street, near
restaurants and bars, the subway and important to Levinson who loved movies,
the Lowes Canal Theatre was nearby. The Lowes Canal was the city's second
largest theater housing 2,300 seats. It was a true movie house extravaganza
designed by renowned theater architect Thomas Lamb to make patrons feel as
if they had entered a European palace.

That sealed the sale, and Levinson agreed to pay the $22,000 asking price
for the house. That pleased Tucker; a pleasant man who had moved his family to Central Park West. In fact, he liked Consuelo and Willie and was so
relieved that the sale went quickly that he agreed to include a second property
as well. Around the corner, accessed by another street, were the former
stables that had a separate deed, and were not attached to the house in any
manner. Thomas Tucker the property owner said, "If you buy an automobile,
you can garage it in the old stable. You really have to keep them indoors during the winter or they won't start. Consuelo had wanted a car of her own
since she drove around with Vanessa in Cooperstown so having a garage for
one was good news. They shook hands and Levinson gave Thomas Tucker his
business card, and asked Tucker to have his lawyer send over the contract for
the properties.

Later that afternoon in bed in Consuelo's Warwick Hotel suite, Levinson
happily exhausted said, "I think we did well today. I mean earlier. We always do
well in bed together. I like the house."

Consuelo replied, "Maybe we should have found out about the neighbor. We
share a wall so it's pretty close living, and if they're not nice people we could
regret it."

Levinson said, "I think we're all right. I have a good feeling about the house." His comment wasn't based on anything in particular, but he hoped he was correct. They continued to enjoy each other's attention to their most sensitive places. Levinson at first in Havana had treated Consuelo as if she would break during lovemaking, but discovered she was strong, flexible and inventive, and he was brought to a level of sexuality that he hadn't dreamed existed.

Finally satisfying each other they showered and dressed. Levinson for the first time noticed the bedroom's decorations and furniture. He was impressed. Consuelo reminded him of just where they were. "Do you know who's in the hotel right now?" He didn't. She continued, "Marion Davies is in the house. The chambermaid told me this morning. When she's in town she's here because when William Randolph Hearst built this place he had an entire floor custom made for her. The staff is alerted whenever Marion is coming here because William Randolph will show up. I think it's romantic like a king building a castle for his consort."

"I think what we were doing is as romantic as can be, and I bought a castle for you today," Levinson said.

Consuelo smiled and took Levinson's hand in hers. "I want to talk to you about our castle. I can buy it. I have lots of money that doesn't get any less no matter how much I spend, and you gave me this beautiful diamond ring so it's my turn."

"No, Molly told me that you insisted that all of the bills for our wedding be sent to the Knickerbocker Trust Company for payment from your account. I'm beginning to feel like a kept man, and by the way who does the buying and selling of your stocks and commodities? They seem to know when it's time to sell. I wonder if that's all legal"

Consuelo answered Levinson's concern. "Of course it's legal. These people were introduced to me by George Gershwin. They're stockbrokers, they would never do anything wrong."

They left the Warwick on 54th Street, and walked to Longchamps restaurant on 46th Street for their dinner, and later saw the new movie *Fury* starring Spencer Tracy and Sylvania Sydney at the Loews Theatre on Broadway.

Levinson agreed that he would spend August with Consuelo in Cooperstown since the courts were closed in New York. She would try to rent a house on Lake Otesaga, and planned to shop at Scribner's on Fifth Avenue for a copy of the *Leatherstocking Tales* for Levinson so he could look out at the lake and imagine the Glimmerglass Lake of James Fenimore Cooper's stories.

Chapter 36

Summer 1936

On August 10 George and Ira Gershwin flew from Newark Airport the region's first major facility for air travel, to Glendale, California on a Transcontinental and Western Airline (TWA) Douglas DC3 a newly introduced aeroplane. Their cross-country trip took over seventeen hours and required stops for refueling in St. Louis, Topeka and Denver. Nevertheless, the DC3 halved the amount of hours that were usual for the flight just two years before. A ticket for the flight cost $160 one way.

Once in Los Angeles, the Gershwin brothers settled into a suite at the Beverly Wilshire Hotel and began work on a new movie score for Fred Astaire the hottest talent in Hollywood. Less than two weeks later, the brothers leased a large house in Beverly Hills that had its own swimming pool and tennis court. They were quickly and firmly ensconced in the movie business accepting offers from several studios to write the scores for upcoming musicals. They adapted almost immediately to the "California quieter creative life," and presented to U.C.L.A. the rights to their hit song, *Strike Up the Band* for the university's fight song.

Consuelo and Willie were spending August on Lake Otesaga in a rented place called Mohegan Cottage. The cottage had five bedrooms and three baths, outside shower, large living and dining rooms, screened porch, and a lakeside dock with row boats and canoes. They decided to have a pre-wedding honeymoon for the month, and get settled in the Greenwich Village house right after marrying in the middle of September. After one week together alone, they invited Vanessa and her family and the Levinson's to Mohegan Cottage.

For the next two weeks, the house was busy with adults and children swimming and boating, cooking out of doors and watching the shooting stars over the lake on clear nights. They all agreed that it was the best time they ever had. For the last week of the month, they were alone together tired from having all of the company. They appreciated being alone not even getting dressed or getting out of bed if they felt lazy or sexual. Consuelo read Louella Parson's column in the Albany newspaper about George and Ira in Hollywood, and wondered if Kay Swift had gone to California as well. Before leaving Cooperstown for Manhattan, Consuelo asked Vanessa to drive her by Dr. Collins-Clark's office to see if her shingle had been removed. They discovered it was no longer hanging in front of the red brick office building.

⊶

Molly had put her heart and soul into her brother's wedding, which took place Sunday, September 13 at Delmonico's. The restaurant usually closed Sundays, but Oscar made it available for his doctor's family wedding. The ceremony was held in the wide hallway that divided the restaurant into barroom and dining room. Chairs were set up for the almost eighty guests, and the room was decorated with yellow and white rose displays designed by Irene Hayes for society florist Wadley Smythe located nearby on Beaver Street. Twelve tables set for the luncheon sported elaborate yellow and white rose center pieces.

A string ensemble played classical selections for the wedding ceremony and during the reception that included: Debussy's *Afternoon of a Faun,* Handel's *Water Music,* Erik Satie's *Trio Gymnopodies* and selections from Vivaldi's *Four Seasons,* which made the affair even more uplifting. Molly had given a great deal of thought to the menu for the luncheon after the wedding ceremony, and had conferred with Oscar and his chef several times selecting some of the restaurant's specialties since Delmonico's was famous for originating several dishes.

Once the ceremony ended, the bar opened and remained so during the afternoon. Molly's order was, "Give them anything they want, and as much as they want." The luncheon's first course was the restaurant's original Manhattan clam chowder a departure from the New England variety because Delmonico's left out the heavy cream. The appetizer course was their new creation Lobster Newberg served in individual clay pots right from the oven, and the entre was of course Delmonico steak a two inch thick prime dry-aged sirloin cooked to each guest's order. When Molly had visited Delmonico's to plan the wedding; Oscar had brought her into the restaurant's meat locker to see the aged beef that he planned to serve for Willie and Consuelo's wedding. The locker; really a refrigerator the size of a small room held the marbled beef for various periods of time to dry-age the steaks placing Delmonico's among the city's most prized restaurants for beef loving gourmets.

Delmonico Potatoes another original dish accompanied the steak. The delicious mashed potatoes were topped with grated cheese and buttered bread crumbs then baked. A Waldorf salad was served, and the elaborate lunch was finished with Delmonico's classic and dramatic flaming dessert Baked Alaska. Tuxedoed waiters served with skill, and the bride and groom cut the three-tiered wedding cake as the last part of the party.

The day went off as planned. Molly wouldn't have it any other way. Consuelo as a bride radiated a sense of contentment that added to her beauty. She wore a gown that was straight rather than billowing and ecru in color rather than stark white. Leo De Pinna personally searched among the designers he patronized to find the perfect dress for Consuelo's wedding day. Cousin Tonya, the maid of honor wore a slightly darker cream colored gown that complimented her café au lait complexion.

Tonya first visited Manhattan in July staying at the Warwick Hotel with Consuelo in order to select a dress, and have a fitting at De Pinna. She was similar in height and dress size to Consuelo so there were many choices for the maid of honor dress. She looked beautiful especially after spending the day before the wedding with Consuelo at Elizabeth Arden's Red Door Salon. Willie and brother-in-law Joshua Kaufman looked resplendent is white ties and tails.

Emil Mosbacher gracefully gave the bride away, and New York State Judge Edward Josephson, a classmate of Levinson at Columbia, was eloquent in his remarks about the couple. Between courses, there were champagne toasts to

Consuelo and Willie from relatives, friends and law partners. Some were serious; some funny and all were encouraging. Consuelo gave Molly a wide gold bracelet inlaid with sapphires as a thank you for all of the planning and orchestration of the wedding that everyone agreed was a wonderful tribute to two good people.

Everyone Consuelo invited to her wedding was there with the exception of George Gershwin. Luckily Ira had returned to New York to help Lenore get ready for their permanent move to California. Levinson's parents had a difficult time believing that Gershwins, Mosbachers and the Harburgs were at their son's wedding, but they were all so friendly and happy for Consuelo and Willie that it seemed completely natural. George Gershwin had sent a wedding gift to Consuelo's Cooperstown address with a note that he was in California and not able to get away due to concerts scheduled for September. Marilyn Arnoff brought the large square box with her from Cooperstown. It contained a fine Danish modern silver tea and coffee set on an oblong sterling tray made by silversmith Georg Jensen.

Consuelo was happy to see Harvey Sparks and James Flynn again along with their wives. It was their first time in New York, and were grateful for the accommodations she arranged for them at the Warwick. Levinson was happy to meet some other reasonable people from Consuelo's past. Harvey reported that the Excelsior Hotel was busy and profitable largely because of the contract negotiated by Flynn with the Civilian Conservation Corps. The federal government's work program had brought several thousand young men to West Florida to cut down trees for fire barriers, plant trees in wet sandy areas and drain mosquito infested swamps to preserve public health. The CCC had set up a hospital and dispensary north of Tampa for Corps members, and the medical and nursing staff stayed at the Excelsior.

Now that they were married Levinson officially moved into Consuelo's suite in the Warwick Hotel where they planned to stay until the new furniture was delivered to their home. Consuelo refused to allow her new husband to bring anything except his clothing from the apartment he had shared with Adele. Everything in the apartment was donated to the New York Foundling Hospital an orphanage for abandoned children. Levinson didn't have favorite things. Objects meant little to him. He didn't even have a favorite chair so giving up the furniture and fixtures in the Tudor City apartment was easy. He had Consuelo now, and nothing else mattered to him.

They made three trips together to the W. & J. Sloane furniture, antiques and home accessories store on Broadway and 19th Street in the center of what was known as "The Ladies Mile" because of the preponderance of stores catering to women. The city's leading department stores were housed there in Beaux-Arts French architectural style buildings. Neither enjoyed shopping for furniture or much else, but Consuelo did like to buy clothing when it was offered in the De Pinna manner.

Consuelo had seen examples of the new Art Deco furniture featured in newspapers and in display windows along Sixth Avenue. She and Levinson decided that their wonderful non-traditional marriage should include the revolutionary designs of the Art Deco movement that had been translated into furniture, and had the appearance of futuristic images that weren't really intended to be used. They strolled around the giant store selecting a sleek lined blonde wood bedroom set, a dining room set designed by Donald Deskey who rounded every corner of his sensuous styled furniture, a dinette table and chairs with a circle pattern on the seats for the breakfast room. Couches, chairs, and tables for the living room that were designed by Walter Von Nessen who introduced colored leather, silk, geometric patterns, and metal into his furniture that while comfortable to sit in, was a bit difficult to arise from since it was lower than traditional living room suites.

After finding the furniture, they enjoyed picking out oriental carpets for all of the rooms, which took the most time because the carpets were masterpieces of the weaving art. W. & J. Sloane was established in 1843 and was the first company to import oriental carpets into the United States so the company was the expert in Persian, Turkish, Chinese and Urals rugs, and had hundreds on display. Levinson liked the deeper colored carpets and Consuelo the lighter shades so they compromised and bought some of each. They also found old delicate silk carpets with flowered patterns that could be hung on walls as works of art, and they discovered large French travel posters for ships and trains that when framed for hanging make interesting decorations. Another afternoon of searching the Tiffany Studios yielded lamps for the living room and their bed-room. "I think we have enough furniture for a while. We should stop now and see how it all fits into the house," Consuelo said. "I'm afraid we won't have room to move around."

Levinson had measured the rooms and assured her that the furniture would fit. "We'll be all right. I can't wait for the comments about the Art Deco stuff. Some of it is pretty unusual." They were having lunch in a Horn & Hardart Automat on Broadway. Levinson said, "I just love these places." Sandwiches and desserts were shown in small windows, and when patrons inserted the correct number of nickels in the slot to the right of the meal item and turned the round knob the door sprung open and the food was available. Coffee was dispensed from the mouths of silver dragons and paid for in the same manner. The restaurants were huge, and tables were cleared and cleaned constantly by the Automat's staff.

Consuelo, enjoying a chicken sandwich, had also selected a piece of apple pie for dessert. She was studying the busy atmosphere and marveled how clean the restaurant was kept. "I like their slogan, 'Less work for mother,' but do you think people will actually take their main meals in places where food is available so fast? It removes the romance from dining out."

Levinson said, "I don't know, but I haven't cooked one meal for myself since Adele left. I get my coffee and a buttered roll at a stand before I go to the office, have lunch with one of my partners at the President Restaurant around the corner on Lexington, and sometimes have dinner at the closest Automat. By the way, do you need me to go to McCutcheons with you today?" Consuelo planned to pick out linens, towels, blankets, pillows and a bedspread at James McCutcheons on Fifth Avenue.

"On no, I'll do that. I appreciate how much time you spend with me picking out what we need." After their lunch at the Automat, they separated agreeing to meet in the Warwick Hotel's bar later. They intended to fill the rest of the house with objects found together in places they haven't visited yet but would share one day. It was the first time in Consuelo's life that she was living like other people, and not a fantasy in which she loved, but her love wasn't returned.

At times she was afraid that something would happen and that an event or a person from the past will emerge and destroy the safe world Levinson offered her. In the middle of the night, Consuelo sometimes sat up in bed at the Warwick Hotel and watched Levinson sleeping and listened to his soft breathing. She marveled at her luck in running into him that day at the racetrack, and thought about the possibility of the existence of a divine plan for her, but quickly dismissed the thought. If there was a plan for her; there must be plans for everyone, and if so why did the plans include disasters, misfortunes and early death?

Chapter 37

29 Grove Street

It was October 10, and furniture, carpets and everything else they ordered from W. & J. Sloane were due to arrive at 29 Grove Street. The McCutcheons order was on its way as well. Consuelo left the Warwick Hotel early that day assuring Levinson that she was able to handle the deliveries and furniture placement. "I'll telephone you if I need help. I promise." The telephone had been installed in their center hall a few days before. The house had been thoroughly cleaned by two women recruited by Consuelo from the neighborhood. At 10: o'clock a black truck with gold lettering on its side proclaiming James C. McCutcheons parked in front of 29 Grove Street, and two men unloaded box after box and left Consuelo with a mountain of linens and household supplies.

At noon two green trucks arrived from W. & J. Sloane. Carpets were put down where they belonged and furniture was placed on them. The unloading and placement took all afternoon, and when Levinson telephoned, Consuelo was having the delivery men move everything around to other places including the oriental carpets. "I can't decide what looks best and where " she told Levinson. He assured Consuelo that he didn't have any strong opinions on interior decorating. After another hour of moving furniture, Consuelo gave up and sent the furniture men away.

Consuelo sank into a Walter Von Nessen chair not certain if she had enough strength to get up out of it. A knock on the front door startled her, and she forced herself to stand, and answer the knocking. On the doorstep was a tall slender woman holding a bouquet of flowers, which she handed to Consuelo. "Welcome to our street," she said. Consuelo took the flowers and then noticed that the woman's other hand was holding the hand of a little boy. "I'm Debra Clyne, and we share that wall," she said pointing to the wall on the westerly side of the house, "and this is my son Herbert. He's two." Herbert was adorable and gave a big wide eyed smile to Consuelo when she knelt down to talk to him, and touch his smooth cheek.

"So you and Herbert live right next door," Consuelo asked. "And thanks for the flowers, they're beautiful."

"Yes, with my husband John. We own the house, and we've lived here for three years. John works for a printer on Hudson Street so he's only a few minutes' walk to the plant. I think I saw your husband a couple of times here with some workmen. I wasn't sure so I didn't introduce myself. I figured I'd wait until the wife showed up. I'm right that you're the wife, aren't I?"

"Oh yes, I'm Consuelo Levinson, and I've been shopping to fill this place so I haven't been around. Herbert is beautiful. He looks just like you."

"Oh thanks, he has John's coloring. They're both a lot lighter than me. More your shade. By the way, now that we met, I'll admit I'm relieved. The Tuckers were nice, but I've never been in here before. We didn't know who was moving in, and what that would mean for us."

Consuelo's mind was whirling. It never occurred to her that their close neighbors would be Negros. She was relieved and elated. She and Debra Clyne were close in age, and Consuelo's first impression of Debra was that her regal appearance was evidence of the ancestry of African chieftains torn from their land by Arab slave traders a century ago. It turned out to be a wonderful turn of events as she too was worried about who was living on the other side of the common wall. Consuelo found a glass vase for the flowers and put them on the new Art Deco coffee table. "They're my first decoration. I'd like to offer some coffee or tea, but we don't have any, and I may have forgotten to buy a teapot," Consuelo laughed.

"That's all right. I'll invite you and your husband over for dinner soon, but when the printing plant's busy John has to work odd hours sometimes. He's the supervisor because he knows how to fix the presses when they break, which happens often. I want to do that soon. I think you and I are going to be good friends." Consuelo was elated as she never had a close girlfriend. Debra said she grew up in western Pennsylvania in the oil region, and had come to New York City ten years ago after taking a secretarial course for Negro girls at the YWCA. "Look I have to bring Herbert home for his nap, but will you and your husband come by later?

"Oh sure, Willie will be home soon. He wants to see what I've done with the place. We bought all this new style furniture and I know he's afraid it doesn't go with the house, but I like it, and I think he will too."

"I like it," Debra assured Consuelo. "We need some new stuff. A lot of our furniture came from John's aunt's house when she passed three years ago. It's really nice and bright in here. The only new furniture we have is in Herbert's room." Consuelo smiled and realized that because she and Willie were so well off she would have to be careful about what she told Debra about how Willie and she lived.

When Willie got home, it was to be their first night there as Consuelo had checked out of the Warwick Hotel that morning, and loaded two taxis with their clothing. He was pleased with Consuelo's furniture arrangement. "Let's go to Chumley's for dinner and celebrate moving into our home," he said.

"All right, but later on," Consuelo said. "We're going to our neighbors for a few minutes. You have to meet them especially Herbert." She smiled and said nothing else. Levinson knew she was up to something. His lawyer's intuition told him there was a surprise in store for him, and he wasn't going to ask anything and ruin her plan.

At seven they walked down their front steps and up the steps of the twin house next to them. A knock with the brass door knocker brought John Clyne to the door with his hand outstretched toward Levinson who immediately understood Consuelo's surprise for him. Levinson shook hands with John and introduced Consuelo and himself. "Please come in. We've been wondering about our new neighbors," Clyne said." This is my wife Debra and our son Herbert." Herbert had been hiding behind Debra, and peeking at the Levinsons who were enthralled by the charming little boy. Clyne asked, "Willie did you buy the place or are you a tenant. If you don't mind me asking?"

"Oh, we bought it. It's ours now," answered Consuelo, "And I know you're owners."

"Yes we own our house," Clyne answered. "Thanks to Debra's inheritance."

"That's a long story for another time," said Debra who had brought a tray of glasses of lemonade with salty snacks from the kitchen. They sat down, and Herbert climbed onto Levinson's lap. They liked each other right away, which made the two families sharing a common wall even better.

Consuelo had longed to return to college and earn her degree. Levinson suggested she apply to NYU since its Greenwich Village campus was just across Washington Square Park, about a ten-minute walk from their home. He had graduated from NYU's University Heights Campus in the Bronx, an easy commute for him from his family's apartment on the Grand Concourse. The Heights campus was a pleasing collection of buildings from the late 1800s that boasted a superior liberal arts and science faculty.

The most renowned building on the campus was the Gould Library where Levinson had spent countless hours studying world history. The Greek Revival building designed by McKim, Meade, and White featured a rotunda with Tiffany designed windows supporting a glass domed ceiling making the Gould library one of the most elegant buildings on an American college campus. However, Levinson realized his sister's influence when Molly offered to accompany Consuelo to Hunter College on Park Avenue in mid-town. He knew he didn't have a chance to convince Consuelo to go to NYU even though as it turned out Debra Clyne had graduated as an English major from the university's Washington Square College. Molly believed that if women were going to emerge as a force for change in America, they should be educated at superior women's colleges. Consuelo applied to Hunter College, which was tuition free, and she was accepted for the spring term of 1937.

Fall became winter, and it was harsh. They stayed indoors weekends in front of the fireplace fueled by logs found in the old stable they owned around the corner. Most weekdays, Debra and Herbert stopped over, and while he napped they told each other their life stories. At first Consuelo was timid about her love affairs, but eventually, she told Debra her most intimate secrets except for the details of her finances. These she kept to herself so it wouldn't seem she was bragging. Actually, the acquisition of her wealth was such an unusual story she wondered if anyone but her husband would believe her. Debra had grown up near Titusville, Pennsylvania in the center of oil well country. Her father had owned a small dairy farm from which he scraped out enough of a living to support his wife and five children.

Debra and her older sister knew they had to get away from Titusville and its roughneck oilfield workers. In their early teen years, they realized they were targets for molestation or worse. Even though no drilling crewmen would talk to a Negro woman in the daylight; it was a different story after dark in the lonely fields that surrounded the oil rigs. "Maddie and I just hated to walk near the oil rigs. They were filthy with black goo everywhere, but the worst was having those Oakies staring at us, and knowing what was on their minds." Consuelo hugged her as the tears ran down Debra's face. "We left Titusville and went to live with our mother's cousin in Allentown. She was the secretary to the Baptist Seminary and found a job there for Maddie, and I enrolled in the YWCA's stenography class."

"I grew up in a small place also, but I was never afraid," Consuelo confessed.

"After I finished the YWCA classes I couldn't get a job in Allentown. My brothers left home too. Two went to the State Normal School at Cheyney, the college for colored teachers, and that's what they do, teach high school in Philadelphia, and my other brother joined the Navy. He's a chief mess steward. One of my teachers at the YWCA told me she was going to New York City to work at NYU in the business department. She said my skills were so good she'd guarantee that I'd get a job there, and she was right. I started as a clerk in the School of Commerce, and ten years later I was assistant to the registrar with a lot of responsibility. I also earned my English degree free along the way because I was a university employee. I lived in a building NYU owned and met John one day when he and his crew were delivering the university's catalog to our store-room, and I had to find places to store about a thousand of them."

"You're a brave woman, and I'm proud to have you as a friend," Consuelo assured Debra. "I almost feel guilty that I didn't face what you did growing up, and that my life, except for some disappointing love affairs, has been pretty easy, but you have a good husband, and Herbert the most wonderful little boy ever, and when Willie comes home every day he can't wait to see him, and a lovely home."

Debra smiled and said, "Thank you. You're right. I do have a good life, and having you as my friend makes it even more wonderful. I want to tell you more about us. I haven't had the opportunity to talk with anyone except John about my family."

"Let me get the coffee that's perking and muffins with French strawberry preserve. I baked the muffins last night. It's the most I've done in a kitchen in years. Willie doesn't seem to care if we eat out a lot. He has breakfast and lunch near his office, and likes to try the new restaurants for our dinners, but I'm trying to make coffee in the morning and bake for him. I may even try to cook dinner sometime." She walked to the kitchen and brought back cups of coffee with a small pitcher of cream and a sugar bowl along with the muffins and jam.

They settled in with the refreshments and Debra continued her story. "As I said, we lived right outside of Titusville, a dirty ugly place. Daddy's farm was forty acres. His grandfather was given the land after the Civil War for fighting with the 6th U.S. Colored Infantry Regiment of Camp William Penn. The land wasn't good for growing. It was hilly, but Daddy raised dairy cows and hogs. We were never hungry."

She stopped, drank coffee, nibbled on a muffin. "One day about five years ago a man from the Jersey Standard Oil Company drove up and asked if his geologist could make some test bores on our land. Daddy said sure, and the men wandered around the farm for an hour or so taking soil samples. When they finished, they said goodbye, and maybe we'd hear from them again. We didn't know for sure, but oil was everything around there so we hoped for the best news that there was oil on the property. Soon after that men from the Vacuum Oil Company came by wanting to test our soil." Debra's smiling face gave it all away. "Well there was oil, and daddy who was a really good businessman, and could do arithmetic in his head asked the two companies for their offers. Soon both had offered around $100,000, but Jersey Standard added shares of stock in the Humble Oil Company and the South Penn Oil Company to the proposition so daddy took their offer."

Consuelo was elated. "That's so wonderful. I'm happy for your parents. Where did they go to?"

"They were so happy to leave Titusville but were worried about living somewhere safe. It's been really bad for us in places so they wanted to live in a Negro community where they wouldn't stand out. First, they thought about Harlem, but neither mama nor daddy has ever lived in a city, and they didn't want to move to an apartment. They heard about a place all the way out near the end of Long Island called Sag Harbor Hills. It was for well off Negros. Most came out in the summer, but there's enough that lived there all year to keep each other from getting too lonely. And it was on the water in a small town with its own beach so they bought a nice house there. We went out last summer by train." Debra hesitated then said, "My folks gave us the money to buy our house. I'm so thankful. It takes a lot off our minds. I didn't want Herbert growing up in Harlem so we came here. He should be with white children also because he's going to have to learn how to live with white people. He'll find out that most are not as good as your husband. John has a good job nearby, and maybe someday when Herbert's in school, I'll go back to working at NYU. I loved it. The students were so nice."

Chapter 38

May 1937

With the advent of spring, life in the city began again for those who survived the years of financial downturns and business failures. The New Deal had provided jobs for almost nine million unemployed people from laborers to artists. Public schools, roads, bridges, post offices, and airports were built and decorated with paintings and murals. The new facilities created more jobs, and opportunities for financial stability. Republicans in the House and Senate fought the Roosevelt administration's work projects and were successful in having some parts of the New Deal declared unconstitutional by the Supreme Court. Consuelo and Willie feeling like bears waking from hibernation began to frequent Broadway and saw productions of *A Doll's House,* As *You like It,* and *Of Mice and Men.* Consuelo brought Debra to Saturday matinee performances of *Brown Sugar* and *Abie's Irish Rose.*

Tonight the Levinsons met the Mosbachers and the Harburgs at 21 for dinner. One of the Kriendler brothers, owners of the 21 Club, sent two bottles of Taittinger Comtes de Champagne Brut Vintage 1930 to their table in celebration of Yip Harburg's marvelous new hit song *Over the Rainbow* written in collaboration with Harold Arlen. Harburg promised a signed and framed copy of the sheet music for hanging in the restaurant's bar room along with the hundreds of items related to celebrities. After some talk about Havana, and Consuelo's guide book, which she was close to completing for Random House, and her finishing the first semester at Hunter College the conversation centered upon the group's favorite topic: George Gershwin.

The Harburgs had seen Gershwin recently in Hollywood. Yip reported that George had put himself on a frantic schedule of concerts and movie score commitments, especially the *Goldwyn Follies,* that had taken up more of George and Ira's time than it should have. "George is different. I believe he really doesn't like it out there. He's distracted, tired and passes up parties and chances to go places. He doesn't eat much. That's not George."

Consuelo not innocently asked, "Why did he move to California. It sounds as if he could have stayed here and done the same work?"

"Because," Gertrude Mosbacher answered, "He wanted to get away from Kay Swift, and thank God he did." There was an awkward silence at the table for a moment, and then everyone laughed and agreed with her except Levinson who was still learning about the characters that had inhabited his wife's life.

Consuelo kept tabs on Gershwin through *Billboard Magazine,* the music industry's weekly bible. The publication, which she purchased at the news stand on West 4th Street near the subway entrance, reported on George's concerts, and new songs completed and published by the Gershwins. She also read Louella Parson's daily newspaper columns and listened to her radio shows for any tidbit about Gershwin in Hollywood. As she suspected Gershwin was often linked with Paulette Goddard, even though it was common knowledge Goddard was engaged to Charlie Chaplin. Photographs of Goddard with Gershwin were published in newspapers when the couple attended Hollywood events or tried to slip away for a weekend in Palm Springs or the Valencia Hotel in La Jolla. There even were rumors that Goddard and Gershwin would marry. It was accepted by the rest of the country that the people in Hollywood were philandering sex crazed libertines, playboys and harlots, as proven by their frequent marriages, divorces, and affairs which everyone loved to know about. In fact, Louella Parsons and Hedda Hopper Hollywood's famous gossip columnists were the most widely read journalists in the entire country.

Chapter 39

Harlem June 1937

Consuelo, Debra, and Herbert were on Eighth Avenue subway line's A train on the way to 125th Street in Harlem. They were going to Sofia's Beauty Shop just off of Lenox Avenue for hairdos and manicures. Debra was going to have her long black hair straightened with a hot comb using Madame C. J. Walker's preparations the only hair products she trusted. "Vegetable" shampoo was one of Madame Walker's top products for Negro women's hair, and Debra loved the way it smelled. She also enjoyed the constant chatter of the women in the shop. There's a loving atmosphere when a group of Negro women gets together. They looked out for each other and their families. It's so natural that it's taken for granted. Consuelo, fascinated, paid close attention to the rhythmic movement going on in Sofia's. It was all new to her. Regina, a stylist was asking if anyone was hungry because she was going to order chicken from Mamie Smith's Fry Kitchen by the Hotel Olga, another stylist was asking about someone's son Johnny a musician while another kid was being reprimanded for messing with the hair products, everyone there watched out for Herbert, and a friendly street peddler came in selling socks, soap, incenses, and cigarettes. Everything was so alive! She felt welcome in this world of which she hadn't been a part. If only Harlem could be as peaceful all the time as it was today, Consuelo thought.

Renee her favorite hairdresser took special care with Debra's hair giving it the attention a mother gives her daughter. Renee loved working with

Debra's long textured hair taming it after the shampooing. This was Debra's favorite part too. Renee parted sections of hair and applied Madame Walker's "Wonderful Scalp Ointment" as she gathered large braids in four sections. The perfume smell was intoxicating each time the hot straightening comb flattened sections of her natural tresses. Debra's was considered "good hair," and fun to style. Consuelo had her bobbed black hair washed, trimmed and set with big hair rollers, and then she was placed under a dryer for 25 minutes. Both Consuelo and Debra enjoyed experiencing their shared culture, which was new to Consuelo, but in which she was completely comfortable.

Consuelo hadn't been to Harlem in the daytime. She had accompanied Daniel Clark and then George Gershwin to the Cotton Club, but that was a white patron's only world. Today in the soft warm June weather she saw Harlem's residents busily shopping, strolling and showing life along the New York streets that had boasted music, art and literature collectively known as the "Harlem Renaissance," which because of the Great Depression, had quietly disappeared. Funny, Consuelo thought. It's different being here today. It's a real place with people doing ordinary things. The men they passed on 125th Street were mostly well dressed in dark blue and gray suits and white shirts with neckties in the Duke Ellington style. Most wore fedoras or derby hats.

Harlem's women were beautiful. Fashionable, wearing dresses that ended at their knees, and silk stockings with seams in back showing shapely legs, their feet in high heeled shoes. The women's hairstyles emulated the lush coiffures of pianist Hazel Scott, Nina Mae McKinney known as "The Black Garbo," and movie seductress Francine Everett, the Negro goddesses of show business. Consuelo and Debra each holding one of Herbert's hands strolled along the Avenue passing people conversing and laughing who appeared to not have a care in the world.

During their lunch, in a coffee shop, next door to Sofia's Consuelo looked at Debra, and said in a low voice, "I want to tell you something."

"Uh Oh, when someone says that to me. I want to say, are you sure you want to tell me something I might not be able to forget?"

"Oh it's not that bad, but I have to talk with someone I trust." Consuelo looked around as if the other patrons were interested in her story. "Lenore

Gershwin, Ira's wife and I write to each other from time to time. "In a letter a few weeks ago she said that George was acting strangely doing odd things around the house staying in bed until the afternoon, and showing a temper that no one close to him had seen before. He also has terrible headaches and vertigo. He even tried to push Paul his butler and friend out of the car Paul was driving. And strangest of all things, he keeps asking where I am."

"Oh boy Consuelo, you do leave a mark on your men. So what's this all about," Debra asked?

"Well, another letter from Lenore came yesterday." Consuelo dug it out of her pocketbook. She writes that George and Paul and a male nurse have moved into Yip Harburg's house in Beverly Hills. Yip's in New York, so the house is empty. I saw him recently and he's worried about George. Paul told Lenore that he has to watch George all the time because he's doing crazy things, and looking for me inside and outside of the house as if I'm hiding from him."

"So what does Lenore want you to do, and is that Yip Harburg you just casually mentioned the one who wrote *Over the Rainbow,* Judy Garland's song?

"She didn't say, and yes it's the same Yip Harburg as if two people could have that name." Consuelo hesitated, but then said, "I think I should go to California and try to help him. What do you think about that?"

Debra pulled Herbert onto her lap so he could snuggle against her. "Consuelo you're still a newlywed married to a nice guy who has you up on a big pedestal. Don't mess it up. George Gershwin left you for Paulette Goddard. I can't believe I'm saying that as if I know them. That's what you've done to me. If you don't know what to do, don't do anything. That's what my Daddy would say"

They returned to Greenwich Village on the A train. Consuelo wrote to Lenore expressing her concern for George, and saying she wished there was something she could do. The Clyne family had plans to spend part of July with Debra's parents in Sag Harbor Hills. They invited the Levinsons but, because the courts closed in August, July was a busy time for Willie. Consuelo had rented Mohegan Cottage again on Lake Otesaga for the month of August, and Debra and Herbert would visit them. Consuelo decided to try to forget about Gershwin, but she hoped he wasn't really so sick, and that someone could help him.

Chapter 40

"I'm on My Way"

Lenore telephoned Consuelo the evening of July 9 a Friday. She reported that George was in a very bad state, irrational at times, angry, then frightfully quiet. He still searched for Consuelo. Lenore asked if Consuelo would fly to California. She would pick her up at the Glendale Airport whenever Consuelo could get there, but the sooner the better. Lenore believed it would help.

When Consuelo told Levinson her plan to go to California to try to help Gershwin, Willie said he understood, or he thought he understood, and wouldn't stand in her way. Consuelo was grateful and kissed Willie passionately. "I promise when I return you'll receive all my attention," she assured him.

Debra was less enthusiastic about Consuelo's trip. "I hope you know what you're doing," was all she said then hugged her. Consuelo kissed Herbert goodbye. He loved his new aunt and uncle, and they loved him back.

The TWA flight at 8 am Sunday morning was the first available plane to California. Levinson reserved a seat for Consuelo and arranged for a taxi to pick up both of them at 6 am Sunday. He would accompany his wife to Newark Airport, and see her off. Early the next morning their taxi drove through the Holland Tunnel to New Jersey and headed west to the airport arriving in plenty of time. Consuelo was too nervous to eat anything or even drink coffee. Levinson assured her she would be well fed on the plane. The passengers boarded at 7:30 and the full flight took off fifteen minutes early. Levinson waved until the plane was far away on the runway. He was unhappy about the situation, but wouldn't have tried to stop Consuelo. She obviously had a great need to try and help Gershwin.

Unlike the luxurious Pan American Clippers that flew to Havana, Rio and Buenos Aires treating passengers to the finest hotel style accommodations that included gourmet meals, lounges with full bars, and sleeping sections the Douglas DC 3 airplanes were designed as the workhorses of the air. The center aisle was narrow, and passengers for most of the flight remained in their seats. Meals were sandwiches and other simple fare. The job of the DC 3 was to move people from coast to coast as safely and efficiently as possible without the romantic image enjoyed by Pan American Airlines that by federal law flew only to destinations outside of the United States. Levinson had gone over to the large newsstand on West 4th Street, and bought copies of magazines for Consuelo to read on the airplane. He picked up *Life, Look, Vogue* and *Vanity Fair* hoping that Consuelo would be able to concentrate enough to read on the airplane, and forget about the flight at least for part of the time she was in the air.

At fifteen minutes after one o'clock, after a smooth flight, the TWA DC 3 landed at Lambert Field in St. Louis, Missouri for a thirty-minute refueling and a chance for passengers to stretch their legs. Consuelo had been worrying about what she would say to Gershwin when she got to California. Had Lenore told him Consuelo was on her way to see him? How would he react? She hoped he'd be glad to see her, and not feel as if she was meddling in his life. After all, Gershwin's friends believed he left New York for a simpler life in California leaving everyone behind. Consuelo took advantage of the opportunity to leave the airplane for a while and walked the short distance to the terminal.

A TWA agent handed out copies of the *St. Louis Post-Dispatch* to the passengers. Consuelo took a paper and walked to a group of chairs and sat down. Unfolding the Sunday newspaper; she was struck by the large typeface of the headline until she realized that it proclaimed: **George Gershwin Dead at 38**. Consuelo couldn't move her body. She was sobbing loudly when the TWA stewardess came to find her. "Mrs. Levinson the airplane is loading for takeoff. Are you all right?"

Consuelo held up the newspaper and said, "George Gershwin is dead. I must go home."

Afterward

In 1975, the newly appointed Secretary of the Navy, a friend of the vice president of the United States, Nelson T. Rockefeller, moved his family into a home purchased from the estate of Clyde Tolson. Tolson had inherited the Georgetown house in 1972 from his friend and mentor J. Edgar Hoover the longtime director of the F.B.I. A dusty leather valise found in the cellar's former coal bin boarded over for thirty years contained within it a Nile crocodile skin briefcase filled with what appeared to be the score for a musical show called "A Time in Ybor City." Eighteen copies of a small red covered book with the same title were also in the valise. After looking through the papers, the Navy Secretary re-packed the valise and put it back in the old coal bin.

For Herbert's third birthday, Consuelo and Willie established a trust fund for him. They deposited two thousand shares of the newly issued Consolidated Edison stock, about 10% of Consuelo's stock position, which was to be held by the Hanover Bank until Herbert's twenty-first birthday.

Consuelo excelled in Hunter College and, after transferring her course credits from the New York State Teachers College, graduated in two years with the Latin honor Summa Cum Laude. She and four other women in her graduating class were accepted to Columbia Law School. She registered at her husband's alma mater as CC Levinson.

The Levinson's purchased Mohegan Cottage on Otesaga Lake as a summer retreat close to Cooperstown. They continued to visit Havana during the winter months until 1958 where the guide book, *A Time in Havana* by CC Levinson was sold everywhere.

The End

Author Notes

Edward Jablonski and Lawrence D. Stewart; George and Ira Gershwin's biographers said it best.

**"On a rainy Sunday – July 11, 1937 – at ten
thirty-five in the morning,
the brilliant flame that had been the life of George Gershwin
aged only thirty-eight, flickered out."**

He passed away without knowing that his great collaboration with DuBose Heyward and Ira that produced "Porgy and Bess" would become America's most beloved opera. Ira continued the Gershwin musical tradition for several decades finally succumbing at age eighty-six in 1983. He enjoyed smoking clear Havana cigars almost to the end of his life. DuBose Heyward died at age fifty-five in 1940 after inspiring the Gershwin masterpiece "Porgy and Bess."

When George Gershwin lapsed into a coma he was brought to Cedars of Lebanon Hospital in Los Angeles. The doctors there agreed that Dr. Walter Dandy of Johns Hopkins in Baltimore should be brought in to do the neuro-surgery. Dr. Dandy was vacationing on a yacht somewhere in the Chesapeake Bay. Calls to President Franklin D. Roosevelt in the White House by George's friends George Pallay and Emil Mosbacher caused two Navy destroyers to set out to locate Dr. Dandy. He was found and brought ashore in Maryland, and a police escort brought him to Newark Airport where he spoke by telephone to the doctors at Cedars of Lebanon Hospital who asked him to fly out to Los Angeles and perform the delicate surgery. Emil Mosbacher had a private plane ready for the doctor's flight to California. However, Gershwin's condition was deemed so critical that surgery was performed with Dr. Dandy in constant touch over a phone line from Newark. George never awoke.

Kay Swift after divorcing James Warburg went on to marry Faye Hubbard a semi-literate, alcoholic rodeo cowboy ten years her junior. They lived for a time in the west on his ranch, in a house without running water or electricity. She, after a few years of marriage, mostly living apart divorced Hubbard, and in 1947 married Hunter Galloway twelve years younger than Kay. He had the look and demeanor of old money families, but in reality was broke and had a limited career as an actor. After their marriage, he never held a job again. Kay was also reputed to have had an affair with the analyst Gregory Zilboorg from which a pregnancy and subsequent abortion resulted. She died at ninety-six years in 1993 recounting her life of love affairs to her grandchildren and anyone else who would listen.

A tall stone marker behind Plant Hall on the campus of The University of Tampa still marks the place where Babe Ruth hit his longest home run.

My mother, Johanna Roth Kase was born in the East New York section of Brooklyn across the street from the brownstone house where the Gershwin family lived. The families knew each other and the children played together until the Gershwin's moved to lower Manhattan's East side. My mother's long-time friend Ida Wolpen was my "godmother," and the Gershwin children's aunt.

My uncle Max Kase was the editor of the *Havana Telegram* a daily English language newspaper owned by William Randolph Hearst. Max worked in Havana during the 1930s observing the spread of the power American gangsters had over the Cuban Capitol. He returned to New York prior to World War II, and was the sports editor of the *Journal American,* the Hearst newspaper in New York where he was awarded a Pulitzer Prize in 1952 for investigative journalism, and is credited with the founding of the National Basketball Association (NBA).

De Pinna after being sold by the family closed in 1969.

John Foster Dulles and Allen Dulles remained on United Fruit Company's payroll right through their time serving as Secretary of State and Director of the Central Intelligence Agency respectively. The concept of conflict of interest didn't occur to them.

Ybor City produced hand rolled clear Havana cigars until the late 1930s. The cigar factories closed one by one due to the effects of the Great Depression, mechanization and extensive marketing by the cigarette companies. It still exists as a tourist destination, and in the old places that hosted the speeches of Cuban revolutionaries from Jose Marti to Fidel Castro one still, can hear the message; "Cuba Libre."

Suggested Reading

The Gershwin Years: George & Ira   Edward Jablonski and Lawrence D. Stewart

The Memory of All That: The Life of George Gershwin   Joan Peyser

The Immigrant World of Ybor City   Gary R. Mormino and George E. Pozzetta

Folly Beach: Glimpses of a Vanished Strand   Bill Bryan

Tampa Cigar Workers   Robert P. Ingalls and Louis A. Perez, Jr.

DuBose Heyward: A Charleston Gentleman and the World of Porgy and Bess   James M. Hutchisson

Nacional De Cuba Hotel: Revelations of a Legend   Luis Baez and Pedro DE La Hoz

Clothes Make the Man: Elliot White Springs

The Cigar Handbook   Mark Stucklin

The Memory of All That: George Gershwin, Kay Swift, and My Family's Legacy of Infidelities   Katharine Weber

Havana Nocturne: How the Mob Owned Cuba and Lost it to the Revolution   T.J. English

The Mafia in Havana: A Caribbean Mob Story   Enrique Cirules

About the Author

Ron Kase enjoyed a teaching, administrative and grant writing career spanning more than four decades that included positions at the New York City College of Technology (CUNY), Fairleigh Dickenson University, Empire State College (SUNY), Mercy College (NY) and Ramapo College of New Jersey. As a sociologist, Dr. Kase is intrigued with the national political process and the influence of religion on elections, which is contrary to the Constitutional guarantee of the separation of church and state, in which the state is protected from organized religion. He also believes that the second amendment clearly does not guarantee anyone the right to be armed except for "members of a well-ordered militia."
ronkase@rocketmail.com

Made in the USA
Columbia, SC
19 July 2018